Christmas
Angels

ALSO BY NANCY NAIGLE

Christmas Joy
Hope at Christmas
Dear Santa
The Christmas Shop

Visit www.NancyNaigle.com
for a list of all of Nancy's novels.

Nancy Naigle

Christmas Angels

ST. MARTIN'S GRIFFIN

NEW YORK

First published in the United States by St. Martin's Griffin, an imprint of St. Martin's Publishing Group

CHRISTMAS ANGELS. Copyright © 2019 by Nancy Naigle. All rights reserved. For information, address St. Martin's Publishing Group, 120 Broadway, New York, NY 10271.

www.stmartins.com

Library of Congress Cataloging-in-Publication Data

Names: Naigle, Nancy, author.
Title: Christmas angels / Nancy Naigle.
Description: First edition. | New York: St. Martin's Griffin, 2019. |
Identifiers: LCCN 2019027834 | ISBN 9781250312624 (trade paperback) |
    ISBN 9781250312631 (ebook)
Subjects: LCSH: Christmas stories. | GSAFD: Love stories.
Classification: LCC PS3614.A545 C46 2019 | DDC 813/.6—dc23
LC record available at https://lccn.loc.gov/2019027834

Our books may be purchased in bulk for promotional, educational, or business use. Please contact your local bookseller or the Macmillan Corporate and Premium Sales Department at 1-800-221-7945, extension 5442, or by email at MacmillanSpecialMarkets@macmillan.com.

First Edition: October 2019

P 1

May the sparkle of the holiday
season bring you joy, laughter,
and fill your heart with bright
moments that carry on forever.

Wishing you and your loved ones
a Merry Christmas, and daily
double-doses of happiness.

Acknowledgments

HUGS AND HIGH fives to my editors, Tiffany Shelton and Eileen Rothschild, for helping me bring sparkle to every page of this book. Marissa, DJ, Natalie, Megan, and the whole team over at St. Martin's Press, thanks for always helping me navigate the marketing, PR, and other opportunities that help to get *Christmas Angels* into readers' hands. Your tireless efforts are appreciated.

A heartfelt thank-you to Kevan Lyon for steadfast support, and for helping me achieve my dreams. I appreciate all you do. You're the best.

And to those who help me daily behind the scenes in ways they don't even know: Andrew, Mom aka Miss Bettie to my friends, Dad and Greta, and my furry four-legged boys, Dakota and Sarge, who give me unconditional love on those very late nights as I write while everyone else is sleeping.

And to all of you reading this, thank you for being a part of this amazing journey.

Christmas Angels

Chapter One

Everything happens according to the timing of our life, and no two lives are the same.

Her grandfather's words echoed in her mind the way they still did so often, even though he'd been a long time gone. Liz Westmoreland had lived her whole life by that philosophy. If there was one thing Pop had taught her, it was not to rush through life or try to force an order to it.

"Things happen when they are supposed to," Pop would remind her when she'd complain about the summer going too fast, or a fishing trip not coming soon enough. It seemed as if her whole childhood had been a lesson in patience. No matter if it was a burnt batch of snickerdoodles or heartbreak, Pop offered the same advice, and Gram echoed the sentiment. They were a united front. Always. If Liz ever decided to consider marriage again, it would only be for the promise of a relationship like theirs had been.

Patience as a life skill had helped Liz in business too, earning her the reputation of one of the best project managers at PROEM Service Group, where she was responsible for launching store openings for the finest chains around the world. Patience and timing were demanded of her daily and she excelled at both. Good thing too, because McKinley was a new client and their project was in the ditch when PROEM asked her to step in and work her magic to get them back on budget and open on time. With the help of handpicked short-term contractors, she'd recouped the overrun, and the store opened on time exactly four weeks ago today. The postproduction period was over and she was ready to submit the final paperwork showing that not only was the job complete, but they had exceeded all stated goals.

It's a wrap.

She smiled with satisfaction as she raised her finger above the keyboard, then hit enter to send the email with the final documents closing out the project. For a moment, her eyes hung on the email her boss, Peggy, had printed and placed on her desk this morning. McKinley was so happy with the outcome that they'd already booked two more new store openings with them. In Peggy's handwriting, "Great job. Thank you!" was scribbled across the bottom.

She twisted a white-gold sand-dollar pendant between her fingers. She'd splurged on the necklace as a memento of the project at the grand opening. Spending time on the beautiful South Carolina coast working on the McKinley store had given her a whole new appreciation for the beach.

Out the window it was a gray and rainy day. The whole state of North Carolina was getting soaked today. Traffic stacked up on the interstate. No ocean here, just a sea of cars crawling through the rain. She hadn't missed the traffic one bit.

Summer was just a hazy memory under the autumnal foliage that now glistened beneath the weight of raindrops. The colorful leaves proved that time had continued to move on while she was heads down on the McKinley project.

She clicked on the bookmarks tab on her computer and brought up the latest bed-and-breakfasts for sale in the southeast. Perusing those pretty places was her favorite mind cleanse. A few minutes imagining that her only job was to host people in a lovely inn somewhere in the mountains was enough to offset hours of untangling project snafus and budget overruns.

For as long as she could remember, Liz had dreamed of following in her grandparents' footsteps running their inn, Angel's Rest, but she'd landed here instead. Not that she was complaining. She'd earned a corner office and a six-figure salary, and since she had barely a minute to spare she'd been able to put a lot of money aside to someday follow that dream. Not an awful problem to have, but some days she wasn't even sure how she might find the time for someday.

A double knock at her door brought her back from the daydream.

"Thanks for the loan." Her friend Dan stood in the doorway about to flip the key fob to her Range Rover across the room.

She jumped to her feet to catch it in midair. "You're welcome. Did you find your clients the perfect home to live out their golden years?" The only time Dan ever borrowed her car was when he had senior-citizen clients who couldn't make the climb into his oversize Suburban. She'd told him when he bought the thing it wasn't practical for a real estate agent, but there was no talking him out of it. So on occasion he begged her to trade vehicles for the day. *What are friends for?*

"Good catch. We wrote an offer on one of the new condos downtown. They loved it." Dan rubbed his hands together. "Only

had to show them three places before they made up their mind."
He pumped his fist. "Sold!" His premature gray made him look
older than he was, which probably made people assume he had
years more experience than he did. It was moments like this, and
in his twentysomething antics, that his real age showed.

"Congratulations."

"A good day, despite the rain." He glanced out the window,
then shrugged. "I've got to run. I'm showing a Bank of America
exec a few places this evening." He turned, then leaned back
into her office. "If I get done early I'll bring Jeb's barbecue. I'm
showing a house right near there. Deal?"

"I thought you had a date with LeighAnn tonight."

"She had something come up at work, so I went ahead and
booked this showing for tonight. We're going out tomorrow for
lunch instead."

"Okay. Sounds good then." But he was already walking away.
Didn't matter. He pretty much showed up at her house as he
pleased anyway, and she was fine with that. He was kind of like
the brother she never had. A good friend, but sometimes a pain
in the butt.

Just as she sat back down Peggy walked in. "Ready to celebrate being done with the McKinley project?"

"Oh yeah!" She leaned back in her chair. "I just sent in my
final reports. Everything is officially off my plate."

"You did a great job. Thank you so much for taking that on
when it was in such a mess."

"You know me. I like the challenge."

"That's true." Peggy peered over the desk toward Liz's computer. "So what are you working on there?"

"I was just doing a little daydreaming over this B and B for sale." She spun her screen toward Peggy. "Look at this place. Isn't it dreamy?"

"Gorgeous. I could spend a week there."

"Me too." This house was a lot fancier than what Liz had in mind, but someday she was going to find the perfect place at the perfect price. "Still dreaming."

"Why would you even dream of leaving all this?" Peggy spread her arms wide. "I mean trading the chaos for tranquility? Are you crazy?"

"Maybe, but someday I want the only thing to overwhelm me to be the joy of a beautiful sunrise, instead of back-to-back meetings that steal my last hope for a good day." She and Peggy had daydreamed about low-stress jobs before, but she was pretty sure that it was all talk on Peggy's part. Someday Liz would do it. "Doesn't that sound like heaven?"

"It does." Peggy leaned on the desk. "I'm not sure the last time I took the time to watch a sunrise. We're going skiing in Boone next week. I'm going to make a point of doing it . . . at least one day."

That sounded wonderful. She couldn't wait to do the same. "I love Boone. It's not all that far from my grandparents' old lodge."

"Do you think it's too early for some holiday decorations to be up?"

Thanksgiving wasn't until next week. "My grandparents used to start decorating for the holidays in October. It was quite the extravaganza. People came from all over to see it. That place was . . . magical." She felt the remaining stress from the McKinley project fall away. Thinking about Angel's Rest always had that effect on her. "I remember Pop and Gram making a big deal of driving over to Boone to get cookies at Boonies."

"Boonies has the best snickerdoodles." Peggy put her hand on her stomach. "You're making me hungry."

"My grandmother's snickerdoodles were even better, and I have her recipe. It's about the only thing I can bake. I'll have to make you some." She could almost smell the buttery cinnamon aroma of those cookies baking in the mountain-house kitchen.

"What are you waiting for?"

"Time, and it just so happens I have a lot of that right now. I'll make you some." She glanced back at the computer screen. Wistfully, she said, "I really can't wait to find the perfect inn and follow in my grandparents' footsteps."

Peggy laughed. "I can almost picture you tottering around welcoming guests into your home with a plate of cookies. Since you sent in the final paperwork on your project why don't you head on out for the day? Take tomorrow too, and make a long weekend of it. We won't be reassigning projects until after the holidays."

She never took days off, but this time she didn't have a project to work on and she did have a ton of banked vacation time to burn. "That actually sounds really good. I haven't even begun my holiday shopping yet." She pulled out the bottom drawer of her desk and grabbed her purse. She liked her holidays simple these days, so she really didn't have much shopping to do except for a few people here at the office, but relaxing at home would be nice. She could do both. "I'll take you up on that offer."

"Great. Enjoy." Peggy headed out the door.

Liz wasn't far behind her. On the elevator down, she made a mental checklist of the stores she could hit on her way home.

Outside, red and gold leaves swept by in a trail toward the

storm drain. She pulled the hood of her coat up over her head, then splashed her way through the ice-cold rain.

She shivered as she slammed the car door. "Whew." She had doubted the meteorologists' excitement over a possible freeze warning this week, but she had to admit it was seeming more likely now.

She pressed the ignition button. The vents blew cool air across her arms. She stabbed at the buttons, desperate to find some warmth.

30 MILES TO EMPTY displayed across the bottom of the dashboard.

"Really, Dan?" *Why do you always do that, and on a rainy day no less.* This was just one more reason they'd never be more than friends. He drove her nuts with his lackadaisical attitude. Why was it so hard to respect never going below half a tank of gas?

She drove out of the parking lot and stopped at the first gas station, grumbling under her breath the whole time she pumped the gas. The wind swirled around her, knocking her hood back and stirring long strands of her hair against her cheeks. By the time the tank was full she felt cold to the bone.

As she jumped back into her Range Rover, all that gusto she'd had for leaving the office early to do some shopping just followed those drowning leaves down the storm drain. She pushed her damp hair behind her ear and headed straight home.

Inside, she peeled out of her wet coat and hung it in the shower to dry. Flipping through the mail, she dropped the junk mail into the trash can in the kitchen, then stopped and reached back down to retrieve a colorful oversize postcard.

A dozen homes lined one side of the card. It was a list of properties for sale at auction, and the one in the bottom right corner looked a lot like her grandparents' inn at Antler Creek. Her favorite place in the world.

Liz grabbed her laptop and set it on the island, typing the URL of the auction company into a browser as she slid onto one of the handwoven rattan high-back barstools. There were several properties listed in the Blue Ridge Mountains on the auction portal.

It took only a few clicks to bring up the information on the property listed on the card. It looked a lot like Angel's Rest, but upon closer inspection it wasn't like it at all. Her grandparents' inn was a true timber-frame home. The one in the listing just had the look of a log home. There were a lot of those around these days. Plus it was only about half the size. The similarity had just been wishful thinking.

She scanned through the other listings. Unlike the properties on the B and B site she usually daydreamed over, all of these were being auctioned, and opening-bid amounts were extremely reasonable. Excitement built as she stumbled upon more impressive-looking homes in the Blue Ridge Mountains.

She scrolled down, zipping through the long inventory of homes being auctioned. She read through the list of requirements to bid. It was doable. Someone else's misfortune could be her gain.

Even more excited with the possibility, she clicked back to the list of homes.

One of the houses caught her eye. She zoomed in.

More wishful thinking? Or could this one really be . . . ?

She double-clicked on the image and expanded the photo.

There was no mistaking that front door. A zing raced from her heart to her fingers as she zoomed in on the next picture. Someone had hand-carved that door for them in exchange for something. Pop was always bartering one thing or another. She was thirteen the summer he installed it.

The place was overgrown and definitely in need of some TLC, but that was easy enough to fix. She gulped back emotion as the familiar sight brought memories rushing back more clearly than ever. From the aerial view she could see that the two cabins, and the old barn out back were still there too.

Dan called out a hello. "I thought I'd beat you here. You're home early." He'd let himself in through the door from the garage.

"Yeah." She was only half listening as her eyes landed on the sale date. *Tomorrow?* If she was going to make her dream come true, she had a lot of work to do in a hurry.

"My clients rescheduled for tomorrow because of the rain, but I brought barbecue anyway."

"Thanks. That sounds good." Liz stood from her chair, and went to help him. "What do you know about buying properties at auction?"

"You mean besides the fact you get what you pay for and there are usually a ton of problems with them?" He started unpacking food from a large paper sack. "Or that you have to plan in advance if you really want to jump in on an auction property." He neatly lined up napkins next to plasticware next to sauce packets. "You need all your ducks in a row. And if you want to buy a place you should work through me. Rain or shine, unlike my clients this afternoon who canceled because of the rain. I hate rain."

He could bellyache about the rain all he wanted, but nothing was going to dampen her mood. "Ducks happen to love this weather," Liz said with a playful flap of her arms. "And I happen to think it's a perfect day for getting my ducks in a row."

Chapter Two

Liz motioned for Dan to follow her to the kitchen island. "Look at this. I'm sure it's my grandparents' old place."

"You haven't been back there in what? Twenty years?" Dan pulled the computer closer and looked at the listing.

"Maybe fifteenish."

"Nice. Yeah. Wait. What are you thinking?" Dan lifted his gaze, then cocked his head. "You're not seriously considering—"

"I've been waiting for this my whole life. Angel's Rest is practically mine." Excitement forced her words out in a flurry. "So, how do I do this auction thing?"

"You don't." He closed the top of the computer, and handed her a barbecue sandwich. "Not without going to see the condition of the house and checking to make sure you're not also buying old liens against the place."

"There's no time. It goes up for auction in the morning. I've read through the FAQ's, it doesn't look that complicated. I need to get a proof of funds letter from my banker before I can bid though."

"You're going to bid on this place sight unseen? I have to

advise against it, Liz. That's just plain crazy." Dan ran a hand through his hair. "You're always talking about situations being a 'sign'; well, maybe this is a sign that you should let this crazy idea go once and for all."

"No. It's not a sign to let it go. Finding out the day before Angel's Rest goes up for auction is a sign it's meant to be." She scooted closer to him and opened the laptop again. "Look at these. The pictures don't look so bad. Okay, so it's overgrown, but that's cosmetic."

"Pictures can hide a multitude of problems. Very expensive ones, and the fact that there are only three pictures total is a red flag, especially since only one shows the house. The other is an aerial. You have no idea what it looks like inside."

"It's rustic. It's a timber home, what could go wrong?"

"Termites?"

He had a point. "Well, the thing is still standing."

"You have no way of really knowing that without going and taking a professional with you to check it out." Dan leaned against the counter. "Why are you so hell-bent on this idea? You're good at what you do. You have a good life here. Why the heck would you want to move to the mountains?"

"I loved spending time with my grandparents. The mountains are like an old friend to me. The nature. The quiet. I always thought I'd rent rooms out to people, and help them enjoy the area just like Gram and Pop. It was a good and pleasing way of life."

"You'd be bored out of your skull up there. No shopping. Probably no pizza delivery. You do love pizza."

"I can make my own pizza."

He cocked his head.

"I could learn."

"You love your job."

"I wouldn't say I love it. I'm good at it. But I could still do some projects if I get bored. I love that place. It's why I've worked so hard and saved for so long. Every bonus, every raise— I've invested it all for this one dream."

Dan folded his arms. "So that's why I couldn't get you to look at a new house last year?"

"Exactly. I told you. I have everything I need here. I've got money socked away for a new place." She raised her eyebrows. "The *right* place. The one that I've had in my heart since as long as I can remember."

"But a person in your position should live in a much nicer house in a much better area of the city. Maybe you'd be happier here if—"

"There's nothing wrong with this house or my neighborhood. Or Angel's Rest."

"I didn't say there was. Your house will be an easy sell, but I just didn't think you were really serious about a house in the mountains."

"You never listen to what I say." Which was fine, really. It would be a different story if he were her boyfriend, but their relationship wasn't like that.

"I do listen. Kind of. I guess I just didn't put two and two together."

"Well, call it four and help me, why don't you?"

He handed her a plate with more barbecue, slaw, baked beans, and corn bread on it. "Do you know how much work a place like that could take?"

"I can take a leave of absence to do the renovation. It won't be much different from what I do on a daily basis, but instead of opening a mega-retail site I'll be opening an inn. I can do contract work from up there and do both for a while until I build up a clientele."

"You really have thought this through."

"I've been dreaming of it for years, Dan." She walked into the living room with her plate and plopped down on the sofa. "You just don't get it. My grandparents owned *this* inn on the mountainside of Antler Creek. What are the odds of me finding this out the night before it goes on sale?"

He sat down in one of the chairs and balanced his plate on his knee. "One in a million, I'm sure."

"Right. Each summer," Liz said, "people came not just to Antler Creek, but to my grandparents' inn for the fishing and fireside cookouts, and every winter they came for the skiing and Christmas festivities. The inn was known for the best Christmas lights around. You could see them from down in the valley. People came from miles around." In her mind she was back there, bundled up and excited as people began to join together. "There were carriage rides up the mountain to see the lights up close. Gram would make hot chocolate and her secret-recipe cookies for visitors. I helped. It was magical."

Dan took out his phone and started typing. "And today the population in Antler Creek is eleven hundred twenty-nine, and twenty-five years ago the population was twelve hundred thirty-four."

So there wasn't much growth. That was just year-round population. "A steady population," she reasoned.

"A stagnant one."

"It's not about the population. Or maybe it is. Antler Creek is quaint. It's the perfect place to relax. I loved spending time there."

"That was a long time ago, Liz. And you haven't been back in years. What's that say about it?"

She shut her mouth. That was a fair point. "It broke my heart a little that my grandparents left it behind. I'd always assumed I'd take it over from them."

"What will your guests do with their time when they stay with you?"

"All the things they used to. Enjoy nature. Fly-fishing. Antiquing. Hike to the waterfall. Pop led hikes and fishing excursions nearly every week." *Am I really brave enough to do this?*

"I guess the waterfall would still be there," he said. "Are you going to take strangers on hikes in the woods? That sounds like a recipe for disaster."

"Why not? And fly-fishing on the stream was amazing in the summer. I used to be quite good at it."

He sighed. "You know I'm not going to wade out in cold water and fish, right?"

She shrugged. This wasn't about the two of them. He knew that too. "You can visit. I promise to have Wi-Fi."

His mouth tugged to the side the way it did when he was disappointed.

"Be happy for me," she said. "Please?"

He sucked in a deep breath. "I'm still not saying this is a good idea, but if you're going to do it be careful. The sale is as-is, where-is, so if you win, you're stuck with it even if it's a hunk of termite-ridden rubbish."

"I hear you. You've made your point, but I'm also stuck with it if it's exactly like I remember, and that would be awesome." She grinned so wide her lashes tickled her cheeks.

"I head to Denver late tomorrow night for my cousin's wedding," Dan said. "Are you sure I can't talk you into coming with me instead? It'll be a great party and a fun long weekend. Could save you six figures."

She'd declined the invitation weeks ago. "No thanks. I've got things to do around here that I've neglected the past couple of months while I was working in South Carolina." She took in a long deep breath, crossed her fingers, and held them up. "Or I might own a new home."

He rolled his eyes, and shoved the last bit of barbecue into his mouth. "I'll be back Tuesday. Keep me posted."

THE NEXT MORNING, Liz had met with her banker, submitted her proof of funds, and finished her entries on the auction portal with little time to spare before the auction began.

Like Dan, her banker had given her a speech about buying a property at auction sight unseen. He hadn't seemed any less concerned when she mentioned that she used to spend every summer and winter there as a kid, and that she had a good feeling about this. It might have sounded like an impulse purchase to him, but she'd been wishing, hoping, and planning for this for years. It was surely meant to be. It didn't really matter what his personal thoughts were. This was her decision, and her money, and she had the proof of funds letter in hand. She was set.

The thought of spending Christmas at Angel's Rest this year made her heart dance. She might even be able to convince Mom and Dad to come for a visit, rather than spending the holiday somewhere warm and tropical, the way they'd started doing a few years back.

Five minutes before the bidding started, a timer displayed at the top of her screen, counting down the minutes and seconds until auction time.

As time ticked down, her palms dampened. Her fingers left wet marks on her keyboard when she refreshed her screen again, just to be sure she was in sync. When Gram and Pop sold Angel's Rest and took off in an RV to see the United States, she'd been crushed. She hadn't had any control over what happened back then, but this was in her hands now. She had every intention of being the first bidder.

When the bidding opened there must have been fifty bids all at once.

Her hands twisted in her lap.

The price climbed quickly. Her heart pounded with each increasing bid she made.

Please. Please. Please.

If the bids kept increasing at this rate, her dream would be over before it ever started.

Finally, the bidding slowed when it got to seventy-five thousand. No doubt there were people who just perused every auction in hopes of winning a hidden gem at a bargain. She could see the appeal. This was fun. Almost aerobic.

She took a sip of water, and watched carefully as more bids posted. Feeling more empowered with each bid, she calculated the time left, pacing her bids to increase her odds of being the final bidder.

It was tempting to make a big leap and just get the bidding war over.

More of Pop's words of wisdom were still playing in her head. *If it's meant to be, it'll be.* So, Liz forced herself to be patient.

With twenty seconds to go she made one final bid, and then closed her eyes and silently prayed.

In those final seconds, no one else countered her offer.

Then WINNING BIDDER flashed across her screen in bright blue, along with a very, very long list of legalese and mandatory steps. On a bright note, even with the gavel fee and other associated costs she wouldn't need a loan. Years of prudent saving had prepared her for this moment.

A swirling combination of exuberance and dread assaulted her. What if, as Dan had warned, the house was a termite-ridden heap? This was her life savings. Every nerve in her body seemed to vibrate.

But then she turned and caught a glimmer of sunlight bouncing from the glass of a picture frame sitting on the shelf of her bookcase, like a tiny angel reminding her that everything happens for a reason, and she knew that it would be okay.

She bounced out of her chair and walked straight over to the bookcase and took the framed picture from its place of honor. In her shaking hands, she, Gram, and Pop smiled back at her from the front yard of Angel's Rest. Wearing the cap Pop had given her, the one with the colorful hand-tied fishing flies on it, she grinned like a freckle-faced jack-o'-lantern with a sunburn.

When they'd taken off for parts unknown in that big honkin' motor home, she'd thought they'd gone crazy. It wasn't until months later, when Pop died, that the whole story unveiled itself. The ugly truth that cancer had eaten away at his body and the year they'd been told he'd have wasn't what God had in mind, and not two months after Pop passed Gram went to sleep and never woke up.

She missed them so much. Angel's Rest had been her happy place. She wanted nothing more than to honor her grandparents by sharing the beauty of Antler Creek again.

She spun around, hugging the memory in her arms, dancing around the house, exuberant at the thought of what lay in front of her.

She wished it were all hers today, but that wasn't the case. There was the matter of fund transfers and deeds and taxes and such. It might be up to thirty days from now before she could call Angel's Rest her own.

Dan was probably getting ready to leave town. She tried to call her parents, but got their voice mail. She was dying to share the news with someone.

She sat down, smiling and letting it all sink in.

There's no reason I can't drive up to see it. The listing had clearly said the property was unoccupied. No one could stop her from peeking in a few windows to get the ball rolling. See how the town had changed. Meet a neighbor or two. There was plenty she could do to get ready to get a plan in place. There was so much to do.

She looked at her watch, then picked up her phone and dialed Peggy.

"You're already bored to tears? It hasn't even been a whole day yet," Peggy teased.

"Hello to you, too." Her insides swirled. "And no. I'm not bored. Quite the opposite."

"Really? What's up?"

"I need the rest of the year off."

There was a long pause on Peggy's end. "Okay, that was

unexpected. But you have the time to take. As a friend, is everything okay?"

"Oh yes. Everything is fine. Wonderful, in fact. Peggy, you're not going to believe this. I don't think I do yet. Remember when we were talking about B and Bs and my grandparents' inn yesterday?"

"Dreaming again. Yes. That would be so wonderful."

"It's not just a dream anymore," Liz said. "Angel's Rest went on the auction block this morning. I bought it."

"What?"

"Yes. I know. It's all crazy, and unexpected, but I found it online last night, and everything has fallen right into place."

Liz heard the heavy sigh across the line.

"I have a feeling you're never coming back," Peggy said. "And as your boss it breaks my heart, but as your friend I couldn't be happier for you. You take all the time you need. We'll work out details after the first of the year."

"Thank you so much, Peggy."

"You've earned it. Send pictures of that sunrise. I'll be living vicariously through you."

"I promise I will." She hung up the phone feeling like a hundred helium balloons were lifting her from the ground.

Liz closed her eyes. "Thanks, Pop and Gram. I'm pretty sure you and a team of angels are looking over me today." She wrapped her arms around herself, feeling closer to them than she had in a long time.

She tossed a change of clothes and essentials in an overnight bag, grabbed a pair of boots from her closet, and prayed it wasn't raining in Antler Creek as she headed out the door on an adrenaline high.

Chapter Three

Matt Hardy sat on his regular seat at the Creekside Café counter—third from the end—the same one he'd sat on when he and his parents would come here when he was just a kid.

"Good afternoon, Matt." Maizey set a glass of sweet tea in front of him. "Everyone is talking about the auction this morning. Speculating."

"No surprise there," he said with a snicker. He didn't have any intention of letting on that he'd bid on it too.

Buck, who owned the Buck Holler Bar, announced, "I heard some Charlotte city slicker bought the place."

Someone else said, "I bet they bulldoze the old place and put up a big house, probably something modern that will stick out like a sore thumb up there."

"Or maybe it's good news and they'll reopen the inn," Maizey said, trying to keep the locals from overreacting. "That would be good news, right? I mean look at all of the places that've sold only to fall into ruin. It's crazy."

Maizey put a hand on Matt's shoulder. "At least you're smart enough not to rent yours out so it stays in good repair."

Nancy Naigle

"Yeah, I'd rather break it in myself." He'd quickly realized that having his house done and not living there year-round was worse than waiting to build it in the first place. "You really think someone might bulldoze the old inn?"

"Who knows," Maizey said. "We'll just have to wait and see."

"It's a shame it was ever bought by that art gallery. They sure did ruin a good thing," another local said. "If they'd have kept it an inn or a bed-and-breakfast I'm sure they'd have been able to keep the clientele coming back. The Westmorelands did a good business up there at Angel's Rest."

"Angel's Rest was a big act to follow. Good people."

"Sure were."

"The best."

"Well, maybe good people bought it this time. You old boys have sure turned into a judgey old bunch. That's enough about that," Maizey said, with a scolding wag of her finger. "Now who's ready for pie?"

Hands shot up in the air. "Coming right up," she said.

Maizey made the rounds with pie until there was only one slice left. "I can't give this last piece away? How about you, Matt? You could use some extra meat on those bones. You work too hard."

"No thank you, but if there's any left I'll get some to go with my dinner."

She winked. "I'll make sure there's a piece left for you if I have to bake another one special."

"You're too good to me, Maizey."

"Your momma would haunt me silly if I weren't." Her laugh carried across the room.

She grabbed his sandwich and slid the plate in front of him, then picked up a pitcher of tea and made a lap around the tables.

How she single-handedly handled this crowd most days he had no idea, but she managed.

The bell at the door jingled and a woman wearing khakis and a blazer walked in.

He heard Maizey stop to chat with her as she took a seat at the table behind him.

The woman's voice had a Southern twang to it, but there was something gentle about it. Behind him he heard Maizey give her the rundown on the specials, and then they started talking about what there was to do in Antler Creek as if she'd be sticking around. He made a half spin on the stool.

She was definitely a city type, but not like his ex, Robyn, who wore shoes that cost as much as his first truck payment, and had one of those pearly white smiles that nearly blinded you from across the street. You didn't see smiles that white in this neck of the woods. That took more than your usual teeth-whitening toothpaste.

He ran his tongue across his own teeth. He'd done the whitening thing once at the insistence of Robyn, who had made it seem barbaric that he'd never considered it before. The next thing he knew he was lying in a reclined position with his lips jacked open and a purple light shining on his mouth in the middle of the mall. He'd never do that again. His teeth had been sore for a week following the treatment. He should've known better than to trust a girl who spelled Robin with a "y." It wasn't that way on her birth certificate. Her mother had made a point of telling him that the first time they'd met. Apparently, Robyn-with-a-"y" liked to be different, and he was just one more thing to add to her list. Country boy. Check.

City girls. A promise for problems. Check.

Not that he really needed a reminder. But if that were true, why couldn't he stop himself from turning around and taking one more look at her?

Even after the self-warning, he did turn and take another look. She was pretty, but he could imagine her looking just as at home in jeans and hiking boots. Most people who came to Antler Creek didn't stay long, since there wasn't a hotel. He wondered what her story was.

He finished his sandwich and settled his bill. When he slid off the stool and started to head outside, he noticed that the woman was still looking over the menu.

He stopped at her table. "I recommend the ham sandwich. It's my favorite." She glanced up and smiled. Without another word, he tugged on the bill of his ball cap. Cursing himself under his breath for the stupid gesture, he turned to leave. Really? Might as well have given her a "howdy, ma'am" to go with the tip of the hat.

Feeling like a total geek, he hustled out the door.

Should have minded my own business.

Elvis lumbered to his feet in the back of Matt's truck. "Hey, buddy, sorry I took so long." Matt took a napkin of leftovers from his pocket, which sent Elvis's tail, what there was of it, wagging so fast his whole body rocked.

While Elvis took his own sweet time snacking on the ham sandwich, Matt noticed the fancy SUV in the parking lot. A black Range Rover. You didn't see many of those around here. Was she driving it?

Elvis plopped down in the bed of the truck, tongue lolling out of the left side of his mouth as if it were ninety degrees out today even though it was a comfortable sixty. At just six months old, he'd already surpassed ninety pounds.

Matt had a feeling Elvis missed Valerie a little. Before Matt finished building his mountain house, he'd been living and working in Raleigh. He'd planned to get a dog when he moved into the mountain house for good, but when he saw the picture of Elvis up for adoption on the news his heart couldn't say no. He'd made the adoption and set up doggy day care arrangements, only Elvis ended up with a terrible case of kennel cough the first week, so Matt hired Valerie to take care of Elvis at home, and take him for walks so he'd only have to be alone a couple of hours a day.

But Matt was staying in his mountain house through the holidays now, and that meant Elvis would have to adjust to not having Valerie around. He'd pouted the first couple of days, but finally was adjusting to being Matt's right-hand man. Matt was thankful to have the big loving pup at his side. It would be Matt's first Christmas without Dad, and he needed time to deal with all of that. Having Elvis made the wounds a little less raw.

It had taken a long time for Matt to get to a place where he could even come back home. But once he did, he realized part of what had been missing in him was the peace this place brought. He felt grounded here now. In a good way.

Matt shifted the truck into gear and drove over to Goodwin's Hardware on Main Street to pick up dog food, and a few supplies to keep the deer from completely destroying his cedar trees.

He whipped the truck into the parking lot, then dropped the tailgate after he climbed out. Elvis hopped to the street next to him. "C'mon, boy."

As they walked through the door of the hardware store, the owner, George, waved a hello and then tossed a dog treat in the air. Elvis nabbed it like a Hoover vacuum after a spider.

"That dog never misses," George said.

25

"Not when it comes to food. Don't ask him to chase a cat, though. He'll just make a new friend."

"I don't doubt that." George came around the counter. "You're a lover, not a fighter, just like your pa, huh, Elvis?"

Elvis lifted his chin and woofed.

"Whatever." Matt rubbed his hand through his beard. "And please don't try to set me up again."

"You have to get over Robyn eventually."

"I'm over her."

"No you're not. She wasn't your type anyway. She didn't even like Antler Creek. All she did when she stopped in to pick up things for you was talk about when y'all would be leaving again. She said no person in their right mind could live in a place without a mall or at least one upscale restaurant."

"Too bad she never let me in on her true feelings about this place. I thought she saw the beauty of small-town living."

"Maybe she did. Maybe it's that scruffy beard that ran her off," George teased.

"I didn't even have this when she was around." He touched his chin. "It's Movember. I'm growing this to raise awareness of men's cancer."

George blanched. "Sorry, Matt. I didn't even think about that. Your dad was a good man."

It was true, but so hard to hear. Choked up, he didn't respond. Cancer didn't always give big early-warning signs, at least not big enough for a man like Dad to notice. It had taken him swiftly. Probably a blessing, not that it brought Matt any comfort. He'd give anything to have Dad back. For a year. A month. Heck, a day longer.

Folks knew and loved Dad, which made moving back a blessing and a curse some days. He changed the subject. "I need some help to deter the deer from completely destroying my cedars. They're making an all-you-can-eat buffet of them."

"I told you not to plant those high-dollar cedars."

"Well, they are planted and there's been no problem until now. When I came around the corner the other day I saw the telltale shape of my once perfectly conical trees nibbled to deer height. I hope I caught it early enough that they only pruned them. I figured a little wire fencing around them would keep the deer back enough to let the trees regain some growth."

"Yeah, but now that the deer have found them it'll be hard to keep them away. They'd get caught in the wire. I have a couple better solutions for you."

He hated to think he might have to replace the trees entirely. As it was, it would take a while for them to regain their former shape. He followed George to the back of the store.

"I've got burlap, or it's a bit more expensive but this polypropylene mesh netting that they used over at the arboretum last year when they had the same problem. This was what was left that they didn't need. I can sell it to you at my cost. It's a better long-term solution and it'll look nicer."

"I'll take it," said Matt.

Elvis finally caught up to them and dropped a tape measure at Matt's feet.

"Looks like your dog's shopping again."

"Funny thing is he brings things I need." He patted Elvis on the head. "Thanks, buddy."

"Now I've heard everything." George walked back up front to the register, and Matt followed with Elvis on his heels.

"He does that all the time. I'll be working and go to get a

tool and he will have already carried it over for me. I'm sure it's a coincidence; I mean, he brings the hammer to me all the time and I don't need that. He must have some retriever somewhere in his mutt-butt bloodline."

"Good thing he has skills. As big as that dog is already he'll need to work to help foot his own food bill." George lifted one of Elvis's paws. "His paw is as big as my hand at just six months? Those giant breeds grow for two years, ya know."

"So I've heard."

George shook his head. "He's going to be huge." He tossed another cookie in the air and Elvis snapped it up. "Remember I'm your friend when you outweigh me, Elvis."

Elvis licked his lips then pushed his nose under George's hand. "You're a good ol' boy." George rang up Matt's order and handed him the ticket to drive around back and load up the purchase.

When Matt pulled his truck around, the guys already had his stuff on a hand truck waiting for him.

Loaded up, he drove straight home and gathered the tools he needed to address the deer problem. Elvis lazed in the cool grass, only getting up to chase the occasional falling leaf and bark at it.

With all of the netting finally in place, Matt gathered up his tools. This time of year the days were so short it was hard to get much done before dark. "Come on, Elvis. You can ride up front. We have to go over to the church and help Pastor Mike." Elvis hopped in the truck. He sat tall in the seat, then lowered his front paws to the floorboard and rested his chin on the dash.

George was right. Elvis was going to be one big dog, but it took a big dog with a heart to match to fill the void in his heart that losing Dad had left.

Chapter Four

Liz sank her teeth into the ham sandwich. She was in a hurry to get to Angel's Rest while there was still some sunlight, but she'd been so hungry she figured she'd better stop first so she wouldn't be in a rush once she got there.

The Creekside Café hadn't disappointed. The lunch was good, and folks were just as welcoming as she remembered, and it wasn't just because of her grandparents either, because no one knew her. Not yet, anyway.

Conversation from the lunch crowd hung in the air, accented by the occasional clank from the flattop grill on the other side of the counter. By the looks of things, this café had to have been here when she was a kid. The old black-and-white floor tiles looked original, and those chrome red-topped stools at the counter looked straight out of the sixties.

She was glad the heavily bearded man had recommended the ham sandwich. She'd definitely order it again.

Maizey, the waitress who'd been kind enough to share some of the local attractions, came back over to check on her. "Everything good?"

"Delicious. You'll definitely be seeing me again."

"That's what I like to hear." Maizey, an older lady with one of those hairdos that look like they were done at the salon, teased and sprayed, rested a hand on the back of Liz's chair. "Besides the new candle factory, and the antique mall, we are kind of known for our waterfalls in the spring and summer. We also have a new jeweler that's working at the gem mine. He can cut and set the stones you find down there, but he does gold and diamond work too. He moved here from New York City. Really nice guy."

"Thanks. I'll definitely have to check that out. Seems like you do a good business around here."

"Locals mostly, but we've been getting more tourists the last couple of years. I think country living has finally become cool again."

"Did that ever go out of style?"

"Not around here, thankfully." The waitress smiled. "My name is Maizey. Anything you need you just let me know."

"I will. Thank you." Liz could tell Maizey's offer was sincere. She could picture herself having meals here at the Creekside Café each day until she got moved in too. Just like one of the locals. "I'm Liz. Very nice to meet you."

"You too." Maizey flitted from customer to customer.

A moment later she was back to refill Liz's sweet tea, and leave the check.

Liz took a big sip of her tea. It was the real deal. Just sweet enough to feel like dessert, like Gram used to make.

The faces at the tables around her were those of hardworking blue-collar folks—most certainly locals, but there were others who, like her, seemed to be passing through for the day. A nice mix. She liked this town.

Liz paid her check and went outside. Her shiny black Range Rover looked out of place with its side-view mirrors all tucked in like a scolded puppy. She hit the button on her key fob. The mirrors moved out and the engine rumbled to life. She climbed into her vehicle and sat there for a moment taking in the surroundings. The cheerful blue awnings over the front windows of the café looked new. The sign was framed in blue, with CREEKSIDE CAFÉ in fat water-blue lettering. On the telephone pole in front of her, a flyer for a bluegrass-music festival that had happened two weekends ago fluttered in the breeze.

I'm going to be a part of this town. Just thinking about it made her nearly light-headed. Antler Creek had always felt like home to her; now it would be.

She picked up her phone and dialed the local contact for the house again. Finally, someone answered.

"Hi, hello. This is Liz Westmoreland. I bought the house on Doe Run Road at auction this morning. I've been trying to get through all morning. I was beginning to think I had the wrong number."

"Sorry," the woman said. "We don't open the office until noon on Fridays this time of year. What can I do for you?"

"I'd like to get a key to the house so I can take a look at it. Can you help me?"

"Oh gosh, the viewing period ended on Wednesday. We don't allow people in once it's been sold. It generally just goes straight to the new owner once all the paperwork has gone through."

She understood that process, but it wasn't what she wanted to hear. "I actually didn't get to see the place before I bought it, and I'm just dying to get inside and look around. I don't mind showing some identification."

"You do realize that the property was sold as-is, where-is. There's no backing out."

"Of course, no I would never." Liz could tell the lady took her rules seriously. "My grandparents used to own the place. You can't imagine how excited I am about this. Can you please bend the rules? I'll sign something taking responsibility. Whatever you need."

"Your grandparents?"

"Yes. They owned Angel's Rest."

"My goodness." The woman sighed. "I guess it don't really matter much. Not like you can hurt anything. And everyone loved your grandparents around here. I'm sure they'd make an exception for you."

Liz could hear the woman rummaging around for something.

"Okay, there's a lockbox on that place. I'll give you the code. My boss is out fishing this afternoon. If he disapproves of me giving it to you, don't be surprised if that code won't work tomorrow."

"That's fine. Thank you so much."

"Got a pen? It's one of those push-button jobs."

Liz pulled the pen from the front pocket of her purse. "Got one."

The woman rattled off the code, which Liz immediately recognized as the address. She could have just said so.

"Congratulations on your purchase," the woman said.

"Thank you again." Liz hung up the phone more excited than before.

With the code in hand she left the café and turned right on Main Street. It was only a short distance to the road up the mountain, which seemed steeper than she remembered. No one else was on the road, so she slowed and took her time around the next bend—a hairpin turn. She white-knuckled the steering wheel, but was relieved to know she was getting close to her destination.

There used to be a big cleared-off area to the left that backed up to a farm with a few cows and a ton of goats. It had always been the landmark that helped her find Angel's Rest, but she didn't remember it being this far.

The leaves nearly covered this stretch of Doe Run Road after all the wind and rain last night. She slowed down, peering over the steering wheel, hoping she was going to be able to stay on the pavement.

"I'm coming home, as soon as I find it," she joked to herself.

Then, she slammed on her brakes to keep from driving right past the mailbox. It had seen better days, but it was definitely the mailbox Pop had built. The concrete pillar with the river rock was still there, although it could use a good cleaning. Most of it was green from the moss that had taken up residency, and the mailbox that had once been a to-scale replica of one of the cabins out back had deteriorated so much it mostly looked like rotted wood that had fallen on top of the old rural-size metal mailbox.

She turned in to the driveway. The property was overgrown in the auction picture, but it was even worse now.

It will be beautiful again.

She tried to ignore the doubt that filled her as she parked and got out. The wraparound porch always looked so inviting lined up with colorful rocking chairs. Now leaves huddled in the corner.

Sadly all of the windows had been boarded over too. It made sense. They certainly wouldn't want vandals tearing up the place when the house wasn't being tended to. On a positive note, she'd have the boards to do something with. Those sheets of plywood weren't cheap. Pop used to cut shapes from big pieces like that with his scroll saw. Put together, they looked like reindeer. He'd even sold a bunch of them to other people in the town. She wondered if she might see some of Pop's artwork on people's lawns this Christmas.

She stepped back and surveyed the house. The metal roof was new. The logs had darkened over the years, but that was to be expected.

On a positive note, the place didn't look like it was getting ready to crumble into a heap of termite dust. Thank goodness, because Dan's comments had kept her up all night.

And no sooner had Dan crossed her mind than her phone rang, and it was Dan's ringtone.

"Hi, Liz." Dan's voice came over the line. "I was going to see if I could use your SUV for the day. I've got two showings this evening with an older couple."

"Sorry. Can't do it this time," she said.

"What? Really?" He laughed. "No, you're kidding, right?"

It struck her that it might actually be the first time she hadn't accommodated him. "No. I've got plans in Antler Creek today."

"Why?" He grunted. "You're not still chasing down that property, are you?"

His righteous tone annoyed her. "No. I don't need to chase it down," she said, determined to not let him get to her. "It's already mine."

"Didn't I tell you that was a horrible idea?" he said, spacing the words evenly.

"You shared your opinion, and you clearly stated it more

times than was necessary, but you'll recall it was *my* decision to make. I made it, and I was the winning bidder."

Silence hung on the line. "Can I ask what you gave for it?"

"No, but I'm happy with it, and that's all that matters. It's a great investment in my future."

"If it was an investment property you were looking for you know I could have sold you something that you truly could have made some money on."

She countered icily. "Why can't you just be happy for me?"

"Fine. I won't say another word about it."

"That's not the same thing as being happy for me."

"Look. I know you're excited, but you can go tomorrow. Let me use the Range Rover this afternoon. What's the hurry anyway? You still have to get through all the paperwork before it's yours."

"Because this is a big deal to me, and if you want to play the told-you-so game I told you when you bought that huge truck that it wasn't practical for the age group of most of your clients. Remember?"

"Touché."

"Besides. I'm already up here." Not really taking any joy in pointing that out, she didn't want to argue with him. "I've got to go."

"I'm sorry. Congratulations, Liz. Selfishly I'm not looking forward to you moving away."

Unfortunately, Dan was always a little selfish, but that was just part of his character. "We'll be friends no matter where I live."

"I know, but I don't have to like it. You *are* going to let me list your house, aren't you?"

She'd thought long and hard about this last night. It hadn't been easy. Her friend Missy was also a Realtor, and though she was closer to Dan, he could be a little spiteful sometimes and there was no sense giving him a chance to sabotage the sale. He was sometimes weird like that, and probably why he didn't have a ton of friends. Exactly the reason they were nothing more than friends.

"I'm going to let Missy list it," she said.

"I thought you might." He sounded disappointed.

"Doesn't mean you can't be the one to sell it, though." The truth was he usually sold houses way more expensive than hers.

"Yeah. True. All right. I'll see you."

The line disconnected. No "best wishes." No "good luck." Not even a less than enthusiastic "I'm happy for you."

She'd better let Missy know she needed her to list the house before she found out from someone else. She leaned against the porch rail and dialed her. She answered on the first ring.

"Hi, Missy. It's Liz. I need to put my house on the market."

"No problem. I'm happy to do it, but what's going on? This seems kind of out of the blue. Are you relocating for work?"

"Something like that. I'll fill you in when we get together."

"Whatever the reason this is great news for me. Finding one-story ramblers with over five thousand square feet is hard these days. I have several older couples looking for places just like yours. This will be an easy sale. Think about what you want for it, and I'll pull the comps. When can you meet?"

"I'm up in the mountains. How about the Monday after Thanksgiving?"

"I'm holding you to that."

"You can." Her dream was now a work-in-progress. Filled with starry-eyed hopes for a future just like her grandparents', she thought this Christmas would be the best Christmas since the last one she'd spent here.

She belted out a fa-la-la-la-la with joy in her heart, then closed her eyes. It was so quiet she could hear herself breathe. A bird called in the distance, probably warning his friends that someone had arrived. She wondered just how long the house had been empty. She had a million questions.

Pine filled the air the way it did right after a big rain.

A twig snapped in the distance. She double-stepped to the door, looking over her shoulder. Probably deer or a rabbit scampering around. Hopefully not a bear, because there were plenty of them too. A thin branch from a holly bush swung back and scraped her cheek. Served her right for not watching where she was going.

Her cheek stung. She patted it, feeling the stickiness that indicated the spiny leaves had won that round.

Off to the side of the door there was a large rectangle where a sign must have once hung. The screw holes were still there, but the sun had bleached the wooden timbers around it, leaving a large dark spot.

She pulled open the screen door and stepped between it and the front door.

The whole house could use a new coat of stain. She rubbed her finger across the dry wood.

Liz pressed the code into the lockbox and then removed the key and opened the door.

The musty smell was only part of what stopped her in her tracks.

She stood there, frozen for a long moment. She wasn't prepared for what she'd walked into. Her eyes adjusted to the darkness.

The entire downstairs had been gutted.

"What happened?" She flipped a light switch out of habit. Of course, the power wasn't on. It was dim inside with all the windows boarded over. Perhaps that auctioneer had been more clever than she'd given him credit for. If anyone had peeked in the window and seen this . . . she'd lay bets that there'd have been markedly fewer bidders on auction day.

She swallowed back a wave of emotion. A lump grew in the back of her throat.

This place—once beautiful—had been torn apart without a care for its former grandeur. Had it been intentional? Or vandals?

Strange faux walls were oddly placed, throughout the gutted downstairs. Apparently to display the art. Others weren't walls at all, but more like cubicle panels. She walked over to where the fireplace had been. A huge panel hung from the vaulted ceiling on chains. She pushed her weight against it and it swung out enough for her to see that thankfully the beautiful stonework appeared to be in decent shape behind it.

"What were they thinking covering this up?" She supposed she should be grateful they hadn't ripped the whole fireplace out.

She turned on her phone flashlight to get a better look at the fireplace. Something reflected in the light. She used her knee to hold the hanging panel away from the wall and reached for it. As soon as her hand grazed it, she knew what it was. She tugged it from the wall and held it close.

How did this fragile angel make it through what must have been one crazy demolition?

A night-light. One of many that used to be here. Each handmade. The clear stained-glass angel held a horn, her dress flowing behind her.

"Oh, Gram. I'm glad you're not here to see this place."

Her heart hung heavy in her chest. She'd prepared herself for repairs—even a lot of them—but this was as if someone had come in and just slashed the life and memories from the place.

She glanced at the glass angel in her hand.

I guess angels can survive anything. She hoped she could survive this too. Someone here in town had made these for Gram. She'd always treasured them.

She knew what every inch of this house should look like. Aside from this little angel next to the fireplace hidden by the tacky hanging panel, she didn't recognize any of it.

Devastating regret assailed her.

She allowed herself to give in to the despair. She wasn't sure how long she cried. But rather than flee, and leave this mistake in her rearview mirror, she gathered her composure and sat there letting her tears dry against her skin until she thought of a bright side.

"It's a clean slate." Another tear slipped down her cheek. She swept it away and concentrated on her last time here.

Where she stood now was the great room. Lodge plaids and jewel tones that celebrated nature had once accented gleaming hardwood floors. Practically every piece of furniture had had a story. Local artwork had graced the walls, along with a few of Pop's prized catches—fish and deer. Also on this level had been the kitchen, dining hall, master suite with an en suite bath, and laundry room.

Disappointment weighed on her. At least the walls looked to be in good shape, although there were tons of wires hanging from them. She'd heard of people stripping a house before it went to auction, but would it really be worth the effort to make a few bucks on a used fixture?

She put one foot on the staircase, but two treads up it was clear that it was in dangerous disrepair—broken balusters and some treads completely missing. Looking up, she saw water damage, probably the culprit of the demise of the once beautiful staircase.

The new roof had given her a false sense of security. On the bright side—she had to think of a bright side or else she'd break down and cry again right here—the roof was one less thing she'd have to fix.

She wanted to see the upstairs, hoping that by some miracle it was in good shape, but one more attempt to step on the stairs was all the warning she needed. She did not want to be stuck here hurt by herself overnight, and her phone was showing only one bar right now.

She walked back into the middle of the room and sat on the floor. She could hear Dan's *told-you-so* as loud as if he'd followed her up here and shouted it into her ear.

She'd let nostalgia cloud her good judgment.

This place would never be like it was when she was kid.

It was going to be a big enough challenge to get Angel's Rest going again, furnishing the whole place and fixing those things that years of neglect required, but now she'd have to renovate before she could even get to that stage.

Her dreams of reopening the inn seemed to be slipping right out of her hands as quickly as she'd held them there.

Chapter Five

Liz steadied herself as her eyes began to sting and a sudden wave of nausea came over her. Hopefully, it was from mounting disappointment, and not from poisonous gas or mold in the house. See, it could be worse.

She stepped outside to get some air. She must have lost all track of time, because now, on top of all the bad news, it was getting dark. She hadn't meant to stay long. She hadn't even figured out where she was staying tonight, and driving down the mountain in the dark could be a little sketchy until she got to know the roads better.

There was no time to dawdle. She hurried to her SUV, glancing one last time back at the house. At least from the outside it still looked like Angel's Rest.

She drove out to the road and turned right. She kept her foot on the brake most of the way down the mountain to keep from picking up speed down the steep grade.

When she got to the bottom and saw the flashing light on Main Street she breathed easier.

She dropped one hand into her lap, and heard the key ring jingle in her pocket. She'd forgotten to put it back in the lockbox.

For the life of her she couldn't remember if she'd even closed the front door. She dreaded the drive back up the mountain in the dark, and really what could possibly happen? Maybe a good breeze would clear out some of the funky air.

Liz had half a mind to just drive straight home, but she still felt a little woozy. She parked in front of the Creekside Café and walked inside. There was a cheerful clatter amid the murmur of conversations.

"You did come back." Maizey recognized her. "I didn't expect you so soon. Just you?"

Just a few hours to be exact. "Yes, Maizey. Thank you."

"I'll tuck you right back here." Maizey led the way to the booth in the front corner by the window.

Liz slid onto the bench seat.

"Are you okay, sweetie?" Her brows pulled together. "You don't look so good."

"I'm fine, thank you." Liz pasted a smile on her face. "I just got some bad news."

"I'm sorry, honey. On a bright note, you're here. Of all the places I've ever been this is the one place that has always done me right."

"I've always felt that way about Antler Creek too."

"So, you've been here before. I mean before the time this morning?"

"Yes, but not in a very long time. My grandparents owned the inn up on Doe Run Road."

"Angel's Rest?" Maizey sat right down with her and plopped her pad and pen on the table. "Wait a minute." She stared a good long moment at Liz. "You are *not* little Lizzie?" She held her hand up about yea high to the table. "Long brown braids, and eyes as bright and big as a day-old calf's. By golly, I do see it. Why didn't you say something when you were in here before? I miss your grandparents. Lindley and Josie were good folks. Everyone felt their absence when they left."

"Then I guess you know my grandfather passed away a few months after they left, and Gram wasn't far behind him. I still swear she died of a broken heart."

"I heard about that, we were all heartbroken by the news. Let me tell you, though, I don't think dying of a broken heart is a joke. I believe that really happens." She placed a weathered hand on top of Liz's. "They did love each other. A real love. You just don't see relationships like that much. Are you married?"

"Me? No. I'm holding out for a relationship like theirs."

"Ain't we all?" Maizey said.

Liz wondered if Maizey had ever been married.

Maizey stood. "What can I get you to eat?"

"I don't even know what I want. How about the special?" And no sooner had the words left her mouth than her mind drifted to the man who'd suggested the special this afternoon, and the door opened and in he walked as if on cue.

He'd spotted her too. His smile was broad, the skin at the edges of his eyes crinkling in a friendly way. He nodded, and mouthed a hello.

She felt her cheeks flush. Glancing quickly down at her menu, she hoped he hadn't noticed.

He climbed onto the barstool at the counter. The same one he'd been sitting on earlier.

Maizey slid a tall glass of sweet tea on the table in front of Liz.

She remembered. Liz didn't get this level of service at the restaurant she went to three times a week. And that just added to her disappointment. She'd had such high hopes that her dreams of owning Angel's Rest here in Antler Creek were going to come true.

She wished now she hadn't shared the news about her purchase with Peggy. Truth be told, half the reason Liz hadn't worried too much about finding a place to stay was that in the back of her mind she'd hoped she could talk the auction company into letting her stay there. It had been a silly notion anyway, but she still could hardly believe the state of the place.

At this point she might as well just go home.

Her heart hung like an anchor in her chest. Saddened by the destruction, she could barely think.

Liz picked up her phone and texted Peggy.

> **Liz:** I'm at the mountain house. It's gutted. Don't count on the sunrise pictures.
>
> **Peggy:** Oh no. Sorry. No big deal though. You can fix anything.
>
> **Liz:** This is bigger than me.
>
> **Peggy:** There's never been a project too big for you. Trust your dream.

LIZ SAT BACK in her chair. Peggy was right. She'd been tossed way worse projects than this to handle that were already over budget and in red status from a timeline perspective. Sure, the mountain house hadn't turned out to be anything like what she remembered or expected, but that didn't mean things couldn't be put right. Better even. Maybe. She just had to put a budget and plan together.

Liz: Maybe I'm overreacting?

Peggy: She probably just needs a little makeover.

Liz: Don't we all. LOL

That was it. Some major cleanup would be a start. Walls would need to be replaced. She'd get quotes on what this would take before she threw in the towel. And definitely before she mentioned anything about it to Dan.

She grabbed her phone and texted Peggy again.

Liz: Not a word to Dan. Don't feel like more told-you-sos from him.

Peggy: My lips are sealed.

FEELING BETTER ALREADY, she took another sip of her tea. Maizey slid the special in front of her. Country fried steak, mashed potatoes smothered in peppery white gravy, and a generous serving of green beans, with a fresh roll as big and fluffy as those she remembered from school days. She breathed in the savory smells. Comfort food was exactly what she needed right now.

"This is perfect. Thanks, Maizey."

The stranger stood up from the counter carrying a paper sack. He must've ordered his dinner to go.

"Have a nice evening, Maizey," he said.

He smiled at Liz, and their eyes connected for an awkwardly long moment. Long enough that she knew his eyes were as blue as a clear spring sky, and his perfect smile was hard to look away from. She forced her attention back to the plate in front of her. By the time she chanced a look back, he was getting into the white pickup truck parked out front.

She ate quietly as he drove off down Main Street. The food was making her feel a little better physically and about the possibilities of Angel's Rest. If the bones of the house were still good, there was still a chance she could bring the inn back to its original glory. She'd gotten a good price on the property, and she did still have a budget.

Peggy was right. It was just another project. *I never say no to the impossible projects, and I always manage to get them done.*

She dug in her purse, pulled out an envelope, and began jotting down milestones.

The problem was she didn't know what she didn't know. She needed a real contractor to come out and assess the situation before she could make a decent plan and prioritize. If she'd purchased this property outright, rather than at auction, she'd have gotten a full inspection so that she'd know exactly what she was walking into.

Okay, so it's a little backwards, but not the end of the world.

A good home inspection was worth its weight in gold. She'd heard Dan say that a million times. She had a sneaking suspicion that Dan got a nice kickback from the home inspector for all the business he sent over, but that didn't change the fact that it was good advice.

"What else can I get you?" Maizey pulled her hands to her hips. "My pie makes everything better."

Liz shook her head. "I'll pass on that pie, but I do need to find a place to stay."

Maizey nodded slowly, as if she was thinking. "You know we

don't have a hotel or inn around here. There's one two exits up on the interstate. I don't know how nice it is."

"Oh, I was hoping for something here in town."

"Well . . ." She pressed her finger to her lips. "It's not actually a rental, but I do think I know where you could stay. Nothing fancy, just a second-floor walk-up apartment."

"That would be perfect. I just really need to settle in somewhere for a few days and get my head right."

"Let me go make a couple calls. I'll be back."

Maizey walked behind the counter and disappeared into the kitchen. Liz was exhausted. The food had helped, but today had been one trying day. She hung her head in her hands, closing her eyes to hopefully chase the headache away.

"So what's got your head all messed up, dear?" Maizey said, startling Liz.

Liz jerked her head up. She wasn't sure if she really wanted to share, but then maybe she knew someone who could help. "It's a long story. I'm not sure I even know where to begin."

"Cut to the chase."

"I need to find someone reputable to do a home inspection."

Maizey's eyebrows shot up. "Are you thinking of buying up here?" She seemed delighted with the prospect.

"Well, that's normally how it would go, but actually I already bought a place." Liz leaned in and lowered her voice. "At auction. Sight unseen, so I need an inspection to figure out just how much work I have ahead of me."

Maizey's lips pulled into a tight line.

"What's wrong?" Liz asked.

"You bought Angel's Rest, didn't you?"

Liz pulled in a deep breath. "I did."

47

"Oh, honey. I'm sure that was quite a shock." She patted Liz on the shoulder. "Well, normally I'd recommend Ronny Ryan. He does the home inspections around here, but he's on a cruise with his wife. Matt Hardy is in town for the holidays, though. I bet he could do it. I wish I'd known sooner, he was just here. I'm sure he can help. If not, he'd most definitely be able to help you find someone. He's helping out down at the church this week. You could probably find him there tomorrow morning."

"Matt Hardy." Liz jotted the name on a napkin. "Thank you, Maizey. You've been really helpful."

Maizey handed her a slip of paper. "Here's the address of the apartment I was talking about. I just spoke with Dottie. They have an upstairs apartment for their boys, Jeffrey and George Junior, but they won't be home from college for a couple of weeks, so you can stay there. I don't think she'll take any money, but I'll let you two fight that out."

"This is amazing. Thank you so much."

"No problem. Glad to help. Once you know what you need done we have lots of handy guys around here looking for work this time of year. I wish you luck with that project. It would be so good for this town to have Angel's Rest back. You take care and keep me posted." Maizey laid the ticket on the table, and flitted off to another table.

Liz paid at the counter. Anxious to gain clarity about her options, she drove back toward the church before heading to the apartment. If someone was there, maybe she could get a phone number for Matt Hardy, and save herself the drive back tomorrow.

Liz parked in the church parking lot, then walked up the four steps that led to the oversize doors of the old stone structure. She put her hand on the heavy iron door handle and gave it a tug. The door swung open easily, welcoming her in.

Inside, the dark wooden pews were empty. She walked down the center aisle between them.

Light shone through the tall arched stained-glass windows. A colorful praying angel looked over her. The brilliance of the colored light sparked an emotion in her. Lately she'd felt like a stained-glass window in a dark room. Like she had something special and wonderful ahead, she just wasn't sure how to make it shine. She blinked back a tear. Her grandparents would delight in the fact that she was back in Antler Creek. Just like Pop and Gram, this town had always been the light in her life.

She'd been to this church before, but it had been a long time ago with her Pop and Gram. She counted the rows to where they'd always sat. The sixth row on the right. Her fingers grazed the top of the worn wooden pew. Pop loved to brag that they'd never missed a Sunday service since the day he and Gram had been married in this church. Maybe that was the secret to their wonderful relationship.

She could imagine Gram as a young bride in a long white lacy veil. She'd been beautiful. A chill ran down her arm.

The last time she'd been to church might have been right here in this one with her grandparents. It had definitely been way too long.

Men's voices carried through the building, followed by hammering from the back of the church, where the fellowship hall had been. She poked her head into the room. Three men worked, while a huge white dog lay sprawled on the floor, looking disinterested. The size of the dog stopped her, but she relaxed a little when she realized the dog hadn't bothered to even lift his head, just his eyebrows above big droopy eyes.

"Hi. Excuse me," she said from the doorway. "I was wondering if anyone here might know Matt Hardy."

Chapter Six

At the sound of his name, Matt stepped from behind the set of cabinets he was getting ready to hang in the church kitchen. "That's me."

Recognition registered on her face. "You again? Hello." Her lips tugged into a smile.

"Hello again." He jostled the cabinet. Pastor Mike took his end. "Thanks, man." Matt walked toward the woman. "What can I help you with?"

"I was talking to Maizey over at the café. I need someone to do a home inspection and she said the regular guy is out of town, but that you might be able to help."

He leaned against the wall and folded his arms across his chest. "You're thinking about buying a house around here?"

"Wouldn't need an inspection if I wasn't, now would I?"

He liked her spunk. "I'm sorry. You just don't look like the type of folks we usually get buying property around here. Where are you from?"

"I live in Charlotte, but I plan to move here. I want to open an inn."

"Really?" Something about her intrigued him, but he knew

better than to get mixed up with another city girl. Robyn-with-a-"y" had taught him that lesson.

"Why is that so surprising?"

He shrugged. He couldn't say what was on his mind. That she would make for a very pretty addition to the town. "The shoes?"

She glanced down at her designer boots.

"And the perfectly matched ensemble."

"So?" She pointed to his black boots and belt. "You match."

"True, but it's the way you match. Like a model in one of those fancy magazines." He regretted it as soon as it came out of his mouth. It didn't even sound like a compliment, although in his head it had.

"Should I be flattered or offended?"

"Neither. Well, probably both. I'm sorry, it has nothing to do with you." *Great, I'm just digging myself in deeper.* "I didn't catch your name."

"Liz."

When her grandparents had left town, he'd thought he'd never get the chance to see her again. He knew it was her. He couldn't believe she was right here after all this time. "Yes."

She looked confused. "Yes?"

Snap out of it. Answer the woman. "Yes, I can help you. I mean, I'm not certified, but I can check everything out for you."

Pastor Mike chimed in. "He's better than the real inspector. He'll give you options you can afford and be realistic about what needs to be done now, and what can wait. Matt has saved us a ton of money, and he can do anything."

"Really?" A flash of relief eased the lines in her face. "If that's true, I definitely need your help."

"Oh it's true." Matt nodded toward the man, then whispered to her. "He's the pastor here."

"Oh? I'm so sorry. I didn't mean to imply—"

"No worries, ma'am." Pastor Mike gave her a nod. "Help the lady out, Matt."

"I'm going to be tied up here for a couple of days, and then it's Thanksgiving. How about we meet early the next week? Maybe Tuesday around ten?"

"More than a week? If that's as soon as you can get to it, I guess it'll have to do."

She'd never make it at a poker table. The disappointment was as clear as a flashing neon sign on her face. "You look disappointed."

"I'm anxious."

"I can meet on Thanksgiving morning, if that works for you."

"Yes. That definitely works for me. I'll see you Thursday at ten." She smiled, and her eyes danced as she spun around and began to head out with a lift in her step.

"Miss? What's the address?"

She stopped and turned around. "That would help, wouldn't it? Doe Run Road. It's the—"

"There's only one place on Doe Run Road."

"Right."

"You're the one who bought it at auction this morning?"

"Yes."

He shook his head; how had he not recognized her at the café? No wonder she'd caught his eye. "You knew it was an inn before."

"I most certainly did. A beautiful inn."

"You didn't see it before you bid?"

53

"No. I know, I know. I didn't get a chance to see it before I bid. Not exactly my best move, but I couldn't risk losing it. The inn is very special to me. Besides, how bad a deal could it be? Location is everything, right? And Antler Creek is one awesome location for an inn."

"It hasn't been an inn for a very long time. The place has been gutted. It's changed hands a couple of times. It was last an art gallery."

"I was up there earlier today. I saw." She raised her hand as if she couldn't stand to hear more.

He couldn't blame her. It was a tragedy what had happened to that place. With a gentle smile, he said, "Okay then. I'll see you Thursday."

"Thank you so much. This has been my lifelong dream. I just hope it's doable."

She wasn't the only one thinking about lifelong dreams at the moment. "Anything is possible. I'll see you on Thursday, Liz."

He stood there watching as she walked out of the room. Her boots echoed through the sanctuary, and with each step his heart did a two-step. Liz Westmoreland was back in Antler Creek.

Pastor Mike cuffed his shoulder, practically giving him a heart attack. "She's a looker."

Matt nodded. "She's more than that."

"You know that from a five-minute first meeting?"

"I've met her before."

"Who is she?"

Matt didn't even hesitate. "She's the woman I'm going to marry."

Chapter Seven

Matt turned over and punched his pillow, trying to get comfortable. I should have told Liz that I was the one she outbid on the old place on Doe Run Road. The thought had tumbled around in his brain for the last two hours.

She might not trust my assessment if she knows.

But he knew that was doubtful, although it was a mounting list of problems. She might think he was just trying to scare her off or talk her out of the property, which wasn't the case. The truth was she'd caught his attention ... again. The last thing he wanted was for her to leave.

She'd looked kind of familiar the first time he'd seen her in the diner, but now that he knew about her connection to the inn he remembered everything about her.

The two of them shared more in common than just bidding on Angel's Rest.

They'd spent a lot of hours together fly-fishing the stream and hiking these hills as kids. Not just the two of them—there was always a big group of kids on those outings—but she'd intrigued him even back then. His first crush.

He only had to remember the one new girl. She'd been a stranger to all of the kids, and her focus had been on spending time with her grandfather, not the other kids. She might not remember him, but he sure remembered her.

If he'd only been up-front with her about the auction, and the fact that he'd already conducted the in-depth inspection, he wouldn't have to wait until Thursday to see her again.

Each day dragged by, and when Maizey told him that she was staying in George and Dottie's apartment, Matt found himself spending more time in town than usual hoping to bump into her, with no luck.

On Thanksgiving morning, Matt rolled out of bed at six o'clock and grunted out a hundred push-ups followed by a hundred sit-ups the way he did every morning. With his blood pumping, he went to the kitchen and preheated the oven. Out the window, the low morning light rose like smoke from the night grass.

He'd had plenty of invitations for a hearty Thanksgiving meal and probably more desserts than he was willing to exercise off, but this year he couldn't bring himself to spend it with anyone. He missed Dad.

Just because he wasn't up to spending Thanksgiving with anyone didn't mean he didn't like a good turkey dinner, though, and he was fine with dinner for one.

Memories of Thanksgivings with Mom and Dad filled his head. It would never be the same now that Dad was gone too.

The oven beeped, letting him know it was up to the desired temp. He hadn't even started yet. His coffee had cooled during his walk down memory lane too. He dumped it into the sink and took the turkey tenderloin he'd picked up at the market yesterday out of the refrigerator.

He gave the tenderloin a rubdown with olive oil, then added fresh thyme, sage, garlic, coarse salt, and fresh pepper before popping it into the oven and setting the timer for forty-five minutes.

Then he pulled cans out of the pantry and placed them on the kitchen island next to the fresh eggs Pastor Mike had given him yesterday for helping out. It didn't take him long to put together candied sweet potatoes and one of those green bean casseroles. He opened the large oven door and slid both dishes on the rack below the turkey. Then he worked up a batch of stuffing and set it to the side. He'd have to make the gravy when he got back.

By the time he'd scrambled a few egg whites and drunk a hot cup of coffee, the timer on the oven was ticking off the final few minutes on the turkey. He shoveled the last two bites of his eggs into his mouth, turned off the oven, and covered the loaf pans that his casseroles were in with foil before heading out to meet Lizzie at the inn.

She had the same effect on him now that she had all those years ago the first time he laid eyes on her serving hot chocolate one frigid winter night before Christmas with her grandmother. His parents had taken him to see the lights.

It had been a cold December night and Mr. Jarvis had hooked up his hay wagon behind his draft horses and chugged a trailer load of locals up the steep path to see the holiday lights. There hadn't been anything fancy about it, just a great way for people to spend time together, and celebrate the holidays with some a capella caroling. It was sort of the unofficial kickoff to the holiday season. There'd been no town tree lighting back then. Other than the live nativity at the church, the Westmorelands' extravagant light display and treats at the inn was the big attraction.

People still talked about those times now. They'd been a part of the fabric of this town for so many years.

Everyone in town participated.

Waiting for her to come back that summer had felt like a lifetime.

Once the inn closed, the town decorated the big cedar in front of town hall the first Friday night of December. It wasn't the same, though.

Matt scooped out a big dish of dog food. "Come on, Elvis. Time to eat."

That dog was never in a hurry. He lumbered into the kitchen, stopping to stretch and yawn. "You be a good boy while I'm gone. I won't be long." He patted Elvis on the head and left to meet Liz.

He was running early, so he took the long way around, back down through town. Antler Creek was quiet on this bitter cold morning. Then again it was still a little too early for people to realize what they'd forgotten at the store for turkey day just yet.

As he passed by, there were only three cars in front of the market—proving his point.

Doe Run Road was a frosty sight this morning. The freezing rain had laid a thick layer of ice along the bare branches, weighing them down so much that they seemed to reach for the other side of the road, forming a glistening tunnel. In places, limbs had fallen into the road. Ice cracking into what looked like shards of glass sprawled on the pavement.

Matt glanced at his watch. He'd planned to be early, but he could see by the fresh tire tracks on the road that he hadn't been the only one up and ready to go early this morning. She was already here.

His pulse quickened. Why? They hadn't really known each

other all those years ago, and she'd had a boyfriend waiting on her at home, so they'd just been casual friends doing things in a group with other kids from the church. But she was different from the girls he'd known. Confident, and unaware of how cute she was . . . even when she was wearing hip waders and a fishing hat.

Matt took in a deep breath. *Get ahold of yourself,* he thought.

Until Liz came back to town he wasn't the least bit interested in getting involved again. He was fine being alone. Completely fine with it; in fact, he preferred it that way. His house was always clean. There was no argument over what to watch on television, or the way he spent his money. He could eat whatever he liked when he liked. A woman was definitely not what he needed right now.

But it's Lizzie.

No. Don't fix what ain't broke. Things were good the way they were. Uncomplicated.

She could go back to Charlotte, and I might never see her again.

"My point exactly," he said to himself. "I sure don't need to make that mistake again." He pulled into the driveway and parked next to her in front of the house. *Just get in there, give her the information she needs, then get out.*

He grabbed the bright orange rechargeable spotlight from his backseat. With his notepad in hand he walked to the door, rapping on it three times before letting himself inside. "Good morning."

"Hey." She spun around toward him, all bundled in a hip-length ski jacket, with the hood up. "Thanks for being on time. It's freezing in here."

Her nose was red, which made her look even cuter as she bounced up and down trying to expend some energy to warm up. He wished he'd thought to bring a kerosene heater for them to at least warm up around as they talked, but he wouldn't need that much time.

"We'll try to make this fast."

She clapped her gloved hands together. "I'm more interested in an in-depth look at what I've got to work with than a fast one."

"Of course. So, I guess I need to let you know . . ."

"What?" Concern danced in her eyes.

"I've already done a lot of this inspection."

"I don't understand." She looked around. "The electricity isn't on, so you couldn't have come last night."

"Right. No. I worked it up over the past few weeks." He could tell she wasn't tracking to what he was saying. "I was bidding on this place too."

"Oh!" Her eyebrows shot up, and a slight smile played on her lips. "You were?"

"Mm-hmm. You were just willing to pay more than I was." He noticed her lips tug to the left, as if that piece of information pained her. He hoped she hadn't paid much more than his threshold had been.

"Yeah, well you clearly had more current information than I had." She scanned the room, shaking her head. "I only stumbled upon it being up for sale on Thursday night. I had no time to check things out. I bid solely on emotion and great memories from my childhood." She raised her hand in the air. "I know that's not a popular methodology. I personally wouldn't recommend it either."

He laughed. He liked her moxie. "Well, it's yours now."

"Exactly."

"So, I've already done the in-depth look at the bones of this place and there are a few problems, for instance . . ." He took her arm and moved her about four steps to the right. "The folks from the art gallery didn't get professional input when they started removing walls, else they wouldn't have removed that one." He pointed above where she'd just been standing. "That used to be a weight-bearing wall. If it's left open it needs a structural beam there."

She took another giant step back. "That's important."

"Yeah, and as you can see there was some significant water damage. Nice that they'd repaired the roof. Too bad they left the huge mess. Rumor has it they took the insurance money and fixed the roof, but decided the building was too much work for the limited foot traffic they got up here. They closed the gallery instead."

"I can see where that could be the case." She walked around the room, then turned and looked his way with her head cocked. "If I'm understanding you correctly, you already have some idea of the extent of the necessary fixes and renovation involved."

"I do, and I'm happy to send it to you."

Her eyes narrowed. "Couldn't you have just told me that when I talked to you about doing the inspection?"

She was right. He could have. "That's fair. You're right, but you know part of the assessment depends on what it is you plan to do with the place. So, let's talk about what your plans are. That will impact the list of what really needs to be done, and the cost to do it."

"I probably should have asked what this inspection was going to cost me."

"I'm not going to charge you a dime for what I've already done as my own due diligence to bid on the place."

"Really? Why would you do that?" She seemed skeptical. "I mean, you have the information. I need it. Simple supply and demand."

That made him chuckle. "Maybe in the city. Around here, we call it the good neighbor policy." Right now was the perfect time to tell her he remembered her from those fishing trips in the stream with her grandfather, but for some reason the thought of saying that as they stood here in the freezing cold in the dark seemed creepy.

"So far all the neighbors seem pretty nice."

"Folks up here are the real deal. It's a good place to be."

"My best childhood memories are from here." She sucked in a breath, smiling as if she was seeing things the way they used to be. "I always dreamed of running the inn like my grandparents had. When they sold it and took off in that RV, I was devastated. I didn't understand it." She looked away. "Honestly, I still don't understand how they could leave this behind."

"I guess they wanted to travel?"

"Bucket list." She nodded. "Only none of us knew what was really going on until it was too late. Pop had been diagnosed with cancer, so they decided to throw caution to the wind. Go for broke, literally, and travel and see the nation until they couldn't."

"Not a bad way to go." Only he knew better. Cancer was a terrible way to go. He'd seen it attack and age his father in fast-forward time right before his eyes. It had been hard to watch. Finally, he'd just pretended he was helping some other person's grandfather. That had been easier than admitting to himself what was happening to Dad, and there wasn't a damn thing he could do about it.

"Somehow I don't think it was as fun as they thought it

would be. How could it be, knowing that any day could be your last together?"

He shook his head. The lump in his throat kept him from offering up any response at all.

"I feel like now I'm getting the chance to do what I was always meant to do." Her eyes glistened. These were clearly the words of her heart. "I want to bring Angel's Rest back to its original beauty."

He shook his head. He admired her dream, but this was a big task. "This place is a long ways off from that."

"You should've seen it back in the day."

He had. Well, not every room, but he'd been inside the living room at Christmas. It wasn't like this. *Tell her.*

"Where do we start?" she said with a smile.

Rain started pummeling the roof.

They both looked up. "Those metal roofs are great, but they can be noisy."

"I love the sound." She closed her eyes and tilted her chin toward the ceiling.

Her unjaded view intrigued him. When was the last time he'd really just pushed every tiny ounce of negativity away to enjoy something at its very core? He closed his eyes and looked up too. "Great sleeping."

Her eyes sprung open. "Yes!"

The gusto of her response jerked him back. He chuckled at how he'd gotten caught up in her moment. Like an otherwise reluctant trout striking a hand-tied dry fly skittering across the stream. "I'm glad to hear you want to turn this place back into the lodge—or an inn as you called it."

"I'm not even sure I know the difference between a lodge

and an inn or a bed-and-breakfast, but I'm going to have one," she said with a laugh. "At least sort of."

"I believe a lodge indicates there's recreation as well as a place to rest your head. Whatever you decide to call it, there isn't any other place to stay here in Antler Creek, and people still have fond memories of Angel's Rest." He walked to the back right corner of the space. "The kitchen used to be over here. Do you know what you have in mind for that?" He walked over to where a blue "W" was spray-painted. "The pipes are still behind this faux wall. It would have to be stubbed back out, but at least the plumbing wouldn't be a complete redo unless you want to move the water to another part of the room."

"It makes sense to keep the kitchen sink under this window. It's such a nice view. I brought a few sketches of what I had in mind." She crossed the room and picked up a leather folio from next to her purse and carried it back over to him. Flipping through a stack of papers, she pulled one out that had the word "kitchen" in bold letters down the left side. "Here you go."

He took it, then looked at her. "You did this?"

She nodded.

"Impressive."

"Thanks. I would have been fine with the kitchen the way it was if it had still been here, but since it's not, I may as well take advantage of a few newer layouts and conveniences." She handed the whole folder over to him. "I put together the original layout the best I could remember using some software I found online. It's not to scale or perfectly formatted, but it might help us assess my needs."

"Not bad." That was putting it mildly. He worked with guys who'd been educated in drawing plans who handed him less professional stuff than this. "You did good here. Really good, and it's reasonable."

Modestly, she shrugged. "You can Google how to do just about anything these days."

"That doesn't always end well, you know. Can't believe everything you see on the internet."

"Don't I know it," she said with a laugh. "I've had a few Pinterest fails. That site sucks me in every time. Especially with recipes, and I'm no cook."

"Then you probably can mark the bed-and-breakfast off of your list. Stick to the lodge or inn."

"True. I'll stick to what I know. At least when it comes to software and planning, I'm in good shape, and I'm no quitter."

"Good, because a project the size of this isn't for quitters." But he didn't for a second think she would quit this project.

The rain spattering along the roof became louder. "That sounds like hail." She raced to the front door, and flung it open. "It is."

"I was hoping that weather system would skirt us. As cold as it's been, it's going to get slick up here in a hurry." Matt motioned her back over. "We better make this fast."

She closed the door, and jogged back over to his side. Her eyes sparkled. "I'm with you on that."

Okay, so maybe I'm more than a little interested.

Chapter Eight

Matt had spent the better part of the week wishing this bad weather wouldn't hit town, but right now he was thanking God for unanswered prayers, because he couldn't think of a better way to spend his Thanksgiving than with Liz talking about the possibilities of the lodge. Or inn. Or whatever she decided to call the place. As long as she called it home she had his vote.

"On a bright note," he said, "most of the tear-out is already done. The only things you'll need to remove are all of these faux walls."

"Yeah. That's the weirdest thing I've ever seen. They even block most of the windows."

"There's lighting run everywhere. I never came here when it was a gallery, so I don't know what it looked like when it was in business, but it looks weird to me too. The faux walls will come down quick and easy." He shook one of them. "Demolition won't even take a day, and you might even be able to reuse some of the wood and Sheetrock for something."

"I like someone who can see the positive in a difficult situation. Thank you."

"You're welcome. We can store any possible salvage in the old barn. It's not pretty, but it's a good sturdy pole barn and it stays dry in there. Unless you're planning to stable horses anytime soon I'd say you can put the barn on the good-enough-for-now list."

"No horses." She shrugged. "Not to begin with. If I had children that would be a different story."

"Do you want children someday?" *None of my business.*

"Yes. Definitely."

She looked a little sad when she said that. He knew how she felt. He thought he'd have a couple of kids by this time in his life. *Focus.* "Here's just a high-level list of the major things that will need to be addressed first."

He could think of a lot worse ways of spending his holiday time off than with the adult version of the cutest freckle-faced girl he'd ever met. He still in all his years coming here hadn't met another woman who could cast a fly rod as well, and she'd only been about thirteen back then.

"First on my list would be to address these load-bearing walls that have been ripped out. They put the integrity of the entire building at risk. You have a couple of options. Either replace the wall that was once here. . . ." He walked the length of the room where the wall had been. ". . . or put in a structural beam."

"We need to put that wall back up," Liz said without hesitation. "Open-concept is nice, but this is a huge space and it loses the cozy feel this place used to have. I liked that there were so many different rooms and nooks to tuck away for privacy. Even when the place was full of guests I never felt like I didn't have my own space."

"Good. The water damage needs to be taken care of. I did

get up in the attic, and the new roof was done well. You don't need to worry about any problem with that, but until the rest of the water damage is addressed the upstairs isn't safe to access."

"At all?"

"No. The whole staircase needs to be addressed and there are two spots that need to be ripped out and totally replaced. You might find other damage below once those boards are ripped up, but there's no way to tell that just by looking."

"It'll be impossible to match the floor. Old, worn, lived-in floors are so gorgeous."

"I know a guy." Matt winked.

Her eyes grew openly amused. "You know a guy, huh?"

"Yeah. He has tons of this reclaimed flooring available. You won't need all that much, but it'll look warm and inviting. No one will ever know that it's been repaired."

She nodded. "I like your guy already."

I'd rather you liked me! The guy who knows the guy. He pushed the playful thought aside. "Repairing the water damage is a priority before you can do anything upstairs."

"I understand that." She rubbed her hands together. "So I can't go up there?"

"You can do whatever you like. The place is yours, but it's not safe. Especially with so little light. I wouldn't recommend it."

She exaggerated a pout, then nodded matter-of-factly. "I don't want to get hurt, but I'm dying to know if they destroyed everything up there too. Each of the named suites had a private bathroom, and the prettiest crown moldings. I always felt like a princess sleeping up there."

"I hate to tell you, but it's worse than this. Sorry."

Liz swatted the air. "I don't even want to see it then. That's such a shame." She ran her gloved fingers under her eye.

He wasn't sure if she was brushing away a tear or not, but he'd never been good with tears. Pretending not to notice, he forged along. "A lot of the wiring has already been upgraded, and there's a new panel box."

"Great."

"But . . . the wiring in the kitchen has been stripped out. You'll need to take a look at all of the electrical and make sure you've got what you need where you need it quickly. On the bright side again, since so much of the place is gutted right now it won't be too hard to get those wires pulled."

"I can make those decisions now. That won't be a problem."

"It'll be cheaper than adding it later." Matt flipped through the drawings she'd given him and walked around comparing what she had to the existing structure. "You'll have some plumbing changes required to add the bathroom you have here."

"Okay."

"The HVAC is practically new. You're lucky this was abandoned here in Antler Creek. Somewhere else someone may have stolen it. If not to have the unit itself then for the value of the copper. The trade-in value of the copper could be a fifth of the value of the whole unit. That's not chump change."

"So, there *is* some good news."

"Plenty of it. There's a lot to do to get this place up and running again, but the really big-ticket items are in pretty good shape."

She looked relieved. "Did you inspect the cabins out back?"

"I did. One is still filled with stuff from when your grandparents owned the place. I don't think it's been opened or used in years. The other appears to have been used as an artist-in-residency rental. Art supplies and modest furnishings, but it's all intact."

"I'd love to see it, but that rain isn't letting up."

"And it's a sloppy mess out there. Not to mention about a football-field sprint through overgrowth in the rain. That's another thing on the to-do list. They have some trenches dug from the house to the cabins. I'd thought at first someone had stripped copper pipe from the house, but when I looked closer it looks more like they were trying to run new water and quit mid-project. From what I can tell that cabin was on its own well but the pump is burnt up. The well could've gone dry. I'm guessing they were just going to run water off the building up here. Who knows?"

"I like the idea of having a separate well on the property. I'd love to grow my own vegetables and herbs back there somewhere."

"Then add a fence to your plan. The deer around here will call your garden their buffet. I'm dealing with that on the new row of trees I planted."

"Good suggestion." She tugged her phone out of her pocket and typed in a note. "How difficult will it be to get power turned back on so we can see what the situation is there?"

"Easy. We're on Valley Electric Co-operative power up here. They can get to you fast. They'll even do a safety walk-through with you, which will be good, because it appears to be the original wiring out there, and it's on its own meter box."

"So I might be able to actually stay there while work is under way if I need to." She rolled her eyes. "Once I get the water problem handled, of course."

"With a little elbow grease, I don't see why not. Be sure to get those trenches covered up. Those can be dangerous, especially once the ground gets covered with snow."

"Right." She let out a deep breath. "Talking through it with you it feels like an expensive and daunting task."

"It might not be as bad as you think, and if you use local workers, they're fair priced. You might have to be a little flexible. Some of these guys take off in the winter to hunt, but if you're patient they'll get it done. I'll get this worked up and get some estimates pulled together for you."

"This is way more than just an inspection. Thank you, Matt."

"I'm glad Maizey sent you my way. She didn't even know I was bidding on this place, but she definitely saved you some time and money by connecting us."

"It worked out great." Her smile was sweet.

"Are you in a hurry for these numbers?"

Her nose wrinkled. "Technically, no, but I'm dying to know if I'm living the dream, or recovering from a rash decision."

"I'm working over at the church all day tomorrow and Saturday morning, but I'll work on it Sunday. Where can I contact you?"

"My cell phone is the best way.

"Maizey helped me find a place here in town. Really nice couple. It's an upstairs apartment for their sons who are away at school. I can stay until they come home for winter break."

"You're staying at George and Dottie Goodwin's place?"

"Yes. How did you know?"

"It's a small town. That's great, though. They're good folks, and this is a safe town, but I'd still recommend keeping a tight watch over the project. These kind of projects are easy to turn into bigger ones that take a lot longer if you don't keep an eye on them."

"That's true on most types of projects. Which is why I'm here." She handed him her business card. "You can call me and let me know when you've got it ready. Then, we can meet up at the Creekside Café and go over it. Or you can email it to me."

" 'Store Development Project Manager'?" *Quite a job title. How the heck would someone with that kind of job have time for a project the size of this?* "Looks like if anyone has the experience to pull together a plan and keep people accountable it's you."

"You could say that."

"I just did."

"Okay, Captain Obvious, just get that inspection worked up and then I can make an educated decision on what my next steps are."

"You really want this to work out, don't you?"

"I do. I really, really do. I've dreamed of this place my whole life. Well, not like this, but how it once was."

The slight smile that played on her soft pink lips when she talked about this place mesmerized him.

"My happiest days were here in this place," she went on. "This town is special to me."

He couldn't argue with that. "Well, I guess you're in a hurry to get to your family for Thanksgiving dinner. I don't want to hold you up. I think I have everything I need."

"No. You're fine. I'm in no hurry today."

"No?"

They walked toward the front door.

She reached for the door handle and opened the door. Frigid wind rushed between them, so cold you could almost see the frost in the air. The wind had piled white pellets in the corner of the porch.

"It's going to be slick going down the mountain."

"I drive a Range Rover. I think I'll be fine." She pulled her coat tighter. "Maybe I'll even stop for some coffee to warm up on my way back." She took out her phone and pulled up the radar app. "That's a big storm cell." She turned her phone toward him. "We're in for a doozy."

"Nothing's open this afternoon around here. You can't spend Thanksgiving alone. Why don't you come over to my place?"

"I couldn't—"

"Look. It's not a big deal. I made a small dinner. Not fancy, but I'm not a bad cook, and I've been told I'm decent company."

One corner of her mouth twisted upward.

Her uncertainty showing, he didn't give her a moment to debate. "We can look at your plans and talk about them in the light with heat. Consider the meal a bonus."

"You don't have to do that. I'm the one who pushed for the Thanksgiving Day inspection. I should be feeding you."

"Didn't you say you don't cook?"

She laughed.

"You've got to be getting hungry."

She placed her hand on her stomach as it growled an answer for her. "I *am* hungry, and I could really go for a cup of coffee or tea. Something warm."

"Then it's settled. Come on. You can follow me." He didn't bother to wait for an answer; if he gave her the chance to say no . . . she would. He opened the door and swept his arm to hurry her outside.

He jumped behind the wheel of his truck, revved his diesel

engine, and drove out to the lane. She followed right behind him.

A feeling of satisfaction filled him as he carefully took the steep curves with her headlights in the rearview mirror. He turned off Doe Run Road and followed the cut-through that wrapped back up and around the mountain. It was only a few miles, but with the hail coming down the way it was it took a while to get there. He put his blinker on and watched her do the same as he turned down the path to his house.

He pulled in front of the porch, and she parked next to him.

Matt tested the steps for ice by kicking his boot against each tread, trying to scuff the ice to make it a little less slippery for her.

"Careful!" He put a hand out to steady her up.

"Thank you." She looked around, blinking.

"What did you expect?"

"I'm not sure, but it wasn't this. I don't remember seeing a house like this up here. It's gorgeous. How old is it?"

"It's pretty new." He looked up at the carefully designed porch. "It was just built to look old." It was everything he'd dreamed of. He understood her passion for her dream.

"They did a great job."

"Come on in." He walked inside and Elvis stretched long, only lifting his eyes until he saw Liz walk in. He slowly rolled over to his stomach then sat up. "This is my buddy, Elvis."

"I remember him from the church." He didn't lift his head. "Not much of a watchdog, are you there, buddy?"

That's an understatement. He took off his jacket and hung it on the coatrack next to the front door. She followed his lead then followed him into the den.

He stoked the fire he'd left burning in the fireplace. The

extra-deep hearth made it safe to leave burning. A must in this area in the winter.

"I love this fireplace." She held out her hands, warming them. Flames flickered to life as he prodded the thick logs.

The soaring two-story rock fireplace had been the biggest project of the house. It had taken painstaking patience to find just the right rock, and then the craftsman to pull off the construction of it. "It's built from all local rock, too."

"It's kind of a piece of art in itself." She looked up, admiring the craftsmanship. "Are all those iron contraptions over the fire for cooking? Or for show?"

"For cooking."

"Like they did in the old West, I guess?"

"Cast-iron cooking is the best."

"That seems like an awful lot of work."

"Not really," he said. "Once you put it in the cast iron it's just a matter of waiting until it's done. No different than an oven."

"That's really neat." She turned her back to the fire and stood there glancing around. "This feels so good. I was cold to the core."

He went to the kitchen and came back with two mugs of tea. "I hope you like the tea. My sister left it when she was visiting. It's her favorite."

She took the mug and hugged it to herself, then took a sip. "It's wonderful. Thank you. It hits the spot."

He hadn't invited too many people over since he'd finished the place and moved in. His sister, Krissy, had given him some unsolicited assistance decorating the place to keep it from looking like a man cave, which he'd thought was kind of a joke at the time. He had to admit that he was thankful for her help now as he viewed the place from Liz's perspective.

"I *really* shouldn't have come over," she said.

The comment caught him off guard, but there was a playful lilt to her words. Before he could ask why, she said, "This place is dangerous. It's giving me a hundred ideas."

He laughed with her. "I get it. Like you, I had a dream about living up here. This place is the product of probably three hundred sketches, and plans finally coming to fruition. So I get where you're coming from with Angel's Rest."

"I'm so glad you don't think I'm totally crazy."

"Not at all. Let me show you around."

"At the risk of blowing my budget with more ideas, I'd like that."

Matt took her through the house, room by room. Ending in the kitchen, which was on the back side of the floor-to-ceiling fireplace they'd been warming themselves by when they came in.

Liz stood in the kitchen with her mouth agape. "Wow." She stepped in and ran her hand along the cool granite countertops, then the smooth cherry finish on the thick legs of the island. The subzero refrigerator and freezer stood side by side as if they were ready for restaurant duty, and across the way was a four-foot-wide Heartland freestanding range. The kind she'd always coveted, with the cranberry inserts. "You must be a *very* good cook."

"I do okay."

"I'm impressed already."

He walked over to the oven and pulled out the Thanksgiving dinner that he'd prepared this morning. "Still warm. Hungry?"

"I am."

"Then that concludes the nickel tour."

"And you're going to feed me too? If that was the nickel tour I can't imagine what I would I get for a quarter."

Matt had a few ideas, but he wasn't so sure she'd want to hear them, so he kept his mouth shut before he put his size 12 boot into it.

Chapter Nine

Liz hitched herself up onto a barstool at the kitchen island while Matt removed the foil from the loaf pans.

She took in a lungful of the sweet and savory spices mingling in the air around them. Memories of Gram's home cooking when her family would come up for holiday dinners came rushing back. Those had been magical gatherings. There'd be so much food. This was more like a sampler platter from those days.

Matt walked over to a cabinet next to the refrigerator. Inside the wooden door, a panel of colorful lights and buttons on a flashy computerized panel looked out of place in the rustic home, but as soon as Matt pushed one of those buttons old country music poured through the speakers.

Alan Jackson's "Livin' on Love" played as he walked back over to the island and removed foil from the last stoneware loaf pan.

She swayed to the music. "You did all of this just for yourself?"

"A man's got to eat."

"Weren't you worried dinner would burn if you didn't get back on time?"

"No. I cooked this morning. I just left it in the oven to stay warm while I was gone so it would be ready for lunch. Didn't take much effort at all."

Says the man who can cook. "Seems like a lot of trouble for one person. Thanks for inviting me to share it with you."

"There's always plenty."

He probably planned for leftovers. He could make light of it, but she appreciated the gesture. He was a nice guy. She owed Maizey a big thank-you for connecting her with Matt.

"Can't have Thanksgiving without turkey, or stuffing, or, well . . . any of this." He pulled out the pan with the turkey tenderloin and drained the juices into a pot. One twist of a knob and a blue flame danced beneath it. In a bowl he added flour and whisked in a little milk, salt, and pepper; then, as the stock in the pan began to boil, he mixed the two together.

He's making gravy from scratch? She pinched her hand to make sure she wasn't dreaming. Nope. This was really happening.

As he continuously stirred the gravy, he said, "I'd rather have had some yeast rolls but that's one thing I haven't perfected, so you'll be sopping gravy with a piece of sandwich bread like me today." He paused, giving her a serious look. "You do sop . . . right?"

"Of course, and I'm perfectly okay sopping my gravy with bread." She should be, because had she been home alone for Thanksgiving there wouldn't have been any of this. If she were forced to eat what she had in the house then she'd have had to eat a low-calorie frozen entree, pickles, or peanut butter and crackers, because most of the time when she was home for meals it was that or a bowl of soup. She was thankful for this spread.

Matt took two plates down from the cabinet and handed her one. "Ladies first."

She put a little bit of everything on her plate. "This really looks delicious." One of these days she was going to have to perfect a few dishes. She'd planned to start putting Grandma's recipe cards to use years ago, but she still hadn't attempted even one of them.

He heaped food onto his plate. "Come on, let's eat in the dining room. It's a special occasion."

She hadn't much thought of Thanksgiving as being special since her folks moved away. Mostly she looked at it as a meal she didn't have to attend. Just a day to herself, and Lord knows there were never enough of those.

He flipped on the light as they walked into the dining room. The table was made of heavy wood with a warm finish. The chairs were big and upholstered in deep-jeweled tones. The chandelier was a mixture of wrought iron and wood—masculine and elegant at the same time.

Liz sat in the chair opposite him.

He hopped back up. "Hang on a second." He left the room and came back with a bottle of wine and two glasses.

He poured two glasses, handed her one, and raised his. "To following your dreams. Always something to be thankful for."

"Thank you, and thank you for sharing this lovely meal with me today." She took a sip from her glass.

"I wouldn't have had it any other way. It's nice the way this worked out." He dug a fork into his food, and she did too.

"This is delicious." She hadn't meant to sound so shocked, but really it might have been the best meal she'd had all year. "What do you know about my grandparents' inn?"

"Angel's Rest? I know that it was once a very popular resort that brought people back to the town over and over. The locals were thankful for all the community ties. The fly-fishing, hiking, things that highlighted the natural bounty of this area. I also know that at the holidays Angel's Rest lit the whole mountain in Christmas lights. People came from everywhere to see them, not that they had to. The glow could be seen from anywhere in the village below, but you had to make it up the mountain for the hot chocolate, cookies, and the special displays."

"Lights at the Lodge." He knew a lot. "Did you ever see them yourself?"

"I did."

She put down her fork. "Do you remember the big steam train that chugged through the yard?" She leaned forward. "Pop loved that thing. He absolutely lit up like a ten-year-old when he was messing with that train."

"I do remember the train." Matt took another sip of wine. "My favorite was Santa's workshop with the mechanical elves, though. Those things were so cool."

"It was quite a show, although only a couple of the elves actually worked. I don't think people even noticed that. Pop tried for years to get them going." Liz remembered it so well. Even now she could hear the tinny sound of the music that came from the speakers Pop had rigged up in the trees. "I wonder what happened to all that stuff when they headed off on their big adventure?"

"No telling. If it was sold around here I'm sure someone would know who bought it."

That thought excited her. What if she could recover that old train? "Do you think there might actually be a chance to find a few original pieces?"

"We could ask around. If not the Christmas stuff, probably some of the furniture. Flossie owns the antique shop and she knows the destiny of about anything you'd be looking for. I'll introduce you two."

"Thank you." She took another bite of stuffing. "How long did it take you to find this place?"

"I started designing the plans before I even really knew what I was doing. Then while I was in college I used it as one of my main design projects."

"You're an architect?"

"I am. It took me longer to design this place than to build it." He laid both hands on the table. "It was a dream that started when I was young. Then I went off to college. It was years before I could really draft a decent plan. I wish I'd thought to keep every version. I learned a lot along the way. Then I'd visit model homes and look through plans and come up with more ideas."

"I know how that is."

"Eventually I settled on one design and it quit changing and it became more refined. When I got to the point that the only things I was fussing over were hardware choices, I knew I was ready to actually get to work."

"That's really exciting. I won't have the luxury to wait like you did, but it has to be amazing to see what you dreamed of in your mind come to be."

"Oh yeah." He scanned the room with a look of accomplishment. "I just got done last year. It was worth every backbreaking moment. It's everything I ever wanted."

"Right down to the option to cook in cast iron in the fireplace?"

"That, and . . ." He leaned forward and whispered, "I've got a tree house out back."

"You do not."

"I do. One day when the weather is better I'll show you."

"Wishing for a son one day?"

"One day."

"That's sweet."

He shrugged. "Don't let it get around."

"Somehow I think this town is already on to you." She laughed and placed her napkin on the table. "This was lovely."

"Thanks for the company." He reached toward her. "I'll take your plate."

"Don't be silly. I might not cook, but I can wash a couple of dishes." She stood and collected the plates from the table and carried them into the kitchen. No dishwasher in sight. Just like a man. She started running water in the sink.

Matt walked in behind her. "You don't need to rinse those. The dishwasher is in that drawer to the right of the sink."

She looked at the wooden drawer. "Here?"

He nodded.

She tugged on the wooden cabinet drawer, and inside was all stainless steel. "This is the coolest dishwasher I've ever seen."

"Perfect when you don't dirty a ton of dishes at once. There's a second drawer below for when there are more dishes."

"Very nice. I might need one of these." She filled the dishwasher, then dried her hands on a red dish towel that had KISS THE COOK embroidered on it. She glanced back up at him.

"It was a gift."

"Put it on my tab," she teased. Liz pulled out her phone and looked at the weather radar again. "It looks like the worst of the storm is about over."

"What's your hurry? Let's take a look at your plans under some light."

She followed him back into the dining room and they spread out all of her drawings. Matt made a few suggestions on the layout, most of which she really liked, and they even laid out electrical-outlet placements while they talked through the usability of what she'd designed.

"I think you've got a really good plan here." He looked up. His gaze connected with hers. "I'm glad I got to be a part of this with you."

There was an awkward silence as her mind reeled. Matt seemed so connected to Angel's Rest that it was a little unsettling, and she wasn't sure if it was in a good way or not.

He cleared his throat. "Do you remember those church outings they used to have at Angel's Rest during the summer?" He sat back in his chair, a thoughtful smile spreading across his face. "Those were great. People still talk about those days, and the hay rides to see the Christmas lights—"

"Of course I remember." Where was he going with all of this? They'd already talked about it.

"And the fly-fishing. I liked that the best. Really memorable," he said. Silence hung between them again. "I remember you from back then."

"You do?" She tried to imagine him younger.

"Yeah, and sadly I have to admit that you outfished me every time. I've never met another woman who could cast a fly rod like you."

She laughed. "Pop taught me. I was fly-fishing from the time I could walk. He gave me this little bucket hat and he put all these colorful lures all over it. It was so pretty, but I'd never use any of the lures. No matter how many I lost or got hung up in a tree I refused to give up any of the ones on my hat. Those things are expensive. Of course, at the time I had no idea. I was just a little thing. I loved being out there with him. He spoiled me, not so much with gifts, but with his time. I was so lucky."

"Your grandpa was a great man. He must've had the patience of a saint to put up with all us kids all the time."

"He lived for that." She looked at Matt. "I can't believe I don't remember you. Maybe it's the beard."

"Yeah. Maybe. I didn't have this back then." He rubbed his hand across his beard.

"A ten-year-old with a beard would've been memorable." He was good-looking, but she'd never been a fan of a beard. Why a man would want all that scruff on his face was hard for her to comprehend.

"I remember you serving hot chocolate in a red coat and Santa hat with your grandmother one Christmas too. Then, you rode back down the hill on the hay wagon and brought enough cookies for everyone."

"Snickerdoodles." Her voice was soft. "It's still the only cookie I know how to make."

"They were good."

"Those were great times. I want to bring that back to this town."

"I hope you will. This town could use that burst of Christmas spirit again."

A tingle of excitement coursed through her, but when her eyes locked with Matt's that tingle turned into a rioting panic.

She glanced at her watch. "Oh gosh. Look at the time. I've taken up nearly all of your day. I'm so sorry."

"Don't be silly. This has been the best Thanksgiving I've had in a while. I'm glad it worked out the way it did."

She wanted to run. To bolt straight out of there. Was she misdirecting her excitement over Angel's Rest toward this guy? She didn't even know him. Didn't even want a relationship. Especially now. There was no time for that, especially if he was going to be working on this project for her. These had been her memories for so long, and she wasn't sure she wanted to share them with anyone else.

His place had some feminine touches. For all she knew he was married. "You know, it's none of my business, but why are you spending Thanksgiving alone?"

He sat there quiet for a long moment. "I lost my dad last year. Cancer. My sister usually spends Thanksgiving in South Carolina. That's where she lives."

"Oh. I'm so sorry."

"I noticed your necklace."

Her hand went to the special sand-dollar pendant.

"Usually it seems like people either love the mountains or the beach. Not both."

She twisted it in her hand. "You're right. I've always been a mountain girl, but I worked on a project in South Carolina. In fact, I just finished it up. I found a real appreciation for the beauty of the coast while I was there. I kind of splurged on the necklace as a reward to myself on the project."

"I guess both have their charms. You couldn't force me to live on the coast, though."

"I don't know that I'd live there, but nature in all its natural glory is pretty amazing no matter what it is."

"True. Well, congratulations on your project."

"Thank you."

He looked around, then sniffed, and a slight grin settled on his lips. "Dad and I worked together on this place. We made a lot of memories in the process. I understand your love of Angel's Rest. Of those things that are special from the past. Come with me. Let me show you something else before you go."

Reluctant for a split second, she followed him into the living room.

He pointed to a reclaimed wood frame hanging next to the fireplace. The wood was rough, some notches deeper than others.

"That picture is the first time Dad took me fishing."

She could see his good looks even in the softness of the little-boy features. He was looking up at his father with so much pride as he held a tiny wiggling fish. "That's so sweet."

"Dad made that frame. That wood was the seat of the old wooden boat we used to take out. Those notches represented the fish we'd caught. How big they were."

Her heart swelled. "Oh my gosh. That's so neat."

"I really miss him. He was a good man."

She saw a tenderness fill his eyes.

"That's the bad thing about love. When it's gone it hurts like the devil. I treasure all of our memories together up here."

"I think you do understand why I hold memories of Antler Creek so dear." Her heart ached for his loss. Matt was clearly a good man too. Probably walking in his daddy's very footsteps. "Thank you for sharing that with me. I think our paths crossed for a reason." *Things always happen the way they should.* Pop's twinkling blue eyes danced in her memory. "I better get out of your hair."

"It's been nice. I'll get right to work on these numbers for you."

"Thank you for everything. Email me the reports and I'll go through them and then call you back with questions." She walked over to the door and pulled on her coat. "Thank you again."

He stepped out on the porch and waved as she drove off.

A gentleman to the end.

Liz shifted into reverse and turned to head toward the road, but her eyes locked on that rearview mirror until she could no longer see Matt.

Chapter Ten

The road down the mountain had been a little sketchy, but once Liz got to Main Street where things were flat it wasn't threatening. He was right. There wasn't one thing open in Antler Creek today. Not even the gas station. The road was empty except for her. Most everyone was probably eating or watching the ball game. There'd be no yard football today because of the weather.

Her mind kept drifting back to Matt, all the possibilities for the inn, and that dinner. He was a very good cook.

Matt had made some good design points today too, and if she wanted to update or make changes to the way the space was laid out, now was the time to do that while the place was mostly gutted.

She was dying to know what the ballpark estimates were going to look like. She'd gotten the place for much less than she'd expected to spend on her dream home, so she had a pretty good budget to work with. But it wasn't unlimited. She might be getting excited over nothing.

Technically, she could continue working while repairs got under way to offset the cost, but if she really wanted to get that inn going again, didn't she owe it to herself to give the project

100 percent instead of what was left of her time while working on opening another store for PROEM Service Group? Her job wasn't a nine-to-fiver. It wasn't even just a five-day-a-week job. It wasn't uncommon for her to be gone for weeks at a time on a project. That would never work.

If she ignored the inn for two weeks, that project could go completely off the rails. It quite honestly could cost her more than she'd make, and she made a very nice salary.

It was exhausting trying to decide whether to gamble on the dream or admit defeat. Dan would be quick with the I-told-you-sos. It was easier tonight to push past all the what-ifs with Matt on her side, though.

Liz parked on the street in front of the Goodwins' house. It was a pretty Craftsman-style home with a welcoming front porch and beautiful stone columns. Twice she lost her footing as she walked up the driveway to the back-stair entrance to the apartment. Thank goodness those stairs were protected from the northerly rain and ice.

She took off her coat and hung it on the thick wooden pegs of the hall tree. It wasn't an original piece, like the one she had at her house, but it did make her think about how inviting that would be in the front entry at Angel's Rest.

She could picture it sitting atop a richly colored hand-knotted Persian rug to anchor the space and give some warmth to the expansive original strip-oak flooring. A good rug could cover up a multitude of problems too, and there were several trouble spots, from what she'd seen in the dimly lit house this morning.

Character, she tried to convince herself.

The apartment had everything she needed, with an extra dose of testosterone. There was no mistaking that this was a young man's apartment. Leather, a couple of deer heads on the wall, and even a kegerator. Not that she minded. She was thankful for the comfortable place to crash.

She filled the teakettle and sat on the edge of the leather couch with her laptop. By the time the water began to boil and emit enough steam to whistle, Liz had added a couple more tabs to her spreadsheet. One she could populate with detailed repairs and cost estimates, and another for the nice-to-haves. She also started looking up contact information for services she'd need, like utilities, inspections, and local emergency contacts. She was a firm believer in planning for any disaster. If you were prepared for the worst, it seldom happened, but if God forbid something did happen the plan to recover had already been created under a cool head when all of the steps could be well thought out. A failure mode and effects analysis also provided a clear view of just how catastrophic the event was—keeping things in perspective.

With the teakettle quieted and her tea steeping in a big mug with an Appalachian State logo on the side, she went back to work.

Without knowing the numbers Matt would come up with, she put together a realistic budget based on her remaining cash on hand and credit available. If Matt's numbers exceeded this budget, she'd have to do the minimum work required to get it back on the market and walk away.

The thought made her stomach flip.

She took a sip of tea, hoping it wouldn't come to that.

She fidgeted with the spreadsheet, narrowing the wiggle room a little, but not putting the project at risk by expecting to work during the project.

Finally, she transferred the figures to her spreadsheet and

locked the cell with her final budget number. It was aggressive, but if she was going to abandon a dream over the number on this spreadsheet, she was going to give herself every opportunity.

The pressure was off of her now. She'd let the numbers decide the fate of Angel's Rest.

She'd either be going all in or be putting lipstick on the old pig to flip it and get out. Dan talked about flip houses all the time. Mostly cursing them for shoddy work, but they did pull in a profit. With the deal she got, hopefully she'd do more than okay and at least break even. Then, she'd just have to come up with a new dream, because if things didn't work out with this family property, she wouldn't have the heart to try with a different place.

Her phone rang, and Peggy's number displayed on the screen. "Hi, Peggy."

"Hey. I'm making my famous potato salad to take to my mom's for Thanksgiving and got to thinking, if you don't have plans why don't you join me?"

"Thank you, but I have plans."

"You do? Skipping Thanksgiving altogether isn't a plan, you know. Turkey has to be involved."

Liz laughed. Peggy knew her so well. "I had turkey a couple of hours ago."

"Was it fast food?"

"No. I met Matt over at the inn to go over the repairs needed. Kind of an after-the-fact inspection."

"Matt?"

"The inspector."

"So you're on a first-name basis with the inspector already?"

"Oh stop. He came highly recommended and I may have pushed a little to get the inspection sooner than next Tuesday.

I'm thankful for the Thanksgiving Day inspection. There was icy rain and hail, so he invited me to share his turkey lunch with him."

"You had a lunch date? I like what I'm hearing."

"It wasn't like that, but we did share lunch. He kind of insisted, and since I was the reason he was out on Thanksgiving I kind of felt obligated." But that wasn't entirely true. Why had she said that?

"Why are you dancing all around this Matt guy? He's cute, isn't he?"

Liz hadn't found him nearly as attractive at first sight as she had once they'd been talking for a couple of hours. He'd really grown on her. "He has a beard. You know how I feel about that scruffy look."

"You can clean him up. Did y'all have a good time?"

"We were inspecting the house. Talking renovation. But to answer your question . . . yes, it was nice."

"Just nice?"

"Okay, it was more than nice. And I can't even put my finger on when the mood shifted when I was at his house—"

"You were at his house? I thought you were inspecting the inn. Go on. Don't leave out a thing."

"It's not like that." *Or maybe it was.* "I almost felt as if I was with someone I'd known forever. Sort of, but also impossible, because he'd said himself that we hadn't really known each other, just been in the same place at the same time, and I didn't remember him at all."

"Remember him from what?"

"He used to go fly-fishing and hiking with my grandpa's group on the lodge outings. He even remembered how good I was with a fly rod."

"Sounds to me like he had a crush on you back then."

"Right, and he's been pining away for me since he was thirteen. I'm sure you're right, Peggy." Liz laughed. "But whatever it was, in a few days I should have some idea of how big this project is. I just set my budget in stone and locked the cell on my spreadsheet. It'll be a go or no-go."

"I really hope it's a go."

"Me too."

"What if your house sells while you're figuring all this out?" Peggy asked. "I ran into Missy at the store yesterday and she said she already had three clients lined up to see your place next week."

That was fast, but that was exactly why she'd listed it with Missy. She delivered results. "I'll add that to my project plan to figure out. Even if it sold the first week, I can eke out at least thirty to forty-five days to escrow."

"So, no problem."

"I guess not. But honestly if I can't restore Angel's Rest, I don't want to move. I like my house in Charlotte. If it hadn't been for stumbling over that auction I never would've considered putting my house on the market." Panic shot through her. She let out a steadying breath. "You know what, I appreciate you keeping me in balance about this, but I'm not going to jinx any of this by getting caught up in the negative thoughts. Once I get all the details from the inspection I'll know for sure what my next steps are, and I haven't signed anything with Missy yet. We don't meet until Monday."

"Good. You have a great head on your shoulders, I know I don't need to worry about you, but please promise me if you get lonely today that you'll call. Okay?"

"I promise." Liz was grateful for Peggy's friendship.

"Great. I can't wait to hear about the inspection. Happy Thanksgiving and I want you to know how thankful I am for our friendship."

"Me too, Peggy." Liz hung up the phone feeling blessed to have such a good relationship with Peggy. She wasn't only her boss, but a true friend. It had been a good day. Yes, there was a lot to be done at the inn, but she was feeling hopeful. In the sky a sliver of a moon hung in the nearly starless heavens tonight.

BLACK FRIDAY IN Antler Creek was nothing like it was in Charlotte. Thank goodness, because Liz had been so consumed by the possibilities with Angel's Rest that she hadn't even picked up groceries for the apartment, and the leftovers from the Creekside Café were running low.

Desperate for a few staples, she'd had no choice but to venture out. Surprisingly, though, things were busy, but not half bad. As she drove by the new candle factory, she noticed that the parking lot was full, but there was no crazy line or anything. She swung in, and by some stroke of luck was able to get a front parking spot. Feeling pretty victorious, she ventured inside.

The retail side of Shining Sol Candles was laid out nicely, with whitewashed wooden stands that played beautifully to the mountain location. A huge Christmas tree soared from the center of the store, a star sparkling from way above them in the warehouse rafters. Even with the number of people here it didn't feel chaotic.

The first candle she picked up was a beautiful spa-like blue labeled SAND DOLLAR COVE. A fresh seaside scent, it reminded her of her morning walks on the beach down in South Carolina. She put one in her basket, then tucked two more in as gifts for some of the people at the office.

She sniffed so many scents that she wasn't sure her sniffer was even working anymore, but her cart was pretty full, so she still considered it a win. She hoped she wasn't jinxing anything by purchasing candles with room themes in mind at Angel's Rest, but at these prices she couldn't help herself.

On the far side a wall of glass exposed the factory. A dozen workers worked at a steady pace hand-pouring the soy candles and placing the wooden wicks just so in the various jars. Seeing the numerous stages from pouring to storing was very interesting. She could see this place being a big draw for the town. She was surprised she'd never heard of it. If the candles burned half as great as they smelled, they had a bright future in front of them.

She loaded up her finds, then drove over to the grocery. At the checkout an older woman peered into Liz's cart. Liz smiled politely and said hello.

"Are you new to town?" the woman asked.

"I am."

"You're the woman who bought Angel's Rest!" she shouted, and by her tone Liz wasn't sure if the woman approved or not.

Liz looked around to see how many people were staring. "I am." She nudged her cart up in the line.

"I'm Beverly. My grandson is the sheriff. Hopefully you won't bump into the wrong side of him." The woman laughed as if she'd told that joke a hundred times. "Ahhh, but seriously, he's single. Are you?"

Liz laughed. "Yes, ma'am. I am, but I'm really not looking—"

"Never are when the right one comes along, dear. You just

keep him in mind. He's handsome, and I think I'm a pretty good judge. He used to play ball for the Washington Redskins too." Beverly made a muscle. "Know what I mean?"

"That's quite a résumé," Liz said.

"He was quite good. Until he hurt himself. I was glad he came home anyway. It was hard to see him get shoved around on the field."

"I'm sure it was."

"I didn't mean to butt in. Maybe we'll see you at the church Sunday."

"I'm sure you will," Liz said. "It'll be nice to see a familiar face, Beverly. I'm Liz."

Beverly took her hand, then tugged her in for a hug. "We're huggers around here, Liz. I knew your grandmother. We're so excited to have you back in town. You let me know if there's anything I can do for you."

"Thank you." Although the conversation had been a little bizarre, it was quite sweet.

She drove down to the hardware store, where boys were loading Christmas trees into the back of trucks and tying them to the roofs of cars.

George rounded the corner in front of her. "Liz. You could've called and I'd have just brought home anything you needed."

"Oh, that's not necessary. I had a couple of errands to run anyway."

"Can I interest you in a Christmas tree? They are on sale today. Your choice tall or small, just thirty bucks."

"That is a deal, but I'm going to pass. I'm sure your sons will want to decorate their own tree when they get home from college. I just need a couple markers, tape, and a box cutter."

"Aisle three," George said, then turned to talk to another customer.

"Thanks." She rounded up the items then got in line to check out, picking up a free calendar to mark down the days to when she might be able to move to Angel's Rest.

People were lined up about twenty deep when she heard someone say that the credit card machine was down. Liz felt bad for George. She'd had that happen in one of the store openings she'd done, and it was a nightmare. It turned out that all it took was a simple reset of the machine and they were back in business. Too bad it had taken them over six hours to find that out. It had ruined their sales for the day.

She turned to the person behind her. "Would you mind holding my spot in line? I want to check something real quick."

The woman wearing a festive holiday sweater looked a little miffed, but agreed.

Liz worked her way up to the register. "Hey, excuse me. I heard you're having trouble with the credit card machine."

"Yes." The girl wearing the name tag with CINDY on it blew her bangs out of her face. "Worst day ever."

"Is it by chance one of the new ones?"

She pointed to it behind her. "Stupid thing just keeps giving an error."

"Do you mind if I try something? I've had this happen before," Liz said.

"Fine by me. It's no good to us like this, and people are getting mad."

She put her things down, went back to where the machine was, unplugged it, then pushed several buttons. She hoped she'd remembered the sequence correctly. Then she plugged the machine back in.

"What are you doing?" George asked.

"Oh, sorry. I heard you were having trouble. I've run into this before, so I—" The machine beeped, and a green light flashed on the front, then turned solid.

"You fixed it?" George turned and asked the customer if they'd been planning to use a card to make their purchase. He grabbed their card and pushed it into the card reader. "It went through." He handed the customer their card back, then put both of his thick hands on Liz's shoulders. "You're a blessing. You just saved my biggest sales day. Thank you!"

"You're welcome." She picked up her things and started back to her spot in line.

"Liz," George said.

She spun around.

"You just carry that stuff right out of this store. You earned it."

"Really?"

"Shoo."

She did as he asked, although it really had been no big deal. She was glad she was able to help, though. He and Dottie worked so hard that even though she was staying at their house she never saw them. They were wonderful hosts, but she couldn't wait to begin living the dream.

Chapter Eleven

Sunday morning, Matt put on his khakis and a sport coat and checked himself in the mirror. This was everyday attire in the city, but now he just saved it for church. It would be hard to go back to Chicago after the holidays. He was becoming quite happy in his current routine.

Every pew had someone in it this Sunday, and people were still exchanging their hellos and getting settled in.

Matt slipped into the back pew, and pulled out the hymnal to mark the hymns they'd be singing today.

"Hey there, Liz."

Matt whipped his head around. Grady Wilson's grandmother stood holding his hooked arm, waving like a prom queen at the woman seated just four rows in front of him.

"This is my grandson. The one I was telling you about. Say hello, Grady."

Grady's cheeks reddened, and he looked like he'd rather throw his grandmother over his shoulder and tuck her in a jail cell than say hello. He dipped his head and tried to keep moving, but Miss Beverly was mouthing, *Isn't he handsome?*

A spark of jealousy gnawed at Matt's gut. He had absolutely no right. He knew that, but the feeling was there.

George clasped a hand on his shoulder. "Good morning."

Matt stood and shook his hand. "Good morning."

"Really? You're just going to sit there," he said in a low voice.

"What do you mean?" He had no idea what George was talking about. He gave Dottie a quick smile and nod.

George tugged Matt into the aisle. "Did you hear Liz saved the day in my store on Friday?"

"Yeah, people were talking about it in the café yesterday."

"Matt, she's a nice gal. She loves Antler Creek, and there's not a 'y' in her name anywhere. Get to stepping," George whispered into the collar of his shirt. "If you don't, Beverly will have wedding invitations made for Liz and Grady before the service is over."

Matt shook his head, but George didn't let up. That glare in his stare was a dare, and Matt moved ahead, stopping next to where Liz was seated. "Anyone sitting here?"

She shook her head and slid over. "Hi. Good to see you."

George cleared his throat as he and Dottie walked by. "Good morning, Liz. Matt."

Before Matt could make any small talk, Pastor Mike stepped to the pulpit with a "Good morning."

"Good morning," echoed from the congregation.

Liz glanced over at him and smiled.

He almost instinctively reached for her hand. Trying to hide the near mistake, he fumbled with the pocket of his sport coat, then folded his hands in his lap. *What was I thinking?*

Pastor Mike preached about Thanksgiving and reminded them that those thanks shouldn't be saved for one day when the turkey is stuffed and so are we. The congregation laughed, enjoying Pastor Mike's relatable style, but still appreciating the strong message sending them out to address the week in a godly way.

After the service, he and Liz walked out together. "Good sermon," he said.

"Yes. Very."

It was polite and damned awkward. "So, I'm going to complete my recommendations today. All I have to do is finish up the estimates."

"Great. I can't wait. I've been speculating since I last saw you."

"I'm sure you have. I'll get them over to you this afternoon."

Maizey and another woman stopped next to them. Maizey grabbed Liz's hands. "It's so good to see you here. You're like part of the town already. We're going over to the fire station to pick up lunch. It's their spaghetti dinner fund-raiser. Why don't you come along with us?"

"That sounds lovely. Thank you," Liz said. "Matt, I guess I'll hear from you later."

"You will." He watched as she walked off.

ALL AFTERNOON MATT had to force himself to concentrate on finishing up the package for Liz. He was distracted, and it was her fault. All he could think about was her. The stupid thing was if he'd just get this done he'd have an excuse to see her. *So focus already.*

He went back through his original notes from his inspection of the house, labeled DOE RUN ROAD. He changed that to ANGEL'S REST, then refined his notes to align with the goals Liz had gone over with him. He cross-checked all of the estimates, then created pivot tables to break out the priority and mandatory work from the things that could wait.

If he couldn't be the one to turn the art gallery back into something wonderful for the community, he was glad that Liz was going to have the chance. The inn had been in her family, after all, and it had been a very active part of this community for a long time. People in the area were going to be very excited when word got around that she was the one who bought it.

He compiled his report, then summarized it along with pictures that he'd taken to show the damage. The list was long, but it was doable if she had the time and money to invest.

Matt emailed Liz the inspection report, including the estimates, then texted her to let her know that he'd sent them and to call if she had any questions. She'd been so anxious, and her enthusiasm was contagious. It hadn't taken that long to work up rough estimates on the changes she'd shared with him, and he'd enjoyed doing it.

In fact, he hadn't felt this excited about a project since he was working on his house.

There were always so many uncertainties in renovating an old home. He didn't envy her for that. It was hard to anticipate what hidden problems were behind walls; then again, there weren't many of those left, with the gut job done on that place. It was a real shame there weren't a few more laws and inspections in place in this community to keep people from doing crazy things like removing load-bearing walls. Liz was lucky the whole house hadn't begun to sag in the middle. If hadn't been for the huge timbers that made up the post-and-timber building, it would have likely been a whole different story.

The Westmorelands had spared no expense when they built that place.

The only reason Matt had taken any interest in the property was to make sure it didn't fall into more disrepair. The back side of that property backed up to his fifteen-acre lot. His reason for bidding on it was definitely personal, but not as personal as Liz's.

He wouldn't mind helping her make her dream of restoring the inn come true.

Matt checked the Sent folder to make sure his email had gone through. Now he'd just have to wait for her response.

He walked into the living room and turned on the big-screen television. The Carolina Panthers were giving the Dallas Cowboys a serious wallop. That was worth watching. He went into the kitchen and grabbed a beer, then settled in for a lazy afternoon.

Dad had always been a Cowboys fan, even though he hadn't lived in Texas since he was five. Mom had a playful rivalry with Dad during football season, and because of that Matt's alliance was to the Panthers just like hers. He hadn't missed a game since she died, and always felt a little like Mom was closer on the days he hung out watching. Now that Dad was gone too, it was even more special—almost a ritual.

He cracked open the beer and sat in his favorite leather chair. During the commercial break, he checked his phone for messages. There weren't any. He tucked his phone back into his shirt pocket, wondering if Liz had considered separating the kitchen a little by adding a butler's pantry. It would make things so much easier for her once she had guests on the property by keeping the mess out of view. He grabbed her plans and a magazine to bear down on and made the changes. He liked what he saw, and he had a feeling she'd like it too. He had no idea what kind of budget she had, so he wasn't sure if she'd be happy or scared off by his assessment.

Somehow, while he was distracted with her plans, the Cowboys had made a comeback and won the game.

He'd expected to hear back from her right away.

The night dragged on, and it bothered him that he couldn't seem to let go of his obsession with checking for an email or text from her. His interest wasn't only in whether she'd do the project or not. He liked the idea of spending time with her.

Worried that he'd scared her with the numbers, he finally went to bed. No good Southern girl would call after this hour anyway.

THE NEXT MORNING, Matt must've walked by his phone three times while getting dressed and making coffee. As was common in the North Carolina mountains this time of year, yesterday there'd been ice and today was going to be unseasonably mild. Nearly sixty-two degrees, but then back to freezing by midweek. It was a good day to get some outdoor things done. He'd promised Pastor Mike that he'd help him finish up the fellowship hall project today, so he got dressed and headed over there.

It was just a little after seven when Matt arrived at the church. He used his key to let himself in and got right down to work. By the time Pastor Mike came in at nine, Matt was almost done.

Pastor Mike looked shocked. "How'd you get all this done by yourself? I was sure it would take the two of us all day to finish."

Matt shrugged. "I'm on a roll."

"How long have you been here?"

"I don't know. A while." Matt put his tools back in his bag.

A line creased Pastor Mike's forehead. "What's wrong?"

Matt shook his head. "Nothing. Why do you ask?"

"You just seem quiet." He gathered some trim pieces and stacked them in a box for the trash. "I saw you in church yesterday with the gal who wanted you to do the inspection. So, I guess you met up with her."

Great. The one thing he didn't want to think or talk about. He took a breath. "I did. Her grandparents used to own the place."

"Speculation was running wild once she left," Pastor Mike said. "Do you have any idea what she plans to do?"

"I know exactly what she's planning. You can tell folks to relax. I think they're going to be very pleased with what she has in mind."

This wasn't helping Matt's plan to not think about Liz or her project today. But he had to answer Pastor Mike. It would be rude to avoid his questions. "She wants to bring it back to what her grandparents once had. Reopen it as an inn and coordinate adventures like the old trout fishing they used to do on the creek, hiking to the falls, even the Christmas lights."

"Too bad she couldn't get the Christmas lights up *this* year. Did you hear they had to cancel the tree lighting at Town Square Park?"

"No. Why?"

"When the water got so high after that nor'easter I guess no one thought to check the storage shed. The boxes of lights and ornaments had gotten so wet and muddy that they were full of fuzzy mildew. Since they were old anyway, the decision was made that it was not worth the health risk for anyone to try to clean them up."

"Why can't they just replace them?"

"There's no budget on such short notice."

"That's a shame." He could probably scrape together some strands he wasn't planning to use. You'd think they could borrow enough strands from folks around town to get the job done, but if he suggested it he'd probably get stuck heading it up.

"George donated one of those big wire-cone trees with the strands of lights that get staked out to the side. You know, kind of like a giant tomato cage with lights on it. Someone was behind on their account at the hardware store and George accepted it as payment. I think he was glad to get rid of it. Won't be the same as a real Christmas-tree lighting, though."

"I guess it'll have to do." Matt picked up a ten-foot stick of trim he'd just mitered. "This is the last one we have to put up and we are done with all the crown molding." He moved the ladder to the far corner of the room and climbed to the top. Pastor Mike handed him the piece of molding.

Roger from the *Antler Creek Chronicle* walked in just as Matt nailed the final piece of trim in place.

Matt came down from the ladder. "You showed up just in time, Roger. We're pretty much done here."

"I've always had pretty good timing," Roger said with a laugh.

"Not so fast," Pastor Mike said. "I've got a long list of to-dos, and you're just in time to help me reload all the pantries. There are twenty-two boxes in my office that need to come back in here."

"Many hands make light work," Roger said, glancing over at Matt.

"You know I'll stick around and help," Matt said.

"You should. I'm late because of you."

Matt turned and looked at Roger. "Because of me?"

"Well, if you hadn't done such a good job with giving that lady the lowdown on what needed to be done on that house she wouldn't be calling me to run an RFP in the paper." Roger rolled his eyes.

"Request for proposal?"

"Yes, and I told her politely that an RFP wasn't going to get much attention in our little paper, but she wouldn't listen. She's very insistent, that one."

"She'd do better to talk to some of the individual guys and piece out the work." Like he'd recommended. "When will it run?"

"Starting tomorrow through December second."

Matt made a mental note to pick up a paper in the morning. There was no online version of the *Antler Creek Chronicle*. If he didn't pick one up at the Creekside Café or the gas station he'd have to borrow one from one of the locals who still had it delivered to their house twice a week and on Sunday.

He might even submit a bid himself.

A little voice in the back of his head reminded him that he'd sworn off getting involved after the Robyn-with-a-"y" debacle, and Liz should be off-limits.

It would be a fun project. One that he had the skills to pull off. This was about the inn . . . not the woman. Mostly.

Chapter Twelve

The sun shone bright, and unlike most Mondays Liz didn't have back-to-back meetings, but she was up and ready to face the day.

After she'd gotten the inspection report and estimates from Matt yesterday, she'd rerun the numbers and even added in some buffer to the project for any new problems they might stumble upon.

Even the inspection she'd paid eight hundred dollars for when she bought her house in Charlotte hadn't been this in-depth. He'd even included pictures. That had been helpful too, because it had been too dark to get a good picture of anything the day she was there with him. Maybe that was for the best.

After carefully working through the entire package, she had no questions at all. He'd left no stone unturned, and there were complete details and hypotheses about all of the elements in the house, along with cost analyses and prioritization of the proposed projects.

Of course, he had no idea what she'd paid for the place, except that it was more than he'd bid.

Even with the additional buffer she'd added to the projected spend, it came in just under her declared budget. Squeaky tight, but it passed the go/no-go gate.

Excited by the possibilities, she exhaled a long sigh of contentment.

I'm going to do this.

She speed-dialed a contact in her phone. "Peggy, thanks for talking me off the ledge the other day."

"What was that all about anyway? I've never known you to balk at a challenge."

"I don't know. I guess there's a first for everything. Believe me, if you'd been here with me when I walked inside, you'd understand."

"That bad?"

"Gutted. Left for dead." And that didn't feel like an exaggeration, but she was here to resuscitate the old place now. "I know we said we'd talk about leave after the holiday, but I wanted you to be thinking about it too. I'm going to request a six-month leave of absence to work on this."

"I'm not surprised. Folks are going to feel like the world is caving in when they hear about it, but they'll get over it. Don't worry. I'll handle things here."

"I know." She hesitated. Peggy knew the whole story, but she still needed to say it. "You know I might not come back at the end of that sabbatical, right?"

"Fully aware, my friend, but that's between us for now. If anything changes, you'll have a job to come back to."

"Thank you, Peggy." She let the last of her concerns drift away. "I've got it all planned out, right to the weather according to the *Farmers' Almanac.*"

"No surprise." There was a trace of laughter in Peggy's voice.

"If all goes according to plan I'll have guests at peak season for the leaves to be changing. The only other dependency is on my house selling by July. If it doesn't I'll have to look at renting it out, which I'd rather not do."

"Hire a property manager if you do. You're too nice to chase down late rent."

"You know that's right, but when I spoke to Missy she seemed to think it will sell fast, so I'm not going to worry about it. Worst thing that could happen is I'd have to cancel my trip out to California to see my parents in the fall, but I've been out to see them the last three years. Maybe under the circumstances they'd like to come back to North Carolina and see the inn."

"Wouldn't that be great? I bet they'd love it as much as you do," Peggy said. "Call me when things get moving. I'd love to come and see it. Until then, you still owe me a picture of the sunrise."

"You got it. I took one this morning. I'm forwarding it now. Thanks for everything, Peggy."

"You're welcome. I'm looking forward to being one of your first guests."

"I'm penciling you in for the first weekend of October," Liz said before hanging up the phone.

She liked the idea of the family being together at Angel's Rest again. She immediately dialed her parents, and her mom picked up after the first ring.

"Liz," her mother answered. "Your father and I were just saying we needed to check in with you."

"Hi, Mom. How are y'all doing?"

"We're good," her mother said. "We spent Thanksgiving with friends on their boat, and they'd like us to join them down in San Diego for the holidays."

"I'm sure you'll enjoy that" was the best she could come up with, because it would have been nice to spend the holidays together in North Carolina for a change.

"You know you're always welcome no matter where we go. Your father says hello. I'm putting you on speaker."

"Hi, Dad."

"Hey, Lizzie," he said. "So, what's going on?"

It was true. She rarely called unless she had something going on or to share. "Well, I bought something."

"A new car?" Dad sounded excited. A die-hard Ford fanatic, he hadn't been a fan of her buying the Range Rover.

"No. Something bigger." She'd planned to draw it out, be suspenseful, but she couldn't hold back. "I bought the inn."

"What inn?"

"Gram and Pop's." The absence of a reaction from them kind of dumbfounded her. "Angel's Rest up in Antler Creek."

"Why on earth would you do that?" both of them said at the same time.

"Because it's the happiest place on earth?"

"Hardly," her mother said. "That place is an hour from anything."

"That's exactly what I've always loved about it. Everyone loved Angel's Rest."

"That was a long time ago, Liz. What were you thinking?" Mom asked. "Don't you remember how much work that place was for Pop and Gram?"

"I remember how much fun it was. They loved it there, and their love for that town is what brought people to it. I've always wanted to carry that on. You know that's been my dream."

"A childhood dream. I never thought you were serious," Mom said. "You have an excellent job."

"Your grandparents loved each other more than any two people I've ever met," Dad said. "It didn't matter where they were. They'd have been happy."

Mom let out an audible sigh. "How will you ever meet someone in that tiny little town? And why would you leave your job behind?"

"I'm not the least bit worried about finding a husband, and I'd leave my job behind because I can. I've worked hard to be in a position to do this. It's been my dream forever." She knew Angel's Rest had something to do with how special her grandparents' relationship was. That place had always made her feel different too.

"Goodness gracious. I thought you'd outgrow that fairy tale," Mom said.

And what's so wrong with a fairy tale? Isn't marrying a prince a fairy tale too?

"Liz, that place has to be falling apart by now."

She wasn't about to tell them it had been gutted. "It'll need some work but I have an RFP drawn up and it'll be in the paper tomorrow." Liz hoped she'd get a good response on the request for proposal she'd run in the *Antler Creek Chronicle* this week. All she needed was a few good craftsmen to get this ball rolling. She purposely kept the list short and succinct.

She could add on to the project later, but right now she just needed to get people lined up so that as soon as she closed on the property she'd be ready to get started.

"Good luck with that," Dad said, as if it were a joke. She

could almost picture them scoffing at her over the phone line. Mom was probably twirling her long manicured Christmas-red-nailed fingers around in circles on the side of her head, indicating that Liz was crazy.

"Mom, do you remember a boy named Matt Hardy from when we used to go to the mountains to go fishing with Pop? He's about my age."

"I remember a lot of kids hanging around and participating in those outdoor activities, but no one in particular comes to mind. Why? Is he working on the property for you?"

"He did the inspection. I don't remember him at all, but he seems to remember me."

"Isn't that cute. Honey, it's not like you were ever there for very long. I'm not surprised you don't remember any of the kids that were around. Your grandparents were quite popular at the church and lots of the kids used to come and help around the place to earn spending money, or to work off the cost to fish or hike."

"I do kind of remember there were always a lot of people around."

"Your grandparents loved entertaining."

"They were always so happy."

"They really were," Mom said. "I hope you find that one day, dear. But if you're going to find love you're going to have to do something besides work. Especially with that no-dating-anyone-from-work policy."

"Squirreling away in the mountains isn't going to increase those odds either," Dad said. "Especially if you want a husband who wears sleeves."

"Dad!"

Her father said, "Nothing wrong with just having fun. Don't go marrying the first redneck you meet either. Maybe you can flip the place and make a profit. That's trendy right now."

This wasn't going the way she'd hoped. Talk about bursting a bubble. "I just wanted to share my news. I'll keep you updated on the progress."

"You do that. Bye now."

She hung up aggravated with them, and feeling more anxious to get the project going if for no other reason than to prove them wrong.

Chapter Thirteen

A week had gone by, and Liz couldn't believe the paperwork on the property had been settled so quickly. Then again, it was a cash deal, which made things a bit easier. All she had to do now was go down to the courthouse and finish her part. The RFP notice in the Antler Creek Chronicle *had ended; unfortunately, all it yielded was two bids, and one of those was from Matt.*

The icy rain had stripped most of the remaining leaves from the trees, and the sky was missing the blue of those perfect autumn days they'd been spoiled with lately. Winter might be officially a couple of weeks off, but it sure looked like it had arrived.

Liz drove over to the Creekside Café for an early lunch. In an hour folks would descend on the place like ants on a picnic and there wouldn't be an empty seat in the joint. She walked in, enjoying the quieter time, and took a seat in the small booth at the front. It was her favorite spot, since she could see people coming and going.

She flipped through the menu, then glanced over at the specials on the wall.

TODAY'S SPECIALS
HAM AND POTATO SOUP
BIG BEN'S FRIED TENDERLOIN SANDWICH
MAIZEY'S LASAGNA - WHILE IT LASTS

Maizey brought her a glass of tea. "What'll you have today?"

"I'd love to try your special lasagna." Liz slid the menu back into the wooden holder near the wall.

"I'm famous for it. Garlic bread?"

"Of course." Liz tapped her flat hands on the table. She loved this place. This town. She couldn't believe she was really going to be a part of it. Her eyes misted over. She dabbed at them with her napkin, then placed it in her lap. She smiled at a couple walking in who sat in the booth behind her.

Maizey came back over. "How're things coming along with the mountain house?"

"Great." Liz leaned her elbow leisurely on the table. She'd gotten used to these chats with Maizey, even looked forward to them. "Right after I eat I'm heading to the courthouse to finalize the deed transfer."

"Congratulations! Dessert is on me today."

"Thank you."

"I'm so glad everything is working out the way you wanted it to. I like having you around."

"I love being here. With the inspection report I got from Matt I was able to prioritize the entire project. I'm planning for an autumn opening. I'll owe you forever for that connection."

"You're off to a quick start."

"That's what I thought, but I only got two bids on the RFP I ran in the *Antler Creek Chronicle*."

Maizey shook her head. "That doesn't make any sense. I know for a fact we have plenty of very talented carpenters, plumbers, and other handymen that could use the work." Maizey tucked her towel in the belt of her apron. "That whole formal RFP might have scared a bunch of them off. Folks around here don't usually work in such a . . . a process-oriented manner. I mean, generally a chat over lunch and a handshake seals the deal."

When Matt mentioned working with the locals he hadn't meant in a formal process. He'd meant more word-of-mouth, she gathered from what Maizey was just sharing.

"Around here folks just want to do good day's work for a fair wage. A handshake is as good as a contract to get what you asked for around here."

Maybe all of her corporate approaches weren't perfect for a job in a small town. *Know your audience.*

"Might've been lucky to get even just two estimates. But you only need one," Maizey reassured her. "Unless they were both way over your budget. What's the problem?"

"No. One was very reasonable, and the other more than double the other."

"Double? I'm sorry. That's just wrong." Maizey frowned. "Some people around here think just because you bought something for more than they could afford, that you have money to burn, or that they are entitled to a hefty slice of it. It's not right."

Liz had a feeling that statement had come from discussion Maizey had overheard here in the diner, not pure speculation. She hoped she hadn't set herself up in the wrong light with folks. That hadn't been her intention. She wanted to be a part of this community the way her grandparents had been.

"That's not the case. I don't have money to burn. My budget is whisper thin. I'm going to have to be very careful."

"Then you will be. It doesn't matter what people think about how much you spent on that old place. This is your dream. You go for it."

"How do they even know what I spent?" Had Matt shared his assumptions with people around here? That was really none of his business.

"It's public record, sweetie, and Rosie who works for the county is married to Johnny Ray who is best friends with Ben and that whole bunch of men that are tighter than any group of old women—don't one of them know anything the rest of them won't hear about."

Liz was still processing the chain of friends two beats after Maizey was done saying it.

Public record. She probably read that somewhere in all the paperwork. Probably would've known it had she let Dan be a part of the process, but she didn't regret cutting that tie.

She wouldn't have expected anyone to care enough to pull records to see what she'd spent. But she hadn't counted on Rosie who was the sister, cousin, or whatever. Geez. Wasn't anything personal anymore? Information about where and what she'd spent on the inn at auction was probably available on the internet too.

"I'm glad you got one good bid. That's all you need anyway."

How was Liz supposed to tell Maizey that she was hesitant to take the lowest bid just because it was from Matt? She was his friend. There wasn't even a good reason to not want him to do the work. He was highly qualified, according to Maizey, and if his house was any indicator of his work the inn would end up looking amazing.

Liz felt the warmth climbing up her chest to her neck, then the burn in her cheeks. "It's not quite as simple as you might think. That bid was from Matt."

Maizey cocked her head so quick it reminded her of playing with those Rock 'Em Sock 'Em Robots with her little brother when she was a kid. A heavily penciled eyebrow practically disappeared beneath Maizey's blond bangs. "Matt Hardy? He bid on your project?"

"Why are you so surprised? You're the one who said he could fix and build about anything."

"He can," Maizey said. "He just doesn't hire out to do work. Ever. Help out? All the time, but never for hire."

That seemed odd, but that wasn't her business.

"Why are you so perplexed when you have a good bid in the hand?" Maizey laughed. "Bid in the hand. Like bird in the hand." She sat down at the table. "Get it. I made a joke."

Liz lightened up. "Yes. Funny. I don't know. I just get a weird vibe around him. I can't explain it."

"Weird? From Matt? He's the nicest man I know. If I had a daughter, he's exactly the kind of man I'd want her to be with."

"He seems nice. Maybe too nice. Or familiar?" She hadn't let anyone be close to her in a long time. Not since the divorce. And all of her friends were work acquaintances, the closest being Peggy, but it wasn't like they were the girls'-night-out kind of friends either. "There's just something about him that nags at me, and not in a totally bad way. I just can't put my finger on it."

Maizey's lips pursed. "The last man I knew that was as nice as Matt was your granddaddy. There's not one thing wrong with nice." She stood and waved as two workmen came in the restaurant, then looked Liz square in the eye. "That city girl brain of yours probably doesn't know how to wrap itself around a genuinely nice man with no ulterior motives." She swished away to wait on the men, who'd just seated themselves at the back table.

Matt did seem nice. Why *did* that bother her so much?

Chapter Fourteen

Unlike in Charlotte, the clerk's office had been a quick and easy trip. Liz took the paperwork in and was back in her vehicle with the stamped paperwork in less than twenty minutes.

Her hands shook as the reality of all of this sank in. *I did it. I really did it.* She looked to the heavens with a clear image of her grandparents in mind. "Every day I work on this project, every day I spend here in Antler Creek is for you. Thank you for all of the wonderful memories. I'm going to bring Angel's Rest back to life and share special moments with others just like you did." *This is what I'm meant to do.*

Overcome by emotion, she took a tissue from her purse. Like none she'd ever experienced before, these were truly tears of joy.

The right things are coming together.

But amid the buoyance of the joy she wondered again why she hesitated to jump on Matt's bid. It was more than fair. He'd proven to be a nice and decent guy, and his house proved he had the skill.

Is Maizey right? Have I become somehow so desensitized to bad behavior that I can't even recognize a nice guy right in front of me?

"Pop," she whispered to the universe. "What am I supposed to do? I wish you were here. You'd remember him. You'd guide me."

A small fluffy white feather drifted down from the tree above. She leaned forward and looked up. A chunky Carolina wren puffed and whistled up a storm, flipping his feathers and chattering at a squirrel busy among the pine needles below.

She got out and picked up the feather from the ground.

"Thanks for the reminder," she said to the bird, who continued to chirp, ignoring her completely, but who had certainly gifted her a feather.

She wasn't going to second-guess Matt or that very attractive bid another minute.

Liz pulled out her phone and brought up the RFP from Matt. She quickly typed a note accepting his bid and asking when they could get together to talk specifics.

The sooner she could start filling in dates to get the first things taken care of, the sooner the real work could begin.

She drove up to the house. Already she was getting more comfortable with the drive up the mountain.

The driveway hadn't eluded her this time either.

She got out and stood in the driveway. Looking at the house as the owner gave her a wonderful sense of pride. The lockbox was gone. She was the only one with a key now. *It's mine.*

She got back in her SUV and took the road that cut back on the mountain—the one they'd taken to Matt's—then followed Underpass Road back down to Main Street.

She saw the town through a whole new lens now.

The parking lot of the church was empty, but as she drove by she noticed they'd hung wreaths and greenery along the front. It looked festive and inviting. Wood was stacked at the edge of the building. She wondered if they were building a live nativity manger. That would be neat. She looked forward to coming back for Sunday service, then meeting and mingling with new neighbors.

Up the block, the hardware store was bustling with customers. Rather than taking the right to turn back on 801 toward the Creekside Café and head for home, she went straight. Ahead a flashing neon sign alongside a towering colorful metal rooster that had to be over seven feet tall with a sign hanging from his beak that read ANTIQUES just barely blocked her view of a red tractor with Santa in the driver's seat waving in visitors to Memory Lane Antiques and Crafts.

Liz remembered Maizey mentioning this place being a couple of blocks behind the café. She wouldn't mind stumbling into a few decorating ideas today. She parked next to the giant rooster and walked inside. A set of horse bells on a leather strap slapped against the door with a jingle.

The scent of cinnamon wafted through the air from a booth near the door filled with handmade brooms and bags of scented pinecones with pretty holiday bows.

"Welcome." A voice came from across the way where a bony wrist waved in the air.

"Thank you." Liz moved forward, trying to take in the vast space. Aisles, both left and right, of twelve-by-twelve cubbies were filled with handcrafted and artisanal goods. A few antiques were peppered in between, too.

"You looking for anything in particular today?"

"Not really." Liz wasn't entirely sure with whom she was even speaking at the other end of the bony arm. "Maybe a few good antique pieces."

"We've got plenty of that. Most of these front booths are the crafters. They are always coming in and out." A tall lanky white-haired woman came out from around the corner. "The big stuff is in the back, closer to the loading dock. Make yourself at home. Holler if you need any help."

"Thank you. I will." Liz meandered through a couple of the crafting booths. There was beautiful horsehair pottery, and there were hand-painted Christmas ornaments.

She stopped and folded back a stack of a dozen quilts. Most of them were hand-stitched too. Jacob's Ladder. Log Cabin. House Block. Bear Paw. Gram had quilted and crocheted too. She wished now that she'd learned from Gram, but Liz had always preferred to spend her time outdoors with Pop. What she wouldn't do to still have one of the quilts Gram had made for her over the years. There wasn't anything more snuggly than a crocheted afghan on the couch in the winter, but a quilt on the bed was a must year-round. She turned back two more quilts, admiring the handiwork, and then there it was.

In blue and white, the soft worn quilt looked just like the one that had been in her room when she was a little girl. The Counting Stars pattern in varying shades of blue and silvery gray. Maybe that gray had once been blue too. A tag was safety-pinned to the corner. King-size.

Liz folded it over her arm. It was highly unlikely to be the same quilt, but it had already jogged good memories and you couldn't put a price on that. This was going home with her. It might be a long while before the inn was ready, but this made it official. She had a starter kit and, with it, the color palette for one bedroom.

The last quilt in the pile was a used Double Wedding Ring

quilt. Age-worn reds, blues, and lavenders. One day she'd have a quilt like this one, and the right man to share it with. But not today.

She stacked all of the quilts back nicely and made her way to the rear of the store. She could spend two days in this place just wandering around.

As Liz cleared the last booth on the aisle, the warehouse opened up and furniture filled it.

The first thing that caught her eye was an armoire.

The tall piece was wide enough to act as a closet, and wouldn't that be perfect for Angel's Rest? She turned the tag over. An 1880 Victorian Walnut Armoire. Someone had taken loving care of it. The wood was in good shape, barely a scuff on it. Large mirrored beveled glass doors on each side opened to a full-length hanging clothes space. The glass was original too. In the middle, a single carved door gave the piece an aristocratic flare over four simple graduated drawers below.

It would be perfect in a guest room. Guests could surely unpack everything they'd need to stay for a week. She was tempted to at least put the piece on hold. It would also allow her to not add a closet to that room, using this piece instead to give it a roomier feeling.

Her phone rang, and she answered it on the first ring out of sheer habit. "Hello?"

"Hi, Liz. It's Matt Hardy."

Surprised to hear his voice, she sat down in the solid pine rocker. "You got my email?"

"I did. I was glad to hear from you. I know you're anxious to get started. What's your schedule look like?"

He had a deep, soothing voice, like someone you might hear

on the radio. She tried to shift her focus from the sound of his voice to what he'd said. "I was just shopping. At the antique shop. I got the deed transferred today and then stopped in here. I was actually just leaving." *Why am I rambling? Shut up.*

"Great. That was fast. I could meet now. I mean, I know it's last minute, but if it's convenient . . ."

"Yeah. No. I mean that would be great. I can meet you now." She got up from the rocker, but was stepping on the edge of the quilt and tripped herself back into the chair. She gathered up the quilt, with the phone between her shoulder and chin, and stood. "Let me just pay for this and I'll meet you."

"We can meet at my place if you don't mind. We'll have plenty of room."

She couldn't very well meet him at Angel's Rest. There wasn't even any place to sit. "That works."

"Do you remember how to get here?"

"I do."

"I'll see you when you get here then," he said.

Liz practically skipped to the register, where the white-haired woman was already waiting on her. "Will this be all for you today?"

The woman wore an oval name tag that read FLOSSIE. Liz remembered Matt mentioning her. "Yes, this will be all today, but I'll be back." She pulled her wallet from her purse. "Someone said you might know where some of the furnishings from up at Angel's Rest ended up."

"Angel's Rest." Flossie spoke the words as if they were special. "Wonderful place. It's been closed a long while now, but I know several of the pieces went to a family in Williamsburg, Virginia.

They were decorating their home and had seen the estate sale advertised. Nice couple. She was pregnant."

Liz's heart sank.

"But the big pieces, they stayed nearby. I know the Goodwins bought two of the bedroom suites. They might still have them."

Wouldn't that be crazy, if some of her grandparents' furniture was under the same roof? "I'll have to ask them about it," Liz said.

"I own the master suite," Flossie said. "I had it in my house up until last summer. Then, when Ben died I didn't need a big ol' king-size bed anymore. He left a big ol' empty spot in that bed. I missed him so much that I switched out to a queen that I had here in the store." She clicked her fingers in the air. "In fact, that bedroom suite from Angel's Rest is in the back room. We haven't moved it out onto the floor yet."

"Really?" She was dying to see it, but it wasn't likely to be going anywhere anytime soon if it was still in the back room. "Could you leave it there for a week or so? I'm very interested in it, but I'm in a bit of a rush this morning."

"Sure, honey. I'm in no hurry to move it. It's a beautiful set. Very ornate. Why are you so interested in stuff from Angel's Rest?"

"I just bought the place."

"Really? You?" Flossie placed her finger on her lip. "You are Lindley and Josie's granddaughter. I'd heard you bought the place. I'm so glad it didn't go to some city dweller who would just tear it down, or darn near ruin the place like that gallery did." Flossie pulled her lips together. "I'm sorry. I hope I wasn't speaking out of turn. Have you seen the inside?"

"I have and I couldn't agree with you more."

"Don't you worry about that bedroom suite," Flossie said. "If you want it I will hang on to it as long as you need. I'd like nothing better than for it to be put back to good use at Angel's Rest."

"Really? That would be wonderful. Yes, please save it for me. Thank you, Flossie."

"Consider it a welcome-home favor." Flossie ran Liz's credit card through the machine and handed it back.

Liz signed the receipt. "Thank you." She bundled the quilt in her arms and tucked it in the backseat, anxious to sleep beneath those stars.

Chapter Fifteen

As she drove, her thoughts filtered back to the evening she'd met Matt at the church. Then, at Angel's Rest in the ice storm. And then again, here at his house warming up by the fire.

She turned into his driveway. A tiny chipmunk poked his head up from the flower bed, then raced across the sidewalk as she parked. Probably stocking up for the next winter storm.

As she walked up the stairs, his big dog watched her through the glass storm door. A fire blazed in the fireplace, orange flames reflecting in the glass. The air smelled of charred wood and spice.

"Hi, Elvis," Liz called out.

The dog's nub of a tail wiggled.

Matt walked toward the door, and motioned to her. "Come on in."

She entered and gave Elvis a pat on the head. "How've you been, Elvis?"

"He really likes you," Matt said. "Look at his tail wagging."

"I like you too," she said to Elvis. "So why'd you name him Elvis anyway?" She placed her hand under his chin. "Do you sing?" She lifted his paws in her hands and hummed a few bars of "Hound Dog," but the dog didn't seem dazzled by her Elvis impression.

"He's been known to howl a time or two, but I named him Elvis because his lip over his left canine will get tucked and hung up under there and it gives him that Elvis lip sneer. Then, if you ever see him get excited you'll see his hip action. It doesn't happen often, but when he gets that little nub of his wagging, his whole rear end helicopters. I'm telling you, Elvis is in the building." Matt made his own best Elvis impersonation. The lip, the hip, and then, "Thank you very much."

Liz couldn't stop laughing. "You two are too much. I haven't laughed this hard in a long time. That was a very good impersonation."

"Thank you very much." Matt ran his hand back through his hair to smooth where he'd shaken it forward. "I've got everything laid out on the dining room table."

She followed him. The amount of paper the two of them had collectively on this project already was a little overwhelming. So much so it made her laugh again. It was like she had a sudden attack of the giggles and everything was funny. "And all of this is before we even get started?"

"I was thinking the same thing when I spread all of this out. We may have to go out and plant a tree this afternoon."

"Good idea." She took her laptop out of her tote bag, pulled out a chair, and sat down.

"Let's get right down to it," he said. "None of the windows are broken in the house, so unless you have any objection, I'd say step one is removing all the boards from the windows so we have some decent light in the place, especially until we get the wiring checked out and some overhead lighting in place. That and clearing out those faux walls and anything that needs to be hauled away."

"That sounds like a good plan."

"I'll have a dumpster on site, so if you can go through all of that stuff in the cabin farthest from the house, and make sure there's nothing you want to salvage, we'll get it all out of there at one time. That'll give us a clean slate to work with, and save you some expense if we do it all at once."

"I can do that. If there's anything that belonged to my grandparents, I definitely want to go through it."

"That's what I figured." He checked off an item on his legal pad. "Have you given any thought about staying up here once the work starts?"

"Yes. The Goodwins have been great about letting me stay, but I'd like to see about getting that guest cabin back in decent order so I can stay there as quickly as possible. I was hoping there might be a temporary or quick way to get the water resolved."

"I noticed that in the RFP. Shouldn't be a problem. I've got a plumber and we'll see if we can get him out there this week." Matt shuffled through some papers and came up with his copy. "Yes, so I'd like to get a crew on cleanup and also get our plumber and electrician out this week."

"If you help me with the timeline and what permits and inspections we'll need," she said, "I'll do whatever I can to keep things moving. Oh, don't let me leave without giving you a set of keys."

"This isn't Charlotte. You'll pull a permit for any new construction, but for the renovations they don't require anything. Once we're done they'll do a new assessment of the property for tax purposes, though."

"No inspections?"

"Sadly no. That's kind of why you're in the pickle you're in with some of the stuff the former owner did. It's nice because you can get things done quickly, but when shortcuts are taken, someone ends up paying for them."

"This time I guess that someone is me."

"Yes, ma'am. Afraid so." Matt suggested splitting the kitchen up a little to add the butler's pantry. "So you can keep the mess out of view of your guests."

"That's a great idea."

"Good. I'll measure it out and get you all the dimensions by the end of the week so you can start working on the kitchen layout design and get the cabinets ordered." He slid a business card toward her. "I've used this guy over the years. He sells high-quality cabinets, and he's great to work with. Tell him I sent you and he'll give you a contractor's price on the cabinetry. They can take a while to come in so I'd recommend getting those decisions made and them ordered. A functioning kitchen will make a lot of things easier, and the bottom line is it'll be better to have the cabinets waiting to be put in, rather than your workers waiting on work to do."

"That's for sure." She tucked the card in the front pocket of her tote bag. "I called the electric co-op, but since there hasn't been electricity to that address in so long they want to come out and do an inspection before they turn on the meter. I'm meeting them tomorrow morning."

"Good. You don't want to burn the place down."

She was ready to relax in front of a fire at Angel's Rest, not watch it go up in flames. "I'll let you know what they say."

Together they filled in a rough timeline and created milestones for the project, breaking it out into two overlapping projects: the guesthouse and the main house were phase one. She had as many tasks as he did the first couple of weeks, with all the phone calls to be made.

"I think we have a good plan. You're good at this." He pushed his chair back from the table. "I made a big pot of chili. Are you hungry?"

"I do love homemade chili. What can I do to help?" She followed Matt into the kitchen.

"You can pour us some tea. Glasses are in the cabinet next to the fridge. I'll get the chili." Matt grabbed two large soup mugs and carried them over to the fireplace. He ladled the chili from the huge cast-iron pot into the mugs and brought them into the kitchen, where he had small dishes of onions, sour cream, and cheese already set up for them.

"That smells great." Her mouth was already watering.

"I thought we'd eat in front of the fireplace if that's okay with you. A little less formal."

"Sure." She set the drinks on the oversize wooden trunk that served as a coffee table. The heavy metal straps, hinges, and latches had aged to a deep patina. It would probably take three strong men to lift the darn thing. It looked like something she imagined you'd find on an old pirate ship.

She bowed her head and said a quick silent blessing. When she lifted her head, he was doing the same. She dipped her spoon into the bowl and lifted it to her lips.

"Do you like the chili?"

"I like it a lot. I'd love to tell you that I'd reciprocate when we get the kitchen done at Angel's Rest, but the truth is I'm not a good cook. I never date anyone I work with either. So there's that." It was a not-so-subtle way to make sure their roles were clear.

"That suits me just fine. As friends, maybe I can give you a hand with a couple of easy recipes so you don't starve up here. There's no delivery in Antler Creek." He tapped his spoon against the side of her bowl. "Add it to your project plan."

"I just might," she said.

After they ate, she collected her things and he walked her out.

When she opened the backseat door to put her computer bag inside, he said, "Wow, you really made quite a haul at Flossie's."

"I sure did." She pulled out the quilt. "Isn't this beautiful? It's like the quilt that used to be in my room at Angel's Rest. I can't believe I found it."

"Nice. Blue is my favorite color," he said.

She hadn't noticed until just now that the quilt was about the same color as his eyes. "It's a Counting Stars pattern." She pushed it back into the car and slammed the door. "I'd be lying if I didn't admit that I'm dying to get moved in. Even if it is just one of the cabins for a while."

"I can understand that. We'll get you in as soon as possible, and we'll get those cooking lessons going too. Pick a night."

"Thanks, Matt." She backed out, waving as she drove toward the road.

He stood there watching from the porch as she drove off. Taking a few lessons from Matt on the fine art of cooking for one wasn't the worst way she could spend her spare time.

Chapter Sixteen

Matt made a few calls to get some workers on board for the Angel's Rest project, then cleaned up the kitchen. With everything from the Angel's Rest project filed away, he rolled up another set of plans and tucked them into a tube. "Want to go for a ride, Elvis?"

Elvis slowly got to his feet and lumbered toward the door.

When Matt got to the truck, Elvis walked around to the back, so Matt dropped the tailgate and let him climb in the bed.

Matt drove across town to the Creekside Café. He carried the cardboard tube and paused to tell Elvis to stay. Not that he ever wandered away; it just seemed like the right thing to do.

Inside, Matt took his usual seat at the bar, and stood the cardboard tube in front of him between the barstool and the counter. "Hey, Barney."

"How're you doing?" Barney said between bites of chocolate chess pie, barely turning to give Matt a second look.

"Good. Getting ready to start a new project."

He nodded and kept shoveling. Barney could fix about any appliance there was, and he was fast. Fast at everything, really. Repairs, driving, and eating too.

Maizey walked over and leaned on the counter in front of Matt. "You're early today."

"I wanted to catch you between rushes. I brought you something." He swung the tube out from under the counter and handed it to her.

"For me?"

"Yep, and it's on the house." He grinned, enjoying the surprise on her face.

"What is this?"

"You were talking about expanding this place someday, but you weren't sure where to begin. I drew up some plans for you."

She took a step back, then placed her hand across her heart. "Are you serious?"

"Sure am."

She popped the end off the tube, pulled out the papers, and spread them out on the countertop. "Scooch over that pie and coffee, Barney."

Barney grumbled but did as she asked.

Maizey pressed her hands together. "You sure did. This is exactly what I was thinking!"

"I know." He tapped his finger to his temple. "I listen. Now you're one step closer to making it happen."

"Thank you, Matt. You're one of the good ones."

"I'm happy to do it. You keep me well fed and happy around here. Always feels like home."

"Antler Creek will always be your home no matter where you pick up your mail, Matt Hardy." She pinched his cheek and then looked back at the plans with tears in her eyes. "Your mom and daddy would be so proud of the man you've become. Thank you for doing this for me."

"Order up," Cook yelled from the flattop, even though he wasn't three feet from Maizey.

Maizey slid the hamburger plate from the window to the counter in front of Matt. "Thank you, Matt. This one is on the house."

"No, ma'am. I worked up those plans because I wanted to do it. I don't expect a thing in return."

"Fine then. Cook, I'm going to need another burger just like the last one." She untied her apron and hung it over the chair, then grabbed a pitcher of water and walked out to Matt's truck with the burger plate in hand.

Matt laughed as he watched her feed his burger to Elvis.

She came back in and washed her hands, then put her apron back on. Cook handed another burger plate to her. "I believe this one is for you," she said with a smirk. "Aren't you afraid he's going to wander off?"

"No. He knows what he likes, and that's mostly lying around."

"Did you know he was going to get that big when you got him? He probably outweighs me already," she said.

"I think he's taller too." Maizey was so short that when she sat down in a chair next to you it wasn't all that different than her standing. Matt liked the amount of feistiness packed into that tiny package, though. She reminded him so much of his mother.

"No short jokes, mister." She wagged a finger at him. "Else that burger plate'll cost ya double."

"Fair enough."

"Speaking of fair, I hear you put in a bid on the Angel's Rest project. Since when do you take on paid work down here?"

He shrugged. "Seemed like an interesting project."

Her brow disappeared under bangs. "Does that mean you might stick around longer than just the holidays?"

"Looks that way. It's a big project."

"We'd like that. This town needs some new blood in it, and you're just the right kind. Elvis too."

"You're just saying that because I agreed to help you put your Christmas lights up next weekend."

"That's only part of it, but I do appreciate your help. Everyone around here does, but I have to ask how much of this has to do with *who* that project is for?"

"You mean Liz?"

"You know I do. Don't play coy with me, boy."

He snickered. You couldn't hide a thing from Maizey. "You know I'm not looking to get tied down again after that misstep with Robyn."

"She doesn't even count."

Easy for her to say. He'd invested a lot of time and energy into that relationship, and until he got working on the house and she realized he had every intention of eventually moving back . . . things had gone along just fine. Still stung, although he didn't really miss her anymore.

He'd been itchy to be here ever since too. Although he'd never planned to move back until he retired, things had changed. He loved his work, but suddenly designing big fancy houses wasn't as fulfilling as it had been. He yearned for something different, and when Liz came along something sparked in him. He wasn't sure if it was the girl, or the project, but either way he'd locked in on the deal now.

That thought—the girl or the project—hung in his mind all the way home, and woke him up in the middle of the night too.

He'd barely slept and it wasn't because of the chili, or the project at Angel's Rest.

What had kept his mind from resting all night was still playing on his mind right now.

Liz.

That woman puzzled him. She was interesting, smart, and a little quirky in a cool nerdy way. She was warm and funny, but turned as cold as ice in an instant. They'd be having a great conversation and then suddenly it was as if she'd put up an impenetrable wall. Not that he was looking for anything serious. It was just kind of nice chatting with her when those icy walls weren't pushing him away.

He'd been perfectly fine by himself. Coming back here to Antler Creek was proof that he was finally okay with everything that had happened and was moving on.

The influx of new visitors to the town if Angel's Rest reopened would be a good thing. The population here in Antler Creek was definitely heavily weighted to the over-fifty-five demographic, and he liked the idea of more people his own age coming to the town. With the inn back in business they might even get more visitors.

"This is about the town. Not Liz." *Great, now I'm talking to myself.* Or was it. Maybe he was lying to himself.

He made himself focus on the project . . . not the girl, making a list of all the materials he'd order in the morning.

It was late when he finally crawled into bed. Liz had made it clear that she didn't date anyone she worked with, so if this was about the girl, it wouldn't happen until after the project and for now he'd best just stay focused on Angel's Rest and let the rest play out.

THE NEXT MORNING, three of the five people he needed for demolition contacted him. They were ready to roll today and could meet him on the jobsite by eleven.

Matt ordered a construction dumpster, then checked his emails before heading up to Angel's Rest to get the project under way. On his way up the mountain road, he passed a pickup truck with the local electric co-op logo on the side. He waved as they passed on the narrow pavement.

When Matt pulled into the driveway, he was surprised to see Liz standing on the porch talking on her phone.

"Hey there." He climbed out of his truck. "I saw the Valley Electric Co-operative truck."

"Good morning. They just left." She gave him a thumbs-up. "We'll have power tomorrow."

"That's good news."

"I like this small-town stuff. The guy who came was the same one who turned off the power when the art gallery closed down, and he remembered everything was in good shape then. He walked through everything with me and said it was safe to turn the power back on. The breakers are all off, so don't let any of your guys mess with them today."

"I'll tape a sign across the panel, just to be sure." Matt opened his notepad and drew a big circle with a slash through it to hang on the box. "I'm meeting my guys here at eleven to get started. I guess all systems are go."

"I thought I'd do a little investigating of the guest cabins today if I won't be in your way."

"You won't be in our way, but could you first do a walk-through with me? I want to see if any of the junk lying around is something you want to save. I'd planned to send you a string of pictures via text, but this works so much better with you here."

"Let's do it." She opened the door and went inside.

"There's not much down here."

"Just don't mess up that fireplace in the demo, whatever you do," she said. "That's the best thing in the house."

"I couldn't agree more." He led her from room to room. There wasn't much down here except a box of paintings in one closet, which she decided to hang on to and take a look at later when they had some light. He marked them KEEP, then led her toward the stairway. "Wait here," he said.

She stood next to the stairs while he went out to the truck to get supplies.

When he came back with his tool bag and a stack of lumber, she was still standing there in the exact spot waiting on him. He placed a tread board on top of each of the broken and rotted boards, with a quick nail at either end to secure it.

"This is just temporary, but it'll do for today." He extended his arm toward her, wiggling his fingers for her to take his hand.

She paused for a moment, looking at his hand, then him, but finally took it. He led her up the stairs to the landing at the top.

Her eyes misted over when she took the last step and looked around. "Oh gosh!"

"I'm not sure why they tore out so much up here, because honestly it looks like they just used it for storage anyway."

She laid her hand across her heart. "It used to be so beautiful up here."

"I can only imagine."

"Each room was different. My grandmother made these gorgeous quilts and throws. She hand-painted little signs outside each of the suites. I can't believe it's all gone." She hugged herself.

"You know my grandmother collected angels." She walked over and took a night-light from the wall. "I found one of these downstairs the other day."

All he could see in her eyes were lost memories. He didn't want to transgress upon them, so he tried to make a joke.

"What came first? The angel collection or Angel's Rest," Matt asked. "Or is it like the chicken and the egg and no one really knows?"

She forced a smile. "I don't know for sure. They always lived here that I knew of, but my grandmother's belief in and love for angels went much deeper than just the name of this place." She turned her back to him. "This was the one place I felt most like myself. My life here felt real."

She was upset. He didn't have to be a sensitive guy to pick up on that. "Hey, let's concentrate on how it will look when we're done. You can re-create all of it."

She nodded quickly. "You're right. I can." Sweeping a tear from her cheek, she recomposed herself so fast he half wondered if it had been an act. "What do we have up here?"

"All righty then. So back here there are a bunch of boxes that look like they may have come down from the attic at some point. I've checked the attic. It's clear. I think some of them could have been your grandparents'."

"Really?" The smile that reached all the way to her eyes looked so much better on her than the worry a moment ago.

"Over here." He led her to the far corner of the room that faced the back of the property.

"That's my grandmother's writing." Her voice rose an octave. "She was so organized. She'd have labeled them like this. Oh gosh, this is good news." She tugged the top off a box labeled SPRING DECOR—GUEST ROOMS. "Throw-pillow covers. She'd change the whole look of every room depending on the season and holiday. I guess these are those little touches that made the rooms seem different. Silk flowers, and colored picture frames in springy pastels. Look at this quilt. Everything has been packed so well." She lifted the quilt to her face and sniffed. "I think it can all be used."

"I'll move any of the boxes labeled like that where you can go through them first."

Liz pushed a few more boxes over near that one. "Definitely." She looked through them and opened one that wasn't marked. "This one seems to be old paperwork from the art gallery."

"I'll get you a marker. You can write 'trash' on any you've gone through so the guys can get them out of here. We'll just work around these as long as we can to buy you some time. I'd hate to assume there isn't anything in them that you want."

"Thank you. If you need me to get one of those storage pods to move them to just let me know. I don't want to slow y'all down or make your job any harder than it is."

"I'll keep that in mind as an option." Matt took her through the rest of the space. "Nothing else up here looks like it's worth saving. Just some old cleaning supplies and art stuff."

"That can definitely all go."

"Okay." He led her back downstairs, stopping to take her hand where the railing was missing. "The first guest cabin is the one they were using for in-residency artists. I think that's your best bet as far as getting something ready quickly to live in. If you can go through that cabin and mark anything that's trash, I'll have the guys move everything to the dumpster for you."

"I'm on it. Once I get it cleared out then I'll have a better idea of what I need to do with that space to make it livable." She turned on her heel and headed to the backyard, calling over her shoulder, "I'm going to get started on that right now."

He watched her walk away. She didn't look worried in the least that she might get that purple peacoat dirty, or that her black leather gloves were way too nice for rummaging through an old dusty building.

Matt realized he was standing there smiling long after she'd cleared the door. He rubbed his hand across his face, trying to jar her out of his mind.

At eleven o'clock sharp three guys in an old blue-and-white Ford crew-cab pickup pulled into the driveway, and tumbled out ready to work. "Hey, boss man."

"Hey, guys." Matt shook their hands. "Good to be working with you again."

"You bet. What do you have for us?"

"Thanks for coming on such short notice," Matt said. "I'm paying you for this demolition and clearing all the trash to the dumpster by the job." He handed them each a sheet of paper where he'd broken everything out so there'd be no questions. "If it takes you three hours or thirty-three you're getting paid the same price, so let's make this time work for us. Get it done right the first time and keep moving."

"We'll do it." The guys looked at one another, nodding. "This is more than fair."

"It's a good project. Big enough to keep you all busy through the winter, and since most of it's inside work, you don't have to worry about the weather chasing away work days."

"Good timing." All three of them were nodding with appreciation. Matt walked them through, using a can of spray paint to mark everything that needed to come out during demolition. "The dumpster won't be here until tomorrow," Matt explained, "but I figure you can get a pretty strong start today, and we can move everything out tomorrow. Plus Bubba and Joe Don will be here tomorrow. They've got the big guns to move some of that heavy stuff."

"You know that's right," the shortest guy said. "Bubba's slow anyway. We'll do the demo and have it piled up waiting for him." The guys nudged one another.

Bubba was kind of a sloth of a guy. The only thing he did fast was eat. Bubba could put away six hot dogs before Matt could finish one. Then again, the guy was every bit of six feet five and probably close to three hundred pounds. He was a gentle giant, though. A little slow, but with the right direction the guy was a good worker, with a good heart.

While two of the guys started pulling down faux walls, Matt and the third of his guys went to work removing the plywood from the downstairs windows. They made quick progress, and once all the windows were revealed, Matt let the guys loose on the rest of the demo inside while he talked to the plumber, Tony, about the overall project.

Matt turned to look back toward the cabins. There was already a heaping pile of junk next to the front door of the first one. He couldn't wait to see what her thoughts were now that she'd spent a little time in there.

"Come on, Tony. Let me introduce you to the new owner. I

know her priority is to get the water running in this first cabin so she can stay here during the renovation project."

If this were his project he'd do the same thing, no question about it, but her being here while he was getting everything she needed done could go either way.

He thought about those signs at the garage that listed the price of repair. Fifty dollars per hour, seventy-five if you watch, and a hundred if you try to help. Hopefully she'd be so busy picking out materials and fixtures she'd stay focused on her fancy spreadsheets and timelines and trust him to do the work.

At least she wasn't staying in the house. With the cabins being about a football field away, they probably wouldn't even wake her up with the hammering.

Chapter Seventeen

Matt and Tony hiked through the thick brush back to the cabins. Matt would bring the Bobcat out tomorrow and clear a path for her. At least this time of year there was no worry about ticks or snakes, but it was hard to maneuver through.

Tony lifted his knees high as they walked. "This place could be a real treasure. I'd heard of Angel's Rest, but I'd never been up here."

"It was a real treasure in its time. Fancy in a sportsman kind of way."

"The cabins are bigger than I expected," Tony said, as they got closer. "I thought they were going to be one-room places."

"No. These are as big as some of the starter homes in town. This one is a one-bedroom. It was used most recently. The other is a two-bedroom from what Liz told me. It's full of storage boxes. I'm not even sure what shape that one is in yet."

"Has to be at least seven hundred square feet or so to the smaller one. The stone chimneys look to be in good condition. The wraparound porches are a nice touch. This could be really good for Antler Creek."

Matt was pleased. He knew Tony would do a good job, but he'd just made himself a little more vested with those observations.

Matt poked his head inside the open cabin door. Partially to keep from barreling in and scaring the bejeebies out of Liz, and partially to be sure he didn't get walloped by the next thing she threw out of there. Surprisingly, she'd cleared out most of the front room. "Wow, you've made great progress."

She spun around. Even with the dirt smudge on her cheek and hair all a mess she looked happy. She used the back of her arm to sweep her hair from her face. "Hey."

"Liz, this is Tony. He's the plumber that'll be working for us."

"Hi, Liz. Great place you have here." Tony extended his hand. "Nice to meet you."

"It's not great yet." Liz shot a look toward Matt. "But it will be." She slapped her dirty-gloved hand on her pants, then shook his hand. "Nice to meet you. I guess Matt told you I'm anxious to get these quarters in living condition."

"He sure did. I'll see what our options are to get some water back here. May as well look at making sure both cabins are back in working order from a plumbing perspective."

"I appreciate that. Come on in." She stepped around a mattress and box spring leaning against the front wall. "Excuse the mess." She turned to Matt. "The mattress and box spring can get thrown in the dumpster. I'll have to see the rest of this furniture in better light to know what's salvageable or not. I'll bring some lanterns when I come back."

"Once we have power tomorrow, hopefully all we need is a few lightbulbs. I'll bring some up tomorrow."

"Thank you. I'll get out of y'all's way so you can get me some water. I need to get a couple things from the hardware store anyway. I'll talk to you tomorrow, Matt."

"Wait and I'll ride with you if you don't mind. I need a couple things too," Matt said.

"Sure. I'll be in the car." She waved as she walked out. "Nice to meet you, Tony."

"That girl is a whirlwind." Tony gestured to the heaping mound of things she'd heaved out of the cabin.

"Tell me about it." Matt had to admit she'd made a pretty good dent in this cabin today.

"You'd better work fast is all I can say." Tony shook his head and laughed. "You go on. I've got this. I'll give you an update once I take a look around. Once you have power I'll be able to prime and run the pumps . . . if they even still work."

"Sounds good. Thanks, man." Matt left Tony to do his thing, and jogged out to Liz's Range Rover. "Thanks for waiting."

"No worries." She backed out of the spot and headed to town.

When they got to the hardware store, they walked inside together, and Matt heard an "ah-ha" come from across the way. George was looking right at him with a big grin on his face. Next to him, Pastor Mike nodded knowingly. Matt was sorry he'd made that comment about Liz in front of Mike now. He might be a pastor, but he and George loved hounding him about his love life. He'd never hear the end of this, even if he'd already told them Liz had made it clear there'd be no dating if they were working together. Of course, George had said that's what Dottie said when she worked for him here in the hardware store, and they'd been married over twenty years now.

Liz cruised through the store loading a cart with industrial-strength cleaning supplies, rubber gloves, and a bucket. She stopped in the pest-control aisle. He hovered nearby.

"Didn't you have some stuff to get?"

"It's at the counter. George had to order a part for the air compressor for me."

"Oh," she said. "I'm sorry. This won't take long."

"I'm not in a hurry. What are you looking for?"

"Spider spray and mousetraps." She picked up a pack of non-toxic mousetraps and frowned. "I'm not sure how humane it is to superglue little mice feet to a cardboard tray. How would you release them?"

"On little snowshoes?" He scissored his fingers in the air and she laughed.

"That seems kind of horrible. Toxic or not this won't end well."

The thought of mice running around with paper snowshoes made him laugh. "I don't think the little guys are going to do much scurrying that way," he admitted.

"Well, they've got to go. They've made a little fortress out of all those boxes in the cabin. I heard one chomp-chomp-chomping in the corner. I swear it sounded like it was the size of a kangaroo." She took a stance as if she were holding a baseball bat. "I had my broom all ready to go after him and shoo him out."

He started laughing.

"It's not funny! I bopped the box expecting this big scary rat or something and this teensy baby mouse ran across the floor."

"Can't have that." He feigned compassion the best he could. Then swiped four packets of old-fashioned mousetraps into her cart. "These always work."

"You're picking them up when I catch them."

"Fine by me." He shrugged and followed her down the aisle. An endcap of foam tubular pipe insulation in eight-foot lengths caught his eye. He snagged one out of the bin and handed it to her. "Or you could fight them off with one of these."

She stepped back and swung it, bopping him over the head.

"Oh, I'll fight something off. Like your bad jokes."

"No fair." He grabbed another one and battled her like a musketeer, playfully whopping her back toward the paint aisle.

She was laughing and scrambling. "Careful what you start."

"Looks like I'm the one finishing here."

"I call uncle! Uncle!"

He tapped her on the butt as she twisted away. "Thought you were no quitter."

"I'm not," she said, pretending to shy away and then spearing him with her noodle again.

George stepped between them. "All right, kids."

They both froze.

"We are so busted," Liz stage-whispered.

"He can hear you," Matt said, and then laughed.

George took the insulation from both of them and then bopped them each on the head. "That actually looks like a lot of fun."

"We're sorry," Liz said. "We got carried away."

"Yeah, you did. So, Liz, I have a question I've been meaning to ask you."

She brushed her hair from her face and caught her breath. "Sure. What's that?"

George glanced over at Matt and grinned. "So, what are you going to do when you've been here a while and miss shopping or going out to fancy restaurants?"

"I won't," she said, "but if I did, then I'd just go online and order what I wanted. Or take a weekend trip. That stuff is fine in small doses, but this . . . this is where nature gets in your soul."

George nodded. "You're the real deal, Liz. A different type of city girl. I knew I liked you from the day I met you." He looked over at Matt. "We all do. Don't we, Matt?"

Matt could've killed George with those foam noodles about now. The question, a mirror to Robyn's comment, didn't escape him. George had made his point, and Liz didn't seem any the wiser, but still. "Yeah. She's great."

Pastor Mike walked up behind him and put his hand on his shoulder. "Is this Q-and-A hour for the new girl in town?"

Liz laughed. "Bring it on," she teased.

"Okay," Mike said. "Do you believe in love at first sight?"

Matt couldn't believe these guys. And they considered themselves his friends?

Liz stood silent for a moment. "I've never experienced it myself, but you know Pop always told the story that the first time he laid eyes on Gram he'd told his buddy that she was the woman he was going to marry. And he did."

"He said that, did he?" Pastor Mike echoed. "How about that?"

Liz looked starry-eyed. "He loved her so much. They had the most wonderful relationship. Maybe that's what made the difference. Love at first sight. I never considered that."

"We better get back," Matt said. "We're losing daylight."

"It was good chatting with y'all," Liz said as they headed to the register.

They checked out and then loaded their things in her SUV. "Mike and George are great."

"Yeah. Good folks." Worse than old lady matchmakers, but he couldn't hate them for that. They meant well.

When they got back to Angel's Rest, the sun was already slipping behind the trees.

"Thanks for the ride," he said.

"See you tomorrow," she said, and then drove off.

The only problem with projects this time of year was that the days were so short. But Matt was happy with the progress they'd made on day one, and that was with only half the crew, considering Bubba and Joe Don really counted as three guys when it came to the heavy lifting.

Matt gathered up the guys. "Since we won't have the dumpster until sometime before noon tomorrow, let's plan to start at eleven again. After that we'll start at sunup each day."

"We'll work until sundown then." All of the guys agreed.

"You might have saved my marriage," one guy said. "My wife is not a fan of me not being able to pay the bills, and Christmas is right around the corner."

"It can be tough this time of year," another chimed in.

"I know. Well, you show up, and I'll keep you busy for a good long time," Matt assured them.

They left, and Matt locked everything up and headed out too.

When he got home, he gave Elvis a pat on the head, then made a beeline for the master bath. He got undressed and dropped his clothes in the washing machine, then stepped into the shower.

He knew Liz had to have ruined the outfit she'd worn today. She'd probably be sore as hell, too, after lifting and moving all of those boxes. He toweled off and put on a pair of sweatpants and a long-sleeved T-shirt.

Elvis was lying in front of the door when Matt walked out. "You ready for some dinner?"

The dog got to his feet and followed him.

Matt chopped onions and peppers, then mixed the ingredients for a meat loaf in a big bowl. Turning the meat into a loaf pan, he drizzled barbecue sauce on top and slid it into the oven.

At the kitchen island, he typed a quick update for Liz. He knew she'd be pleased with the start. There was a lot to share. A call would be so much easier.

Picking up his phone, Matt punched in Liz's phone number, but stopped short of connecting it. He'd never called someone to give them a daily update before. It was day one. He really hadn't uncovered anything that wasn't already on the plan. Why was he so inclined to call her?

Elvis looked at him with quizzical eyes.

"What?" *If he answers then I will have problems.*

He turned his phone facedown and reopened his email and typed a quick note telling her the plumber was on board and the guesthouse was priority. As long as the power was connected tomorrow, there was no apparent reason there wouldn't be water to the guesthouse by the weekend. He hit send, and then fed Elvis.

After dinner he put his dish in the dishwasher, and cleaned up the kitchen. Then he sliced the rest of the meat loaf in sandwich-size pieces and wrapped them in foil. Nothing better than a meat loaf sandwich for lunch. He wondered if Liz liked meat loaf sandwiches.

THE NEXT MORNING Matt took Elvis with him to Angel's Rest. When they got there the Valley Electric Co-operative bucket truck was already there, and Tony's truck was parked in the field in front of the cabin.

Tony walked out of the house as Matt walked up. "We're going to be in pretty good shape. Believe it or not the pump on the well to the house is still in working condition." He put his hand out for Elvis, who didn't bother to even sniff it. Instead, Elvis stretched out on the porch in a sunny spot. "I wouldn't count on that pump long-term, but it fired right up with minor coaxing. We can use it until it has to be replaced. I'll price out the new one so you'll have everything you need when it's time to order it."

"Great. Even if we can eke out a few weeks while you're getting everything in place that will be good. Then you can replace the pump last."

Tony said, "Those trenches need to be filled in, but since we won't be running pipe in them do you just want your team to handle that when they do the landscaping?"

"I was worried someone might step in one and get hurt, but that does make more sense." Matt hadn't considered that, and it would be a cost-saver. "Can you flag the area for us?"

"Yeah, I've got some flags in the truck."

They walked out back to take a look at the area, and Elvis plodded along behind them, then stepped down in the wide trench and lay down, leaning his chin on the heaped dirt at the top as if it were a pillow.

"Now, that's a lazy dog," Tony said.

"He works hard at it."

Elvis's short nub of a tail wagged as he looked up at the two men, his eyebrows shifting up and down like blinkers.

"He looks pretty comfortable." Tony stepped over the trench

and went into the cabin, and turned on the faucet in the kitchenette. The water ran clear.

MATT AND HIS team worked fast, and once Bubba and Joe Don
joined in things started moving at a noticeable rate. It took only
two days to finish all of the plumbing that could be done until
the cabinets and fixtures were there. Inside walls were already
going up and the place was beginning to take shape as an inn
again.

While the guys worked inside, Matt went out to the second
cabin to see what he might be able to clear out, since they still
had room in the dumpster.

That unit had been packed tight.

He wedged himself between a headboard and a row of big
cardboard boxes to get back to the master bedroom. At least in
there the boxes were neatly lined around the room. Floor to ceiling, but you could get around in there. Everything was labeled
too. Not like the great room, where it was just an unending wall
of unmarked boxes.

Elvis came in to explore, slamming against a stack of boxes
that scared him so badly he ran back outside.

Matt discovered a slew of boxes labeled CHRISTMAS in the
smaller bedroom. There were boxes upon boxes of outdoor
lights. Elvis tiptoed back in, found a red ribbon, and ran back
outside and lay down with his chin on it. For a puppy he had a
lot of quirky habits already.

A box labeled HERMEY had a red "X" on the top and the word
"HOLD" written on the side in red marker.

No way. If this was one of those elves, he'd just hit the jackpot.

Matt opened the box and carefully pulled out wads of newspaper. Whatever was inside . . . it was heavy. He lifted the taped paper bundle out of the box, then he flipped his knife open and cut the paper away.

"I'll be darned." It wasn't actually Hermey the elf who wanted to be a dentist from *Rudolph,* but Matt could see the resemblance between the two. This elf was about two-feet tall, and someone had been working on him. There was a bag of screws and wires taped to the back of the doll with careful notes of what still needed to be done. This had probably been one of Liz's grandfather's projects before they packed up and left.

Mr. Westmoreland had the best Christmas decorations around. Better than some of the fancy setups Matt had seen in the city even. Mr. Westmoreland had bought them in a liquidation sale after they'd been on display in one of those big department store windows. Only a couple of them actually moved when they were on display here in Antler Creek, but according to the rumors they once had waved and hammered and even hung ornaments.

Matt looked for more boxes like this one. Like a man on a treasure hunt, he found four more in various boxes labeled with names. All of them had the same "X" and "HOLD" written on them. Matt could only assume it was because they were being worked on, since they were all in similar stages of disrepair. He couldn't wait to tell Liz what he'd found. Having these as part of the Christmas lights would be epic.

Elvis barked and Joe Don called out Matt's name.

Matt looked at his watch. He hadn't realized so much time had passed. He noticed a couple of boxes toward the front with the lids off of them. That crazy dog had probably been doing a little more ribbon hunting.

Chapter Eighteen

Liz pulled into the driveway at Angel's Rest at eight thirty the next morning. Pickup trucks lined the front of the house. She got out and the sound of power tools and demolition filled the usually peaceful surroundings.

The dumpster at the edge of the driveway was nearly full. It was hard to believe there'd been that much junk to get out of here before the real work got going, and they weren't even done yet.

She walked up on the porch, nodding a quiet hello as a guy strolled past her carrying four studs on his shoulder.

Liz caught the door and held it open for him until the boards cleared, then followed behind him.

Country music came from the corner of the room as three men used nail guns to rebuild the wall that should have never been taken down to begin with. She could almost recognize the way things used to be now.

She walked in farther and stopped. The fireplace had been revealed and it was as beautiful as it had always been.

Yes, things were moving along even faster than she'd hoped. At least now the long list of tasks didn't feel as daunting, with some of the former beauty revealed. She knocked on one of the wooden timbers. So far, there hadn't been any huge surprises to disrupt the budget. In fact, the news had all been good.

Project status today was bright Christmas green.

"I thought I heard someone drive up," Matt said. "What do you think?"

"I'm very happy."

"Good." Matt took her by the arm. "Come on. I want to introduce you to the guys." Once they got within earshot he added, "After all, these guys will be your neighbors. This is Liz." He then pointed to each of the guys. "These two giant guys are Bubba and Joe Don. They both were born and raised here in Antler Creek. Then there's Billy, George Junior, and Glenn."

"Hi. Thank you for being a part of the team. This is a very special place to me." She did a doubletake at George Junior. "Are you one of George and Dottie's sons?"

"Guilty."

"Oh my gosh. I'm in your apartment."

He shook his head. "Don't worry about it. Mom and Dad didn't even know I was back yet. A bunch of us are bunking down at Mill Hill. We'll get your place ready soon enough."

"Are you sure?"

"Definitely. Already talked to my parents about it. It's cool."

"Thank you." She felt awful displacing him from his own home, though. She was pretty sure his mother would prefer he was under her roof, even if he'd rather hang out with his buddies.

Joe Don spoke up. "My parents know all about this place. They're really glad you're going to reopen Angel's Rest again. A lot of people in town are."

"I'm so glad to hear that." She clapped her hands. "I don't

want to hold y'all up. Get back to work. I'm going to stay out of your way."

Matt followed her toward the back door. "Want to see the cabin with the running water?"

"Already? Yes! I can't wait!" She couldn't contain herself. *Did I actually just hop in place?*

Matt had mowed a path to the back. It was much easier to get back there now.

"Watch out for the trench," he said. "We've put up some flags, but you don't want to step in that."

What did he think she was? Careless? She maneuvered over the trench with a giant step and went inside the cabin. "This place looks so much bigger with all that stuff out of here."

Matt flipped the light switches, and in the light it looked even better.

"Light! Thanks for bringing the lightbulbs. Wow." She went over to the kitchenette and turned on the faucet at the original enameled cast-iron farmhouse sink. It was in great condition. A little worn in a couple of spots, but so charming. Thankfully, water pummeled the sink with good pressure.

"Tony installed a tankless water heater, so now you've gained a closet too." Matt's phone dinged. He checked the text, then tucked the phone back in his pocket. "So far only very minor tweaks to the budget based on what we've found."

"Good news or bad news?" She bit her lip. She had no idea how much those tankless water heaters were, but they sounded expensive.

"Actually, right now the good and bad are a wash. No impact."

"That's great news. You had me worried there for a moment." She put her handbag down on the counter, and took a tape measure out. "So I have everything in here that I need to spend the night as far as utilities, right?"

"You do. Water and electricity. There's the fireplace for heat, or you could bring up an electric heater. I might have one at the house you could borrow."

"I can pick up a couple. Never a bad investment to have a couple handy."

"True."

"I need to measure some things." Liz stretched the tape and began measuring windows. Curtains might seem like a frivolous thing at this point, but if she was going to be staying up here while workers were coming and going they were a necessity.

"Need help?"

"Nope." She penciled numbers onto her notepad. "I've got it. I'm going to take some measurements and then get down to some deep cleaning so I can start staying up here."

Elvis came bounding into the cabin.

"Look who's here!" She clapped her hands, and Elvis shoved his nose beneath them. "What do you have there, buddy."

"He found that ribbon the other day when I was going through the other cabin. He even slept with it."

"That's so funny. I wonder if this was one of the bows my grandmother made and had stored away? She was known for her bows. Not that you could tell by that thing."

"It looked better when he first found it."

Elvis lay down and put his paw on top of the red, and probably once velvety, ribbon. He didn't look like he was about to go anywhere. "He can keep me company while I'm cleaning," Liz said.

"Text me if he gets in the way."

"He won't."

Matt turned to leave. "You know, until we get all the materials up and the trench filled in it's kind of a safety hazard around here. I wouldn't recommend coming up alone. I mean if something happens you want someone else around."

The comment caught her on the wrong side of a good mood. "I can take care of myself."

"I didn't mean it like that. We'll get this stuff cleaned up and the trenches filled in in the next couple of weeks. Or I could rearrange the schedule—"

"Absolutely not. You've got the priorities. I'll be careful."

He looked unconvinced.

"I promise," she said, raising her hand to God.

She felt a little bad for the tone she'd used, but boy did she hate it when men treated her like she didn't have good sense. She was pretty sure he hadn't given his workers that speech. In all fairness, he had a good point, though. Especially since cell reception wasn't that great up here, but it defeated the purpose if Matt was going to spend his time playing chaperone over her just because of a trench.

Matt left, but Elvis hung back until Liz went to get the bucket and box of cleaning supplies. He trotted alongside her with interest, even sticking his nose inside the open door of the Range Rover.

"I don't know what you're looking for. There's nothing in there for you." She leaned in and jotted "dog treats" on the page in her notebook. Wouldn't hurt to have a stash of goodies for her new buddy. It was the neighborly thing to do, after all.

Elvis went back to the cabin with her, lying in the trench outside while she cleaned. She worked straight through, not bothering to even take a break to get something for lunch. She'd just finished cleaning the bedroom and bathroom and had walked back out to get a clean sponge when she spotted an angel figurine lying on the hearth.

She hadn't noticed it there before.

Carefully picking it up, she turned it over in her hand and wiped the coating of dust from its little wings. Gram used to have a huge collection of angels. Some were small and collectible like this one. Others were fancy, with detailed gowns and soft feathery wings.

"I bet this was yours, Gram." She held the tiny angel in her hand, and then set it up on the wooden mantel above the fireplace to watch over things.

BY THE END of the day Liz almost felt at home in the one-bedroom cabin. She had a list four pages long of things to purchase and projects to do. Most of which she could handle herself. If she had a bed and a lamp she could've stayed tonight.

"Hey, Liz," Matt said with a quick double knock at the front door before walking in. "They're calling for snow tonight."

Elvis hopped to his feet and woofed.

"Does he like snow?" She pictured him more like the dog that carried the keg of brandy down the hill to help stranded skiers.

"It's his first winter. He's so big it's easy to forget he's just a puppy. I guess we're getting ready to find out."

"It's my first winter here in a long time too, Elvis. We'll figure it out together," she said.

"I'm curious. What's your favorite time of the year up here?"

"Summer I guess. I got to spend more time here then, but that was a long time ago."

"I figured with the sand-dollar necklace you wear it would probably be summer."

"I do like the fishing and hiking in the summer, but I'm really looking forward to Christmas."

He leaned forward and touched her necklace, then lifted the pendant and looked at the back. "This is like a real sand dollar. See, if you turn it over, it kind of looks like a poinsettia."

"Hmm. Really?" She unclasped the chain and looked at the pendant. "You're right. I hadn't even noticed."

"There's a legend about sand dollars. Part of it goes:

The Christmas Poinsettia
Etched on the other side
Reminds us of His birthday
Our joyous Christmas tide."

She held the necklace in her hand, looking at him. "That's really beautiful."

"Yeah it is. I thought you'd like it. I'll have to download the whole thing and send it to you."

"I'd like that." A quiet fell over her. She couldn't take her eyes off of him. "Umm. So . . . is there anything else you need me to shop for while I'm out and about?"

"No. I don't think so, but I'll text you if anything comes up."

"Yes. Do that. That would be good." She pushed her hair behind her ear and rushed, gathering her things. "I'm going to let Dottie and George know that I'll be back on Saturday to stay the weekend."

He looked worried. "You don't even have a bed. Or a refrigerator."

"I've got that figured out. I'm going to pick out furniture from Flossie down at the antique store. She said she can have it delivered and set up in the cabin for me. She has some great pieces that I think I'll be able to use long-term. I'll set up for delivery of the mattress and box spring for Saturday. I already ordered the refrigerator and it's supposed to be delivered Saturday too."

"Then I guess we're officially ahead of schedule on the cabin."

"Yes we are." She raised her hand and high-fived him. "Let's keep it that way. Shall we?"

"Count on it." He held the door for her to leave and he locked it before joining her out in front of the cabin. "I have a couple things for you."

She grabbed her purse and followed him back to the house, where his truck was parked.

He went to the passenger side and pulled out a stack of paper. "Here are the plans for the kitchen with all the exact measurements. Same for the downstairs bathrooms. If you can pick out the cabinets and fixtures, and get all of that ordered, that would really help."

"I can do that."

"Do you still have the card I gave you?"

"In my planner."

"Of course you do," he said with a wink. "If you have any questions at all, just call me. Once we get the upstairs framed back out, I'll have those bathroom measurements for you too."

"Sounds good. I probably won't be back here until Saturday, between the shopping and with all of this to work on."

"Then, I guess I'll see you Saturday," he said.

"You don't have to come just because I'm going to be here."

"I know, but the weather is so iffy this time of year we want to work Saturdays when we can to stay on or ahead of schedule," he explained. "We never work on Sunday. That's just a rule of my own."

She smiled gently. "I like that rule." It was nice to know some people still held Sunday as a day of rest. She could get used to that.

Chapter Nineteen

The next day, Liz drove back to Charlotte to pack necessities. It was odd to see the FOR SALE sign in her front yard, and to have to use the lockbox to get in. A few real-estate-agent cards were on the counter. A good sign that the house was being shown.

She'd thought she'd just pack a suitcase or two and be done, but since the endgame was to be in Antler Creek forever, aside from her business attire it made sense to pack all of her winter clothes and take them with her. She also packed her coffeemaker, and then in an effort to declutter the kitchen she went ahead and took everything that was out on a counter. A plus for staging. She went through the house and collected all of her personal pictures and put most of them in a box in the back of her closet, taking only two of them with her. One of her with Pop and Gram at Angel's Rest, and one of her with her parents last year at a vineyard.

By the time she was done packing, her vehicle was filled to the headliner. When she was ready to leave, she had to rely on the onboard cameras to see behind her.

She'd planned to try to stop by and visit Peggy and Dan, but it had taken her so long that she didn't have time.

Luckily traffic was light and she got back to Antler Creek before Flossie's antique shop closed for the day. "Hi, Flossie," Liz called out as she walked in.

"You're back," Flossie said. "I knew you'd be back. Are you here for the bedroom suite from Angel's Rest?"

"Not this time, but I still want to see that one. Today, I need a queen bed and dressers to be delivered as soon as possible. I know it's almost closing time. Do you mind?"

"Of course not. Come on. I've got some beautiful pieces." Flossie led the way. Liz racewalked to keep up with the long-legged woman's strides.

An hour later Liz had purchased a beautiful wrought-iron bed with an open scroll pattern along each side. With the log-and-chinking walls, the open design of the bed would really lighten the look in the room. She found a tall dresser, and two bedside tables that complemented the design of the bed too. It wasn't what she'd had in mind when she went in, but as soon as she saw it she knew it was the answer. On her way out she found a large wooden chest she could use to store blankets in that could double as a coffee table, and a rocking chair. "I'll take them too."

Flossie added up all the purchases, and while Liz swiped her card, Flossie made a couple of calls to find someone to deliver Liz's purchases.

"All set," Flossie said. "The boys will meet you over at Angel's Rest at eight tomorrow morning, and move everything in."

"Great. The mattress and box spring will be delivered some-time between nine and one." She grabbed Flossie's hand. "This is so exciting. Tomorrow I can spend the night there."

Flossie scribbled something on the back of one of her business cards. "You tuck my number in your purse. If you need anything at all, or you get scared, you call me."

"That's so sweet." What did this little old lady think she was going to do? Chase bears away?

Liz stopped at the grocery store and picked up a bottle of wine and a bag of white cheddar popcorn to celebrate. Tonight she was going to kick her feet up and watch Hallmark movies until she fell asleep.

THE NEXT MORNING, Liz cleared out the few things she had at the apartment and left the key under the mat with a thank-you card for Dottie and George. They'd been such a lifesaver. It would have been miserable burning up the road between here and Charlotte all week long.

She drove up the mountain to Angel's Rest feeling like it was the first day of a whole new life. She was surprised when she pulled into the driveway. It was incredible how much difference even just a day made.

The dumpster had been taken away, and now she could drive back to the cabin. She parked, got out, and grabbed as many bags as she could handle. She was relieved to see that Matt had laid a solid wooden door that had seen better days over the trench as a makeshift bridge so she didn't have to hop over the trench with her hands full.

It took four trips to get everything inside. Unfortunately, the clean cabin was now a mess again, filled with boxes and bags full of stuff lined up against the wall out of the path the folks from the antique shop would need to bring in her furniture.

She found the bag from the grocery store and emptied the contents of the dog biscuit box into a clear glass jar she could leave on the counter for when Elvis came.

No sooner had she put the lid on the jar, there was Matt's familiar knock at the door.

"Matt? Come on in."

He swung the door open and stepped inside. Elvis pushed past him and ran up to Liz. She loved on him, then went to the cookie jar, and tossed one in the air for him. He snapped it out of the air. "You do tricks." She applauded. "Did you know that?"

"I did."

"Well, how about that, you smart boy." She rubbed his ears, then went back to putting away the cleaning supplies and paper goods she'd picked up.

She took a heater out of its box and handed it to him. "Can you plug that in over in the front of the room? It says it'll heat a hundred and fifty square feet, so I bought one for each room. Once we get the central heat and air fixed, I can just use these for backup."

Matt unwound the power cord and plugged it into the wall closest to the door.

She plugged another one in in the kitchen. "I guess this will test the circuit breakers."

Both heaters started whirring. Matt held his hands in front of the unit he'd just plugged in. "It's putting out some good heat."

She did the same. "You're right. I might get run out of here. At least they have thermostats on them. It should keep things comfortable."

A truck rumbled outside. "That must be my furniture." She jumped over a box and ran outside.

Four young men, maybe not even out of high school, were lined up at the door with the bed frame. "Come on in, guys."

Matt slipped out while they moved in her furniture. She dug in her purse for tip money. It was the least she could do. She had no idea what Flossie was paying them, but they'd shown up on time and that was worth something.

The guys put the bed together, and it wasn't thirty minutes after they left that the truck with the refrigerator, mattress, and box spring showed up.

The new refrigerator fit perfectly. She'd measured carefully, but the cabinets were years and years older than standard appliances were built for now and finding the biggest refrigerator for the space hadn't been easy. She'd gone back and forth on what color to get, too. She was glad she'd gone with the white, because it also brightened that whole corner of the kitchen up. With so much wood in the cabin, any reflective areas were a bonus.

As she watched the delivery truck head out, she noticed Matt and his crew beginning to pack up too. Matt waved from the house.

She waved back.

He walked toward her with Elvis. When he got within earshot, he said, "We're getting ready to head out for the day. Are you sure you're comfortable staying here tonight?"

"I'm looking forward to it."

"Call me if there are any problems. You know I'm just up the road. I'll be right here if you need anything."

"I won't need you. I'm a big girl."

Elvis walked past her and plopped down in front of the heater in the living room.

"Someone is making himself at home." Matt looked embarrassed. "Elvis. Get out here."

Elvis didn't even lift his head.

Matt slapped his hand against his thigh and whistled in an attempt to get the dog moving, with no luck. "They're calling for snow again tonight."

"They call for snow every day around here. Haven't had much yet." She walked over and wrapped her hands around Elvis's soft muzzle. "Your daddy's going to get jealous if you keep playing favorites."

Matt shoved his hands in his pockets.

"Go on, Elvis. Time to go with your daddy." She snapped her fingers, and the dog slowly got to his feet and headed for the door. "I'll see y'all in church, or Monday morning."

Matt lifted his hand to his ear.

"I know. I'll call if I need you. Don't worry. You're like an old woman." She was complaining, but she did appreciate his concern.

Once Matt's truck turned onto the main road, she closed the door and locked it behind her.

She had everything she needed right here. She rummaged through the bags until she found the one with the new sheets. Robin's-egg blue. Okay, so it wasn't exactly a winter color, but when she'd seen them she immediately thought of snowflakes and icy blue skies on a snowy day. *And Matt's eyes.* It seemed perfect, and now that she was fluffing the fitted sheet to tuck it beneath the mattress, she realized it was even prettier against the deep wood tones of the timbers and contrasting chinking of the cabin than she'd imagined. Stunning, really.

She made the bed, hospital corners and all just as Gram had

taught her all those years ago, then layered a thin cotton blanket, followed by the quilt she'd bought from Flossie. The bed looked fresh and inviting, and cozy enough for any season.

Knowing that a staged house sold much quicker than a lived-in one, she hadn't hesitated one moment in raiding her own favorite things to bring with her. She hadn't been sure where she'd use them, but removing a few lamps and a few special pictures and decoratives had made her house in Charlotte look even neater and hopefully would make this one feel homier.

She looked over the lamps she'd brought with her and settled on a tall colonial-style lamp for the bedside table. She'd be able to read until she was sleepy. No television meant no problem as far as she was concerned—she had some movies saved on her computer if she got bored.

Propping up the pillows on the bed, she folded back the blanket and quilt for later.

Liz walked to the door, then turned around. The ornate footboard brought an elegant balance to things without looking too feminine. If she were checking into an inn and staying in this room tonight, she'd be quite pleased.

An hour later she'd hung pictures in the bedroom and set up a plant stand under the southern-facing window, where her favorite violets could thrive.

All the furniture arranging combined with those little heaters had warmed the tiny cabin enough that she was glad she hadn't gone ahead and tried to make a fire. It would have toasted her out of the place. Once she turned down the thermostat on the heaters, it was so quiet that all she could hear was her own heartbeat in her ears.

She wasn't used to that, but she liked it.

She grabbed her jacket and walked outside. The sickle moon from the other night was a no-show, leaving only the brilliance of a new moon and a million vibrant stars. It seemed like the perfect night to spot a shooting star. "Gram, I love this place. I haven't seen this many stars since the last time I was here with you and Pop."

A shooting star crossed the sky, as if they were smiling upon her. "I love you too."

That was all the reassurance she needed to go back inside and know that she was going to have a good night's sleep.

She changed into a new pair of pajamas—a black long-sleeved top, and black yoga-style pants with tiny golden polka dots—then crawled between the sheets, suddenly feeling weary from the busy day. She didn't even bother trying to read, instead switching off the bedside lamp. The only light was a soft glow from the stained-glass night-light that she'd bought this morning on a whim.

Liz set her phone alarm to eight o'clock. If she slept in that late on Sunday, it would be the first time in years, but she didn't want to risk sleeping the day away either.

She snuggled down under the covers and then reached up and turned off the alarm on her phone. She wasn't on anyone's schedule all weekend but her own. Sunday was supposed to be a day of rest. Maybe it was time she figured out her own body clock.

Back under the crisp linens, she was hit by the scent of warm snickerdoodles and bacon, even though nothing had been cooked in this cabin in years. It was just like Gram tucking her in and placing a soft whisper of a kiss on her forehead. Her eyes fluttered open in the darkness. She knew it was her imagination, but it felt real in a very comforting way.

Her body relaxed and she fell asleep in her cabin beneath the beautiful Appalachian stars.

Chapter Twenty

A rapid rat-a-tat-tat at the door woke Liz. She jolted out of bed a little confused. Who could be here?

She raced to the door. After catching her toe on the corner of the new chest in the living room, she hopped the rest of the way to the door, grimacing as she swung it open.

"Hi."

Two short round women stood side-by-side, grinning. They looked alike except for the color of their coats. The woman holding an old-school cornflower Pyrex casserole dish wore a forest-green coat, and the other clung to a huge plastic bowl the same color as her blue jacket. "Welcome!" they sang out.

The blue-coated woman paled. "Oh goodness. We've woken you." Panic in her eyes, she swung her gaze toward the other lady. "I told you it was too early."

Liz raised her hands. "No. It's fine."

"Are you sick?"

"No. I'm just getting settled in. I'm . . . uh . . ." Liz wasn't sure what exactly the right answer was in this circumstance.

The woman wearing green offered a reassuring smile. "I'm

sure you're beat with starting to get things moved up here and all. I'm Joe Don's momma. He told me all about you and your plans to bring beautiful Angel's Rest back to life again."

"Hello," Liz said. How that tiny little woman ended up with a boy the size of Joe Don was anybody's wonder. Her husband must be a mountain of a man.

"Her name is Donna Beth, and I'm her sister Sonja, but everyone calls me Sonny. We brought you a little something for while you're getting settled in. I made you my famous chicken and biscuit cobbler."

Liz liked the sound of that. "Thank you." She accepted the casserole dish from Sonny. "Please come in." She shuffled back from the door and they stepped inside. "This sounds amazing."

"Oh it is," Donna Beth assured her. "Sonny makes the best chicken and biscuit cobbler around. Her biscuits are second to none."

"Thanks, sis." Sonny blushed.

Donna Beth made herself at home, walking right past Liz to put a bowl of beans on the counter. "I hope this will feel like a little taste of home for you, Liz. Pinto beans the way your grandma made 'em famous when she ran the inn. Not just fatback, but extra garlic and some jalapeños to give them a kick."

Liz couldn't believe it. "You didn't!"

"Yes I did."

"I'm not even sure *I* have that recipe."

"We'll get together and I'll teach you then," the woman assured her. "This was one of those recipes that made eating up here a special treat. I sure miss Josie."

"Me too," Liz said. "This is unexpected. Thank you so much. I'd ask you to sit, but as you can see I haven't gotten that far yet.

All I have is the trunk and the stools at the bar in the kitchen and they still need another good scrubbing. Can I offer you a cup of coffee? I do have coffee and cups."

"No, thank you." Donna Beth nudged Sonny. "We're not going to stay. We just wanted to let you know how happy we are that you bought this place. That art gallery was never welcome in this town. That's why they closed down, you know."

"That's not entirely true." Sonny elbowed Donna Beth.

"It is," Donna Beth said. "Ain't nothing going to survive in this town if we don't get behind it. You know that's true, Sonny."

A little jolt went through Liz.

"They were their own worst enemy," Sonny said. "They didn't really care about this town or being a part of it. It all worked out for the best. Even though it sure did take a long time. We're so glad you're here to put it back to right again."

Why had she just assumed she'd be welcomed back? It had never occurred to her that she might not be. Thank goodness she seemed to be starting off on the right foot. A happy accident indeed.

"You and me both," Liz said. "Would you mind if I get your phone number and addresses so I can be sure to get your dishes back to you?"

"We taped them to the bottom," Donna Beth said. "You can just bring them to church on any Sunday morning if that's easier. No hurry."

Liz picked up on the unsubtle recommendation. Or maybe they were just probing to see if she was a Christian girl.

"That's a very good point." Liz followed as the two ladies let themselves out the door. "Thank you again. I know I'll enjoy all of it."

"You take care now." The two sisters crossed the makeshift door bridge over the trench.

Liz watched them trek through a light layer of frost toward their car, looking like a couple of Christmas elves in their blue and green matching coats.

The aroma of the two dishes already filled the room. Her stomach growled.

She popped a butter toffee–flavored coffee pod in the coffeemaker and stood there still smiling from the thoughtful visit until the coffeepot gurgled. It took only a couple of big swallows for her to finally wake up. She opened up the goodies Sonny and Donna Beth had left for her. A quick bite from each had her remembering Grandma's cooking. "Mmm. Good stuff."

With her coffee in hand, she dragged one of the boxes from the front corner of the room and slid it under the light. The tape had lost most of its sticky and came right off. She pulled out the newspaper-wrapped contents one at a time. Carefully she unwrapped a cobalt-blue bud vase. The paper was an old copy of the *Antler Creek Chronicle*. She recognized the hardware store in one of the ads. The candle factory had been set to open the following year. It might be fun to decoupage something with some of these headlines. Rather than wad the paper, she smoothed the sheets and stacked them as she went through the boxes.

A lot of the items were just small knickknacks that could be sold down at Flossie's, or donated to a church rummage sale. She unwrapped the next piece and sat back on her heels. She remembered the angel. Gram had used it as a table decoration, but the cone-shaped bottom made it easy to use as a tree topper. The angel was every bit of fourteen inches tall, and her clothes were still in good shape too.

Christmas Angels

Liz tugged on the fabric gown, straightening it.

The angel's shiny blond hair hung straight. Liz could picture this angel sitting at the edge of the big wooden chopping block, reigning over Gram's baked goods. Liz got up and carried the angel to her kitchen island. Until she had a butcher block of her own in the main house, this angel could live right here.

The sound from a diesel engine with some serious exhaust issues sent her rushing over to the window to see who was here. It didn't sound like Matt's truck.

She pulled back the curtain and peered through the slats of the blinds. A big four-wheel-drive pickup truck painted in camouflage rumbled right up the driveway toward the cabin. Only a local would even remember there'd been a roadbed that led back here at one time.

A big man in coveralls got out of the truck.

She grabbed her coat and tied the belt around her waist, then walked out to see what he wanted. "Hello?" She might consider buying a gun. There were crazies everywhere in the world. Walking out like this might not have been the smartest move.

"Hey there. Was hoping you were home." His grand smile made his cheeks look rosy and red. "George and I used to hunt with your grandpa."

A friend of George and Dottie's. She relaxed a little.

The huge man had a well-trimmed beard that was graying and the kindest eyes she'd ever seen. "Really? That's neat."

"He was a good man. Fishing, hunting, that man could do anything and was happy to share his love of our outdoors here in the mountains with anyone who would give him the chance to share it."

"I agree. I spent my summers up here fly-fishing with him."

She'd never gone hunting with him, though. Taking a deadly shot at Bambi didn't seem fun at all. And sitting out in the cold for hours just to look at a deer wasn't a good alternative. Besides, if you sat on the back porch at dusk you were almost always treated to a glimpse of a family of deer cutting through the property on the way down to the stream.

I haven't thought of that in years. I've got to make a point to sit quietly out here at dusk. I bet there are still deer crossing this land every evening.

"Brought ya something to welcome you, and wish you good luck with this place."

"Thank you." How many casseroles could a girl eat? Good thing she'd ordered the big refrigerator.

He opened the back door to the crew cab, and his body half disappeared into the truck for a minute. Then he stepped out from behind the open door, and what to her wondering eyes did appear but the front half of a big old twelve-point deer mounted to a slab of wood the size of a good snow sled.

"Oh my?" escaped from her lips before she could hold it back.

"I know," he said proudly. "It's a nice one. Hard to part with, but it's the first twelve-pointer George ever shot. He's been keeping it at my place. We shot this on a trip with your grandfather. It belongs here at the inn."

"Thank you." *"I couldn't"* was what I should've said, because what the heck am I supposed to do with this thing?

She stepped forward, but there was no way she was going to be able to carry the monstrosity. She and the big man kind of tangoed back and forth until he realized his gift was too big for her to lift.

"I'll carry it inside for you. Where should we put it?"

"Gosh. It's too big to hang in the cabin, but I'd hate for it to be in the middle of construction in the house. Let's put it over here in the cabin for now." *There goes the space for a dining room table.*

He placed the huge taxidermy piece in the corner, then dug a business card out of his wallet and handed it to her.

"I'm George Goodwin's cousin. I'm Buck. I work with him over at the store."

"Nice to meet you, Buck."

"You just call me if you need anything. We might not be able to match those big-box store prices, but we've got anything you'd need and you don't get charged shipping either. I'll even bring it over if you need me to."

"Can't beat that," she said.

"That your vehicle?" Buck pointed to the Range Rover.

"It is."

"You single?"

That was a little personal. "Yes."

"Nice SUV."

She'd never really considered it an SUV. It was pretty luxurious to be classed as one, and it had more bells and whistles than most cars. She wasn't even sure why she'd bought the thing, except that it was such a great deal and fancier than the car she'd been driving. Dan had talked her into it.

"I heard Matt Hardy is working on the place for you. Good man, and he'll use the locals to get the job done right. Good choice."

Good thing. She hadn't had many options. For a minute, she'd been afraid Buck was connected to the high bid she'd gotten from the RFP. She couldn't even recall who'd submitted that now. If she hadn't gone with Matt, no telling what kind of chilly reception Antler Creek might have given her.

"Are you staying up here tonight?"

"Yes. I'll be here most of the time now."

"Do you have a weather radio? You been following the weather?"

"No, but I have the weather app on my phone." She glanced up at the sky. It was a chilly winter day. Gray, but then weren't most days gray this time of year?

"Calling for snow. You got wood for the fireplace?"

"I've got a couple of heaters."

Buck shook his head. "That won't do. If the power goes out you need wood on hand, young lady."

"I guess I'd better get to town and get some." Being stranded in the cold was not on her project plan.

"You won't need much to get through the next couple of days. You know how that is. If you've got it you won't need it."

"I hope you're right."

"I'll send one of the boys up with some wood and matches for you. I'll reopen the inn tab. My grandparents and your grandparents did business together for years. It's like family."

"Thank you, but I can pay you. I can just go get my purse."

"Don't worry about it right now. We can settle later." Buck got back in his truck and rumbled off.

She probably should have a snow shovel and ice melt around for the winter, too. She went back to the cabin and started a winter supply list. She hadn't budgeted for that. A generator was probably a good idea. Long-term she wanted one that ran on propane and was attached to the house so it automatically kicked over if the power went out. For now just a small one so she could plug in a heater would do, and if the coffeepot would run it would be a bonus.

Liz had her doubts it was going to snow.

She spent the better part of the afternoon unpacking boxes, repacking the things that could be sold, and bagging up what could be thrown away.

A little stir-crazy from being inside all day, she walked up to the house. Inside, good progress was being made. She could more readily see and believe her vision now. A small echo carried with each footfall as she let her imagination go wild, competing with the memories of what it once was. In between there was something special.

A few minutes later, Matt drove up.

"What are you doing here," she asked.

"Buck told George you were out of wood, and he asked me to bring some up for you."

She could kick herself for not insisting on getting it herself. She thought he'd be sending up one of the kids that worked for him, not taking up Matt's time.

"I'm sorry. I could've gone down and gotten it."

"Don't be silly. You don't need to be loading wood in the back of that fancy Range Rover. There are plenty of folks around here happy to lend a hand."

He backed up to the cabin and unloaded the wood, stacking it in a crisscross fashion that made it look like a giant game of Jenga.

Just in case, she grabbed two logs from the top of the stack and laid them inside next to the fireplace.

Matt came inside. "Here." He handed her a long wooden box of fireplace matches, and a bundle of newspaper rolls to use as a starter.

"Oh? Thank you." Sort of a bouquet of them. Almost romantic.

"Want me to start the fire for you? It's way easier to keep a fire going than to start one if you haven't done it before."

"No thanks. I can handle it." She wasn't sure what made her think she could start a fire, but she was sure she could find a video about it online and figure it out.

He said goodbye and left. She lifted her phone to search for tips on starting a fire, but the data connection was so weak that she finally gave up.

She didn't really need anything at the market, but a quick drive to town would give her a chance to at least connect to the internet, plus she liked the feeling of being part of this town. Besides, she could use some more cleaning products to finish up those saddle stools at the island.

The lot at Spivey's Market was full, but there was an open spot right along the curb. She pulled into it and went inside. Pushing the basket up and down the aisles, she was happy to see that this small-town market was still thriving, with plenty of choices. The meat case looked better than the one in the fancy store down from her house in Charlotte. If people were going to keep dropping in, she was going to at least have something to offer. She stocked up on a few things that would be simple to put together quickly, then bought more packing tape and Magic Markers. On a whim she bought marshmallows. The big ones. Perfect for roasting.

A woman pushing a shopping cart with a toddler in the seat

stopped her. "You're the lady who just bought Angel's Rest, aren't you?"

They were probably about the same age. "I am. Your little girl is so cute." She couldn't wait until the day she had a little girl in hot-pink cowgirl boots riding in her own buggy.

"Thank you. Can you say hello, Lily?"

"Lello."

Liz thought she'd bust. How adorable. "Hello, Miss Lily. I'm Liz."

"I'm Abigaile. My friends call me Abby. I work down at Dr. Flynn's office. He's the dentist."

"Then I'm sure our paths will cross. I'll need a local dentist."

"Great. Until then, if you've got free time a bunch of us will be at the church Tuesday night. We're putting together stockings for some of the kids in the area."

Liz loved the idea of the town caring for its own. "I'll be there. What time?"

"Six."

"Anything I can bring?"

"We'd just appreciate your help."

"Count on it." Liz waved to Lily. "Bye, Lily."

"Bye-bye." The little girl's fingers flapped, chased by a self-entertaining giggle and squeak.

Liz drove home excited to have something to add to her calendar other than things from work.

Chapter Twenty-one

Matt was fairly certain little miss Liz was going to be over her head if this storm system came through like the animated Van the Weatherman had predicted. A few hours ago Matt had scoffed just as Liz had earlier, but now things seemed to be really lining up to be a humdinger that could blanket this town.

He called Liz to make sure she had the fire started, but she didn't answer.

Her phone connectivity had been spotty at best. She needed to go ahead and change cellular providers. There was only one that the locals used with pretty good success.

Matt took an old photo album off the bookcase next to the fireplace. His mother had been fanatical about archiving their lives. Every year, every trip, every occasion. He flipped through the grainy pictures of him, his sister, Krissy, and his parents. Mom would have loved the new technology and digital photography nowadays.

He came across some old summer pictures. Among the group in a trout-fishing picture he was pretty sure he could make out Liz. Waders and all. That fly-fishing cast of hers had been something he would never forget. He remembered going home and practicing for weeks trying to look as adept as she had out there. Not only had she looked good, but she always caught something.

Among Christmas pictures the year he was fourteen there were pictures from the family trip to see the lights at Angel's Rest. Liz and her grandmother were in a candid shot serving hot chocolate next to a Christmas tree. A train chugged by behind them. He lifted that picture out of the album. Liz should have it, since it was of her and her grandmother. The light displays had been so spectacular, but he'd forgotten the specifics until now looking at the pictures. Reindeer, Santa, and snowflakes hanging from the tall trees.

Matt flipped the page, and there were Hermey and the other elves in a scene that looked like it was straight out of Santa's workshop. He counted them. He'd found four with "X"s on the boxes. There were five more somewhere. Hopefully they'd find them among the things in the other cabin.

He laid the album down on the floor next to the couch and closed his eyes. Thoughts of Christmases past rolled in. Years of morning races to the tree with his sister. Mom's cooking. Dad spending the whole day with them playing. Christmas was the one day they could count on him to completely put work aside and dedicate to the family. If he ever had kids, he hoped he'd be able to give more time. Dad gave them everything they needed, but time had always been a premium.

When Matt woke up, it was almost eleven o'clock. The dark night sky had been replaced by tons of tiny snowflakes falling so fast it was nearly a whiteout in the middle of the night, and those tiny flakes had already piled into quite a heap.

He pulled on his heavy coat and went out to the porch. Leaning against the rail, he closed his eyes and let the flakes fall against his face. It looked like Van the Weatherman had known what he was talking about after all.

Matt dialed Liz again, then tried to text her. Maybe she'd already gone to bed.

He went back inside and sprawled out on the couch. Elvis lay on the floor next to him. When he was just a kid on this mountain, nights like this were the best. He still kind of got excited when there was the threat, or promise, of a real winter storm.

The lights flickered.

Things were fine for about five minutes, and then the electricity went out.

He'd been around here long enough to know that happened sometimes, and the Valley Electric Co-operative guys didn't normally take too long to restore power.

Matt lit the oil lamps on the sideboard in the dining room.

When it was close to midnight and the power was still out, and he still couldn't get ahold of Liz, he gathered Elvis and drove over to check on her.

There was already at least three inches of snow on the ground, making it hard to tell where the road ended and the shoulder began. If he didn't know the roads so well, it could have been some dodgy driving.

He pulled in front of Angel's Rest. He trudged through the piling snow carrying two portable spotlights. One for him, and one to leave with her. A large doe took off into the woods, kicking snow behind her, twigs cracking and snapping as she fled.

Matt knocked on the door of the cabin. "Hello? Liz. It's Matt." He knocked again.

She pulled open the door. "What are you do—" Her mouth dropped open. "Snow?"

"Lots of it and more to come."

"I thought they said we *might* get a flurry. I swear there were stars out when I went to sleep a few hours ago. This is no flurry."

Elvis shook hard, making his tags jingle.

"No, it most certainly is not," Matt said.

"What time is it?"

"Midnightish."

"What are you doing here?"

"Being a good neighbor." He shrugged. "Power's out. I was worried."

She spun around. He was right: the little night-light in the kitchen was dark, and the heaters weren't whirring. "Thank you."

Matt grabbed a couple of logs from the stack near the door and carried them inside. "I didn't want you to freeze to death else I might not get paid."

"I see your point."

"So I figured you could come back to my house, or I could build a fire for you here."

"Build the fire. Elvis and I will watch and learn."

Elvis woofed.

Matt gave her step-by-step pointers as he began to build a fire that an Eagle Scout would be proud of. He kind of impressed himself with it.

"You make it look so easy," she said.

He lit the match, and the rolled newspaper caught immediately. "Just lay the lit roll right between the logs like this." The flame licked the air, then the smaller log, and began to spark and sizzle the edges of the bark.

"Thank you," she said. "My first big snow."

"It's the second this year. We had our first snow the week before Thanksgiving. Totally unexpected."

"It's the first snow for me."

"But the first one doesn't count. Do you have a big pot? Or bowl?"

She cocked her head suspiciously. "I do."

"Get it."

She went into the kitchen and pulled a blue four-quart Le Creuset pot from underneath the counter. "Here you go."

In the luminous glow from the fireplace he noticed her necklace. She had it on backward—on the poinsettia side. He wondered if it was intentional. "Wait a minute. You don't cook and *this* is what you have for cookware?"

"Mm-hmm. They're pretty."

"Pretty nice." He shook his head, laughing as he walked outside and set the high-dollar pot on an old tree stump. "Tomorrow. Snow cream."

"Oh my gosh. I haven't had that in . . ."

"Too long."

"I don't know how to make it."

"You can leave that to me. It'll count as your first cooking lesson." Before she could argue, he added, "Is your phone charged?"

"Oh. I don't know." She jogged back to the bedroom and brought it back. "I'm at about thirty percent."

"I tried to call you earlier, but the calls weren't going through."

"My cell reception is lousy."

"We all use the same carrier up here. I wish I'd mentioned it sooner. It's the only one that works. I'll help you get that set up this week. Meanwhile, let me at least charge this one up in case you need help." He walked out and left Elvis with Liz in front of the fire. He put the phone on charge in his truck, then walked back to the cabin. The snow was coming down so hard that he had to stomp off his boots and brush the snow from the shoulders of his coat before going back inside.

Liz's eyes lit up. "It must be snowing even harder." She went to the window and pulled the curtain to the side. "It's so pretty."

Elvis walked to the door and woofed.

"I think he wants to go out." Matt opened the door and he barreled out.

"We should walk with him." She seemed as excited as an eight-year-old on a snow day. "Give me a second." She raced back to the bedroom and closed the door behind her. When she came out she was dressed in layers, wearing a bright red and white toboggan with a giant white fuzzy ball on top. "Get your coat."

He slipped it back on while she put on hers along with a scarf and gloves. "I'm ready!"

They went out and Elvis raced past them.

They walked out across the land toward the edge of the property. It was quiet, and walking with her seemed so right as they broke the pristine landscape with their footprints.

"You should be able to see all the way to Main Street from over there." Matt grabbed her hand as they stepped over a log and he led her to a clearing between the trees.

"It's so quiet out here."

"I love that about this time of year," he admitted. "Look." He extended his arm, pointing toward the opening in the tree line. "It looks like a Christmas card."

Below them Antler Creek was nothing but snow and rooftops. Not a single light disturbed the scene, and even with no light the town seemed to sparkle down there, showing off the simple joy of its people.

Her eyes glistened. "This place brings me such joy . . . right down to my freezing toes."

He laughed. "You're going to need warmer boots."

"You're right about that. I hate to leave this view, but we better get back." She turned to head home. "Come on, Elvis."

Matt walked beside her, and Elvis romped next to them, biting at the snow.

"He's going to get a brain freeze if he keeps that up." She'd never seen Elvis expend so much energy. "I think he's definitely a snow dog."

"He does seem to be in his element, doesn't he?"

Back at the cabin Liz put down a bowl of water for Elvis, then made coffee. She carried two mugs over to the fireplace, and sat on the floor next to Matt.

They warmed up by the fire, letting the crackle of flames take the place of conversation as they sipped their coffee. It was nice just sharing the space with her.

"It doesn't seem like the electricity is going to come back on anytime soon," she said.

"Yeah, doesn't look good. I should probably go so you can get some rest." He got to his feet. "You should be plenty warm with this fire."

"Yes. Absolutely," she said with a smile. "I promise I'll keep adding logs, just like you showed me."

"And be sure the screen is in place so any sparking embers remain in the firebox. You don't want to set this place on fire."

"No. One project is enough. Thank you so much for getting the fire started for me. It was really nice of you to come over here in the middle of the night to rescue me."

"You didn't need rescuing," he admitted, "but I'm glad I didn't miss sharing your first big snow."

"Me too."

"I'll go get your phone, then Elvis and I'll head on out." Matt didn't want to overstay his welcome, but he really didn't want to leave. "And snow cream tomorrow. My treat."

Her face lit up. Tomorrow couldn't get here fast enough.

Chapter Twenty-two

The next day Liz could hardly believe how beautiful the snow was. All of the footprints they'd made last night were completely covered over this morning. As if it hadn't happened.

But it did.

Planning to treat herself to a hot Creekside Café breakfast, she bundled herself up and got into her four-wheel drive. She tried to pull out, but all she did was spin. She got out to look and realized the snow had drifted almost up to the bumper. It wasn't likely she'd be going anywhere anytime soon.

As she stood there looking at the hopeless situation, Matt drove up.

She waved. He always showed up at just the right time.

He rolled down his window. "Where are you going? I told you I'd make snow cream this morning."

"I was going to go to the café for breakfast."

"Maizey doesn't have power down there either. I made biscuits and sausage gravy."

"Have you taken me to raise?" It was a joke, but it was

beginning to get a little ridiculous. "I don't remember the weather ever being this extreme."

"That's because as a kid you don't have to do anything except play on a snow day."

"That's true," she said, and then an idea hit her. "We should build a snowman!"

Matt looked at her like she was crazy, but then he smiled. "Really?"

"Yes! Sure!" She ran over to a wide patch of smooth snow. "How about here?"

"Yeah. We can do that." He bailed out of his truck and raced over to her side. Together they scooped and mounded snow, and it didn't take long to get the huge base of the snowman heaped into place.

"The snow is wet enough to pack," Matt said. "It's perfect for snow building."

She pushed her wad of snow, trying to roll it into a bigger ball. "It's heavy." She let out a puff of frosty mist.

"Yeah. It is."

There has to be an easier way. She jumped to her feet, ran over to pop the back hatch on her Range Rover, and took out a bucket. "Reinforcements!" She quickly fashioned the head for the snowman.

"Nice job!"

"Thank you very much. Plus, the bucket can double as a hat. Here, help me do the middle one."

He took the lead, and finally they had the perfect-size tummy layer for Mr. Snowman.

Matt lifted the middle section to sit on top of the bottom layer, giving it a good shove to make sure it wouldn't roll off.

She wandered off in search of something they could use for the eyes, nose, and mouth. With so much snow, it was slim pickings to find anything, but she did come back with two medium pinecones for eyes, and a row of small ones to use for the mouth.

Elvis lay nearby in the frosty yard biting at mouthfuls of snow.

"What is he doing?" Liz asked. "Do you think he needs water?"

"No," he said. "He seems to believe it's his job to eat *all* of the snow."

"That's hysterical."

"He's still a puppy. Hopefully, he'll figure it out."

She stuck the pinecones in place, then removed her scarf and wrapped it around the snowman. "It's great. All we need is a hat." She lifted the bucket.

Matt took off his cap and placed it on top. "Mine looks better." He stepped back, taking stock of what they'd built. "It's missing something. . . ." He jogged over to the tree line and came back with a small pine branch. He tugged his pocketknife from his pocket and trimmed it down to nearly nothing, then pressed it just above the mouth of the snowman for a nose. "He's one handsome dude now."

"I guess he deserves a name."

Matt thought for a second, then raised a finger in the air. "I've got it. How about Flurry?"

She wrapped her hands around Matt's biceps. "I like it." She snuggled in close for a moment, then pulled away. "I'm getting cold. You want to come in for some hot chocolate? I think I can get water hot enough in the fireplace to make some."

"Sounds good."

She grabbed the breakfast bag he'd brought. As they walked

back over to the cabin she wished they'd built Flurry over here where she could enjoy him.

It was a bit of a comedy of errors trying to get a pan of water close enough to the fire to warm up the water without spilling it, but eventually with Matt's help she got it done.

She went to her bedroom and dragged the quilt from her bed. The king-size quilt was plenty big enough to reach between them without being too awkwardly close.

"This is the quilt you got at Flossie's, isn't it?"

"Yeah. My first Angel's Rest purchase."

He tucked his feet under it. "A good one." Elvis plopped down on the floor and put his chin on the quilt. Matt took his phone out and took a picture of him.

They sipped hot chocolate in front of the fireplace, and Matt played old country Christmas music from his phone. Willie Nelson crooned "Pretty Paper." Gram had always loved that song.

The two of them talked about music, favorite books, architecture, even most embarrassing moments.

She got up and checked the time on her phone. "I can't believe how much time has flown by with us sitting here talking."

"You're easy to talk to," he said.

"It's been fun. How long do these power outages usually last? I guess it could take a long time."

"No. Actually, it's just the opposite," he said. "It's rare we are down for more than a day even in the worst of storms. I think this time we just had so much heavy ice it seems to have the whole town out."

"So, you don't consider this a bad storm?"

"No. I consider it a perfect storm."

"For what?"

"Oh, you just wait." His eyebrows waggled in a goofy way. "Are you warm yet?"

"Mm-hmm."

"Dry?

"Yes. What are you up to?"

"Get your coat. We're going for a ride." Matt stood. "I want you to see something. Antler Creek at its finest, actually."

"Great." She didn't even hesitate, hopping to her feet and heading for her coat.

"Do you mind if we leave Elvis here?" The dog licked his lips, but one side of his lip stuck on one of his canines.

Liz and Matt both laughed. "See. He looks like Elvis."

"He definitely does."

"We'll be back in a bit, buddy. No sleeping on her bed."

"You do whatever you like, my sweet Elvis." She and Matt walked outside, and as soon as they crossed the makeshift bridge over the trench in front of her house, they both broke out into a run toward his truck, laughing.

Matt jumped, pretending to high-five Flurry as they dashed by him.

The sun was beginning to set, and with the temperatures dropping the snow was crunchier than it had been earlier.

They got in his truck, and he pulled out of the driveway.

"Where are you taking me?"

"You'll see."

She was beginning to like his surprises, but she was dying to know where they were going.

He took the road straight down the mountain, then headed across town. When they passed the turn toward the interstate, there were pickup trucks lining one whole side of the street.

"What's going on?" It seemed as if everyone in town knew about wherever it was they were going, but she didn't remember anything being in this block.

He pulled along the curb between two trucks. A rainbow of colors dotted the hill.

Her mouth dropped open. "Every kid in town must be sledding here tonight."

"Probably every dad too. When the power goes out, and there's snow . . . this is where everyone comes."

"Oh, my gosh. How fun."

"Mill Hill is perfect for sledding, plus they have hot chocolate and that old barn has heat. A place to warm up and visit until the power comes on. If there's one thing the people of these mountains know, it's how to bring the community together when things go wrong. In this case, when we lose power, there's always Mill Hill."

"Is there a mill here?"

"No. The Mills own the land. Generators offer light, fun, and hot chocolate. And there are firepits for s'mores."

"I love s'mores. Pop used to make the best s'mores over our firepit."

"I remember that," Matt said.

"Are we going sledding?" She wasn't sure how much she liked the idea of flying fast down an icy hill on top of a board with metal railings. She'd never been much of a daredevil.

"No."

That put her at ease. "Watching sledding is fun too."

"No, ma'am." Matt shook his head. "I'm more competitive than that, and something tells me you might be too."

"Cool." She clapped her hands. "What do you have in mind?"

"Follow me." He walked to the top of the hill where kids were sledding, then veered off to the back side, where people were going down a gentle slope on what looked like giant plastic trash can lids headed for three-foot-tall bowling pins.

"Human bowling? Oh no." She wagged her finger, and took a giant step backward. "You're not getting me to do that."

"Chicken?"

"It's crazy."

"Crazy fun," Matt said. "Seriously. The pins are inflatable and made of soft rubbery bouncy stuff. It doesn't hurt one bit."

"Then, you go first."

"You're on." He paid at the shed, then brought two plastic saucers over to where she was standing. "We're on lane five."

"I have a very bad feeling about this."

"Don't worry. So, here's how it works. We each take a turn being the ball by sitting on the saucer sled and gliding down to knock over the big blow-up pins." Matt waved to someone at the bottom near the pins. "Wave to Flossie."

"Flossie? As in the old lady from the antique shop Flossie?"

"There's only one Flossie. Her family owns all of this. Well, she does now. She's the only one left. She's been running this snow bowl for years."

"Snow bowl?" She laughed. "Fine, so how do we keep score?"

"Just like bowling. We make ten runs, and Flossie handles all of the official scoring."

Liz took the blue saucer. "Okay. You first."

He sat in the red sled, bunched his knees up tight against his body, then bounced his butt to get moving. On the way down he leaned to the left and right, trying to aim for those big pins, but in the end he only knocked the left four down.

A brightly lit scoreboard showed his total of four on the left. Her score was still blacked out.

"I can beat that," she said. Of course, he couldn't hear her from all the way down there. She got in her saucer and slid down the hill. The tighter she bunched the faster she went, and it made her scream, but it was fun.

Plowing right through the middle of those bowling pins, she ended up with a 7–10 split, but she still beat his glide. "You're on, Matt!" The scoreboard updated. Eight to four.

With each glide, the smack talk got a little sillier. It was an absolute blast. People started gathering at the top of the hill, watching and rooting them on.

An air horn blew. "That means it's the last frame," Matt announced.

He'd have to do something pretty spectacular to beat her now. She wasn't even worried.

Matt slid down the hill again and got all ten pins. He leapt to his feet whooping and hollering, then ran back to the top. "A strike in the tenth frame means I get two more slides."

Liz was trying to do the math in her head. He probably could beat her. Especially if she choked on her slide. *I've got to beat him.*

Matt went down the hill again, and, just as before, he hit the pins right in the middle, knocking all of them down. He walked up the hill looking a little like Mick Jagger strutting off some satisfaction. And darn if Matt didn't get one more strike on his next glide.

"No fair. You've done this a million times," she said.

"Don't be a sore loser," he teased.

"I haven't lost yet." She went right to the starting line, then slid her sled up and down a four-foot path up to the line trying to slick up her descent. She jumped on the saucer, squatted, and went flying down the hill. She'd never admit it to Matt, but her eyes were closed half the time. She was lucky she hit the pins at all, and luckier that all of them went down. She didn't even realize they had until she heard everyone clapping and yelling.

She eked out the win by sliding a five and a four—winning by two points. Matt jogged down the hill to where she was still jumping around doing a victory dance.

He caught her hand and spun her, then pulled her in close.

Her breath caught as he held her close for a two-count. She blinked snow from her lashes, and for a moment she could feel the warmth of his breath, and the pounding of her heart.

Flossie announced Liz the winner over a bullhorn. People clapped, and the next set of bowlers started their game.

She pulled out of his arms and brushed the snow from her clothes, a little embarrassed by the public display of affection . . . or whatever that just was.

"Don't try to tell me this is the first time you've ever snow bowled," he said.

"It was."

Flossie walked over to them wearing a warm coat with a giant bowling pin embroidered across the back. "Aren't you full of surprises, Liz Westmoreland," Flossie said.

"Thank you," Liz said. "But speaking of surprises, how did you ever come up with human bowling? It's crazy!"

"I'm one of the few whose family was from all over. My favorite cousin lived in Wisconsin. He once told me about someone who had done it up there to raise money for their fire department. I thought it sounded like a good way to make a snow day fun." She spun around and showed off her jacket. "My cousin had this jacket made for me after the first year I hosted this. Ain't it grand?"

"It is."

"You're a natural, Liz." Flossie waved her clipboard in the air. "As of right now, you have the high score. At the end of the night the high score gets a five-pound decorative tin of birdseed from Goodwin's Hardware."

"Oh, my gosh. There are prizes too? This is serious business."

"Nothing serious about it, but it sure is fun." Flossie placed a gentle hand on Liz's shoulder. "Your name will stay up on this board until someone outscores you. So come on back. The bowling proceeds go to the Main Street beautification fund. Last year we made enough money to get the Christmas flags down the street. We're trying to get enough for lampposts and benches next."

That was going to take a lot of bowling. "I'll do my best to help," Liz told her.

When she and Matt walked back up to the top of the hill, the bowling line wrapped all the way around the hot chocolate shed.

"There must be forty people in line. How did you get us right in?"

Matt grinned. "I paid extra. Fund-raisers don't mind bribes. All for a good cause."

"Main Street is a great cause."

"No," he said with a snicker. "I meant bowling against you."

"You were pretty sure of yourself, weren't you?"

"Fat lot of good that did me. You swabbed the deck with me." Matt gave her a sideways glance. "I *was* undefeated."

"Until now."

"You know I'm going to want a rematch, right?"

At this rate the town might get benches and lampposts both.

Chapter Twenty-three

Liz was almost sorry the evening had to end. She hadn't had this much fun in she didn't know how long. Maybe ever.

Matt pulled into her driveway.

"Thank you for the fun night." She wished the night wouldn't come to an end.

"You're welcome."

She opened the door to get out of the truck.

He got out too, and her hopes soared.

"I'll stoke the fire when I get Elvis," he said.

Elvis. Right. She'd almost forgotten they'd left him behind. The snow crunched beneath their feet all the way to the cabin.

She opened the door and warmth rushed out. Inside, Elvis was sprawled out in front of the dwindling pile of glowing embers. "I don't think he missed us," she teased.

Elvis stood up and shook before walking over to put his nose under Matt's hand. "That's my boy."

He was so easy to be with. It was as if he and Elvis had been part of her life and this place forever.

"I'll just get this fire going and be on my way."

A million clever comments fled through her mind to get him to stay a little longer.

Matt put two more pieces of wood on the fire, then brought in a few more and set them on the hearth to dry out. "So the trick to keeping your fire burning longer is giving your logs a little space between them so they can feed off the heat of each other. They'll actually burn longer that way." He scooched one of the logs a little farther back with the poker. "Leave a couple of inches between two logs and then place a third caddy-corner across the top. Leaving room for oxygen."

"So, that's the trick. I was wondering why your fire burned so much better than mine."

"It's not hard to master once you know the secret. That's a skill you'll need living up here."

Living up here. That had such a nice ring to it.

"Good night, Liz. I'll see you tomorrow."

He paused, and her heart fluttered with hope.

"The crew will be here at sunup, around seven fifteen." He slapped his hand against his leg, and Elvis bounded to the door. "Hopefully, you won't even be able to hear us from way back here. Especially with the thick blanket of snow."

"I don't mind. Really. I love the sound of progress." She held the door as they left. "Goodbye. Thanks again. For everything."

Liz closed the door behind her, and leaned against it replaying the day in her mind. She had so much fun with him, and she must've been getting used to the beard, because he was very good-looking tonight. Too bad they were working together. She had a zero-tolerance rule about dating people she worked with, and in this case her whole dream could go down the tubes if something went wrong. He was handsome, nice, and funny even, but it didn't matter. Her dream, this place, was too much to risk.

She went to her bedroom to change into her pajamas. If only there were electricity, it would've been the perfect time to test out that new on-demand water heater.

As if all she'd had to do all along had been to ask for what she wanted, the lights came on.

"Nice." She went into the bathroom and twisted the handle on the faucet over the tub. She held her hand under the water. It was already hot. Good thing too, because she remembered how cold these old cast-iron tubs were.

She went to get her pajamas, and when she came back into the bathroom steam drifted above the tub. She swished the water around, then stepped in gingerly.

The hot water felt good. She might be sore tomorrow after that snow bowling, but it was so worth it. She stretched and ducked under the hot water up to her shoulders. She was pretty sure she'd used muscles she hadn't used in a while. She smiled knowing her name was at the top of the leaderboard, even though it had to have been beginner's luck.

She got out of the tub and grabbed one of her new Egyptian cotton towels. The hot water had left her skin bright pink. She'd just wrapped the towel around herself when her phone rang. Assuming it could only be Matt at this hour, she grabbed it without looking at the caller ID. "Hey."

"Hi, Liz."

Not Matt. "Dan?" She wrapped her towel tighter around her. She hadn't expected to hear from him until at least after the holidays.

"How's it going?" he asked.

"Great. We've gotten a good start on things already."

"I've been calling and texting for hours." He sounded annoyed.

"Sorry. I have lousy reception up here." *Why did I apologize?*
"I didn't have my phone with me anyways, though."

"You always have your phone."

"Not today." And she liked the feeling of being unplugged
for a while.

"So things are okay?"

"Yeah. Great."

"I was worried. I heard y'all were getting a lot of snow up
that way."

"We are. I'm fine. The power went out, but I have a nice cozy
fire and things are good. Better than good, it's beautiful here. It
looks like a Christmas card out my window."

"We had nothing but rain."

He hated rainy days. Come to think of it, he complained
about a lot of things. "We had enough snow to build a snowman.
I'm going to have to stock up on snowman accessories. I had
to make do with pinecones instead of coal, and my own scarf,
which I could have used today." A giggle slipped out. It had been
fun.

"That's not like you. Doesn't sound like you to settle."

Settle? It was a snowman, for goodness' sake. "It turned out cute,
but I'm definitely going to create a couple snowman kits for the
future. Guests would have a blast with that."

"Guests? You're still seriously planning to invest your money
in that place?"

"More than ever."

"I thought once you had time to think about it you'd come to
your senses. I mean, if you want a B and B, open one here in the

city, where you can charge a premium for it and have a steady stream of customers."

"That can be your dream. I feel very good about my decisions. So much so that I'm taking a six-month leave of absence to make sure it goes without a hitch."

"You're going to take a leave of absence? You love that job."

She realized she hadn't told him about that. "I love this more. I'm excited about it."

"Why would you risk mucking up a great career? This isn't like you at all, Liz."

"This has always been my dream. Who knows when an opportunity like this would arise again? It's like new energy has been breathed into my life."

"It just sounds like a lot of work to me. Next thing you know you'll be canning vegetables and chopping wood."

"Would that be so bad?" She rather liked the idea. "Actually they deliver the wood already chopped and stack it too. You know, Dan, this is why I didn't list my house with you. You still think I'll fail, or I'll come back. I don't think you'd really try to sell my place."

"Might've been the biggest favor I ever did for you."

"Stop it."

"I sold that house over on Silverleaf Street today."

Now, the real reason he'd called. "That's great." It was always about him. Every time he closed a deal he called her, and they'd go to his favorite bistro to celebrate. "Congratulations. That's great. Wait a minute, this busts your myth that no one buys a house in the rain."

"It also busts our pattern of celebrating when I sell one. I miss having my buddy around," he said.

Her heart squeezed. They'd had a lot of fun together, but that's all it ever was and all either had wanted it to be. "I want more, Dan. From my life, and myself. Antler Creek is where I want to be."

"Forever? Come on, Liz, once you get the project done you'll be ready to move on to something else. That perfect little Hallmark-movie town is going to get old once that project is complete."

It was true that as soon as she finished one project she was ready to move on to the next, but this was different. It wasn't just a project; it was a lifestyle change. A way of life that really made her feel whole again. "Not this time. This is the real deal for me, Dan."

"Thanks for letting me share my news."

"Anytime." And she meant that. She treasured his friendship. No, he wasn't perfect. He was self-centered, bossy, and sometimes lazy, but they'd been friends for a long time. She'd miss him too.

Everything in this town seemed as perfect as a Hallmark movie. Even the people in the town were amazingly quirky and good. No, she couldn't believe this would wear off.

She stoked the fire the way she'd seen Matt do, and it flamed up. Placing the logs that he'd left on the hearth a couple of inches apart as he'd taught her, she stood back and let the fire do its own magic. Then she put on her coat and stepped outside to grab a couple more logs to lay by the hearth for the next round. Tiny snowflakes fell again.

What was it Gram had always said? *Big flakes will go away, but tiny flakes are here to stay.*

That never made sense. It seemed the big flakes would be the ones that would add up to accumulation, not the other way around.

It wasn't even Christmas and there was a lot of winter ahead of her. She carried the logs in and set them on the hearth, then added firewood to her supplies list.

She turned off the lights in the living room and kitchen, then went to her bedroom.

She knelt beside the bed, folding her hands on top of the quilt the way she'd done when she was a child staying in the main house. She bowed her head.

"Heavenly Father, it's been a long time since I got down on my knees like this. Please forgive me for letting myself get ahead of your plans. You know every decision I need to make, and your will should be my way. I'm feeling tugged by nostalgia, but warned by friends, and I want to do the right thing. I need your guidance, and I believe you've placed new people in my life to help me on this path. Fill me with peace in knowing that even if I take a wrong turn, your purpose will prevail. In Jesus' name, Amen."

She stood, tired and content from the long day. Peace washed over her.

Something caught her eye in the corner of the room. She walked over and picked up an angel made of silk and feathers with tiny beaded adornments and a golden halo. Once white, the fabric had yellowed. Her long lashes were lowered as if in prayer, her hands pressed together. This had to be from her grandmother's collection too.

How could I have missed this earlier? She picked up the angel and held it to her heart.

Eyes closed, she smiled and lifted her chin. "You sure work fast." Her heart felt full, and contentment spread through her body.

If this isn't a sign that I'm on the right path, I don't know what is.

Chapter Twenty-four

After a great night's sleep, Liz was ready to tackle the cabin again, only she really didn't have the clothes for this kind of weather. Or that dirty work. One of the many things that had been on Liz's to-do list had been to become more active. Working on that cabin had been a good workout. She could feel the soreness in her arm muscles today. At least there wasn't a budget or timeline for activity, and she didn't have to rely on anyone but herself to succeed.

She googled the closest clothing store that might sell some suitable work attire. There was a farm store in the next town. She put the address in her GPS. It didn't take but about twenty minutes to get there.

She grabbed a shopping cart and started browsing. They had a great selection of flannel-lined jeans, thick socks, and hiking boots to keep her warm, and the price was sure right.

An aisle of bird feeders caught her eye. She turned and added one to her cart, along with an outdoor thermometer to hang outside her window. It would be nice to know just how cold or warm it was outside. She tossed a couple of dog bones in her cart for Elvis. Maybe someday she'd get a dog of her own. She imagined a little Yorkie for a moment, then replaced that idea with a friendly, outgoing Labrador retriever. Maybe a chocolate one. A Lab would be a much better choice. She could even make him part of the hiking excursions.

She pushed the cart to the checkout, liking the idea of a job that didn't require her to be on the road half the month.

A woman with beautiful red hair stopped her cart right next to Liz. "Hi. You're Liz, right?"

"Yes." Liz looked around. The stranger had to be talking to her. "I am. Yes."

"You bought the old inn over in Antler Creek, right? I heard you were related to the original owners."

"I was. Did you know them?"

"I didn't, but my husband grew up in Antler Creek. He's over there getting horse feed for his folks. He said he recognized you from church. It's all he and his parents have talked about. If you need any help let me know. My name is Ginger. I live in Antler Creek. Right in the middle of town."

"Nice to meet you."

"My kids are in school until three, so I could help during the day if you need me."

"Oh, well I've got a contractor working on the house," Liz said.

"I didn't mean for a job, I meant just to help. Ya know, run an errand for you. Talk? Whatever. I'm crafty and pretty good at putting things together. I've got time."

"Thank you. That's so nice."

Ginger shifted from foot to foot. "You know what, I'm sorry. You must think I'm crazy just walking up and offering that. My husband is always saying I don't know a stranger. Sorry."

"No. Not at all." *Well, maybe a little. It definitely caught me off guard, but it's sweet.* "It's nice. Neighborly. I appreciate it, actually."

"What am I thinking? I know!" The woman rolled her eyes, but then grinned. "The kids and I are baking Christmas cookies this afternoon. Why don't you come over and help? A couple of the other moms are bringing their kids too. It'll give you a chance to meet some neighbors."

Liz's first inclination was to decline, but really there was nothing holding her to the house today. "You know what. I'd love to come."

Ginger squealed as she jotted down her address, then gave Liz turn-by-turn directions.

"What can I bring?"

"Just yourself. We'll have so much fun."

"I'm really looking forward to it." Liz felt more at home here already than she did in Charlotte the whole time she'd lived there. And it wasn't just the house and the surrounding nature anymore. It was the people.

She swung by the market on her way home and headed for the baking aisle to pick up a few extra cookie decorations for the kids. You could never have too many decorations for cookies. Plus, those little silver dragées had always been her favorites.

LATER THAT AFTERNOON, Liz drove down to Ginger's house. It was a well-maintained house with beautiful holly bushes at each edge of the wide welcoming porch, and a cheerful pop of bright red on the front door. She gathered her bag of cookie decorations and walked to the door.

The wreath was a hoop of shiny Christmas ornaments in silver, gold, and green with a fluffy shimmering white bow. She pressed the doorbell, which promptly responded with the instrumental of "We Wish You a Merry Christmas." Ginger opened the door, revealing three children peeking out from around her hips.

"Come on in!" She swept the children back to clear the way and led Liz into the kitchen. Four other women were already there, with bowls of dough and cookie sheets in front of them. The kids must've ranged from two to twelve. They were moving around so much she couldn't even do a head count. *And this is before the sugar,* she thought, as she held her bag of additional sugary decorations.

For two hours, moms took cookie sheets in and out of the oven in eight-to-ten-minute intervals, and the kids decorated in an assembly line like little elves at the North Pole on steroids. Colorful decorated cookies were piling up all around them.

Liz had never seen so many fresh baked cookies in one place in her life.

"It's almost time to start delivering cookies!" Ginger announced. The children bounced with excitement, but they seemed to have the drill down pat. Each grabbed a paper plate. They lined up single-file, then marched around the table taking one cookie each lap until they had six on their plate. Then, one of the moms wrapped each plate with plastic wrap. The final step was to put a sticker with a picture of Santa on top.

Ginger brought in two laundry baskets lined with towels. The children placed the wrapped plates in the baskets one at a time.

"Hello," a man's voice came from the front of the house.

Liz had expected to meet Ginger's husband, but instead it was Matt who walked into the kitchen. He was everywhere.

"Oh?" He did a visible double take. "Liz? Hey. I didn't know you knew—"

"She didn't," Ginger said. "I saw her at the store this morning and told her she had to come."

Liz waved to him from across the room. "Hi, again."

"Well, let's get this show on the road, how about it?" Matt clapped his hands. "Who's ready?"

The kids cheered so loud it tickled Liz's ears.

"Let's go then," Matt said. The kids swarmed him, and he looked like he loved every minute of it.

He stacked the laundry baskets one on top of the other and headed outside with a parade of little bodies following behind him.

Liz took out her camera and snapped a picture. *Absolutely precious.*

He piled everyone into the back of his pickup, including the moms, but Ginger rode up front with all the addresses, and Liz climbed in the seat behind Matt.

Matt honked the horn, which apparently was the signal that they were getting ready to take off, because the kids hit the deck.

"Merchants or homes first?" Matt asked Ginger.

"Let's do the merchants first. That'll give people more time to get home before we get there."

"Here we go." Matt pulled the truck out of Ginger's driveway and headed for Main Street.

At each stop the moms spotted the kids as they tumbled out of the truck to go in and wish the merchant a Merry Christmas, hand over a plate of cookies, and then sing one quick round of "We Wish You a Merry Christmas" before racing back to the truck in a fit of giggles.

Matt stood at the truck bed lifting the kids one by one back into the truck and securing the tailgate.

At the end of the evening they'd covered a pretty good bit of the town. Ginger and her team of little ones and friends had definitely spread good cheer here tonight.

When all was done, Liz helped Ginger clean up her kitchen. It took some elbow grease to get up all the dried sprinkles and icing, but together they made fun work of it.

"Thank you for inviting me over," Liz said. "I've had such a great night. Count me in on this tradition next year too."

"Thanks for not thinking I'm some kind of crazy nut. I really enjoyed spending time with you too. Everyone really likes you. We're glad you're going to be around."

The kind words poured over Liz in a way she hadn't expected. "Thank you." Her own words came out quiet. "I'm going to head out, but if I can ever help out you let me know."

"Ditto." Ginger walked over and gave Liz a big hug. "Welcome to the neighborhood." She turned and picked up a little red tin that was sitting on the kitchen counter. "This is my own special recipe. Just for you."

Of course it is. I love this place. "Thank you."

It was late when Liz got back home. The snow was slick and shiny under the bright moon and stars tonight. She stepped carefully, trying to keep her footing.

The fire had fizzled out while she was gone, but it was still comfortable in the cabin.

It was still early on the West Coast. She called her parents. "Hi, Mom."

"Liz, everything okay?"

"Yes. I just helped a group of kids bake cookies and deliver them all over Antler Creek. It was amazing."

"Awww." Mom sighed on the other end of the phone. "You

really are just like your grandmother. That would've made me crazy. All those kids running around."

"Just the opposite. They were so sweet. Yeah, hyped up on sugar, but still . . . I can't believe how alive I feel up here, Mom. I love this place."

"You always did," she said quietly. "Want to talk to your dad?"

"No. Just tell him I said hello. I love you and miss y'all."

"We love you too, Liz. Good night."

She hung up the phone, glad that for once Mom hadn't turned the phone call into a lecture of some sort. She warmed up a plate of Sonny's chicken and biscuit cobbler in the little microwave while she set out to try to build her first fire on her own.

It wasn't quite as easy as Matt made it look. She ran through quite a few of those rolled newspapers before one of the logs finally caught fire. But finally one spark led to another and the fire started licking the air in pretty orangey-red flames.

She settled on the floor in front of the fireplace with the savory cobbler, wishing she'd done this two years ago.

Chapter Twenty-five

The next morning Liz walked up to the house to see how things were going. It was amazing that from inside that cabin, she really couldn't hear all the commotion of the work going on. Matt was giving instructions to a couple of the guys, while others were busy putting Sheetrock up on the new wall.

"Good morning," she said when he finished with the guys.

"Hey there." He spun around. "Did you have fun last night?"

"So much fun. Ginger is really sweet."

"Yeah, she is, and she's great at pulling people together for things like that because she's almost impossible to say no to."

"I know! But I'm glad, because I would have really missed out if I hadn't said yes." She stepped aside as one of the workers carried another piece of Sheetrock inside.

"It's nice that you drove them around last night like that. You were so good with the kids."

He shrugged. "It's nothing. They need a way to deliver good cheer, and I've got a truck. It works for everybody. What *they're* doing is nice. I'm just making it easier for them. Plus, they hook me up with cookies."

"Wait a minute." Liz turned to look him in the eye. "I could've paid you in cookies?"

"Yep."

"Man, you're right." She threw her hands in the air. "I really don't know how to operate in a small town." She offered him a playful smile.

"I think you've got potential as a small-town girl."

"Thank you." *You're a good coach.*

He grabbed her hand and gave it a squeeze.

Tingles rose all the way to her heart. *Where did that come from?* She stood unable to move for a moment, or maybe not wanting to.

"I've got to run down to Goodwin's," he said. "Need anything?"

"Um. No. Yes." She gathered her thoughts. "Yes. I need an extension cord."

"For inside or outside?"

"Inside. A brown one. Ten foot maybe?"

"Okay. I'll be back in a while." They walked toward his truck.

Elvis dropped to the ground, not looking eager to get back in the truck.

"He can stay here." Liz patted her hand on her leg. "Want to stay with me, Elvis?"

He bounced to his feet and shook, then raced to her side.

"Don't you steal my dog!" Matt warned her as he got into his truck.

"Not my fault if he falls in love with me and never wants to leave," she teased.

Matt shook his head as he drove away.

She and Elvis walked back to the cabin. Her door looked so

plain now compared to Ginger's. It might be fun to paint the front doors of the cabins. Maybe she could paint this door a pretty blue to match the bedroom. The other could be a rustic red, forest green, or even an autumnal gold. It wasn't a priority, but she liked the idea. She'd add it to the later nice-to-haves list.

The wreath on Ginger's door had been pretty too. She'd said she'd made it out of old ornaments. Liz preferred the fresh-greenery-type wreaths, though. Some fragrant pine in a nice fluffy ring, with maybe some sprigs of glossy holly and berries. There was plenty of that right here on the property. It couldn't be that hard to make one.

She gathered a trash bag and a pair of scissors to collect some materials to give it a try. Her phone was almost out of battery, so she set it on the charger, then called Elvis to come outside with her.

Around the back of the cabin the snow was still pristine except for a set of deer tracks from the woods to the middle of the field. The world seemed so quiet back here.

She walked to the edge of the woods and snipped long thin pine boughs that would be easy to arch into a circle for the wreath. She'd seen a spool of old fishing line in one of the drawers in the kitchen. She should be able to tie everything together with that, and it wouldn't even show.

Unsure of how many pieces she'd need, she clipped just one from each tree to keep from stealing all the new young growth from any single tree.

Ahead, a bright green holly bush with shiny red berries and glossy leaves looked like it would make pretty accents on the wreath, so she headed deeper into the woods. As she walked through the snow, she looked up at the grand height of the trees. Some of them had to be at least thirty or forty feet tall. Big, strong, old trees that had probably been here long before her grandparents had even lived here.

Three huge bunches of mistletoe hung in the tree over her head. Why was it that mistletoe was always so high in the tree? She wished there were some way to get some of the mistletoe down. She picked a pinecone from one of the low limbs and tried throwing it to hit the mistletoe, but she couldn't even throw that high.

She stood there staring at it. *If Matt had been here, would we have kissed here under the mistletoe?*

Elvis licked her hand.

"Thanks, Elvis. Your kisses are good, too." Mistletoe would have been a cool addition, but that wasn't going to happen. She meandered a little farther into the woods. Birds flitted from one tree to the next, their feathers puffed up against the chill.

"You're so fortunate to live among all this beautiful nature, Elvis. Look around. It's magnificent."

He panted as he walked next to her. In some places the snow was clear up to his belly, so he had to kind of leap to move ahead.

The drifts were higher through this part of the woods. She was pretty sure this path led down to the stream where she and Pop used to fly-fish. She wished she'd taken the time to dress more appropriately for the hike. She balled her freezing hands into fists and rubbed them together. Even blowing into her hands didn't seem to help.

"Come on, Elvis. We better head back." She turned around and followed her tracks back. Elvis loped ahead, then came back to do it all over again. The way the snow crunched under her boots, it sounded as if she were a whole group of hikers.

Something scampered off in the bushes nearby. Maybe a bird.

Could've been a rabbit or young deer too, but she didn't see anything but a chubby brown bird sitting on a branch.

"If I put seed out for the birds, do you promise not to eat it?" Elvis looked at her as if he couldn't make any promises.

A clump of something green lay in the snow about twenty yards to her right. She left her trail to see if it was mistletoe. It very well could be, because there was a big bunch in the tree right above it. It was a large pile. It might even be enough to use on the wreath and make a mistletoe ball.

In her excitement she sped up to a jog, but her foot caught on something, and she flung forward into the snow with a thud.

Her hands smacked the ground, and her trash bag of clippings went flying in front of her.

She lay there for a second trying to gather herself, unsure if she was hurt or not.

Sucking in a breath, she lifted herself up to her hands and knees. "I'm okay. It's okay," she said, convincing herself to try to get up.

Pain seared through her body when she tried to pull her foot forward.

Her ankle had caught in a root or something. She swept at the snow, revealing a gnarled mass of roots above the ground that had been completely hidden by the smooth snowdrift.

"No." *Oh no. No.*

With the help of a tree limb lying on the ground nearby, Liz managed to free her foot, then used the stick for leverage to stand. "Please be okay." She took a careful step forward onto her foot, but it wouldn't hold her. She gasped and stood there heaving, tears falling down her cheeks. She couldn't walk back.

Getting back down on the ground with a bad foot wasn't easy. Finally, she just dropped down into the snow, grabbed the trash bag, then rolled over and began crawling back toward her original path.

Elvis ran over to her and licked her face, then ran a large circle around her.

With each movement forward, pain shot through her whole leg. Her pants were now soaking wet, and her hands stung. She tried to catch her breath, then tucked her hands inside her coat to warm them.

Elvis didn't understand what was going on.

He thought it was some kind of game, and he was loving every minute of it.

He kept running around her in circles, then stopping and bouncing in the snow close to her. Then he'd woof and do it all over again.

She crawled as far as she could, until her hands burned.

How will I ever get back?

She rose up on her knees and inched forward. Her foot throbbed from the swelling.

Just keep moving.

All she could see was snow and trees. No one would be able to see her either. Trying to keep her hands from being so cold, maybe even frostbitten, she grabbed the trash bag to wrap her hands. That offered some relief.

I can't believe I came out without my phone. Matt warned me.

Alternating between walking on her knees and crawling, she finally made it to the cabin. Inside, she lay on the floor in front of the fire and cried.

Her skin stung, and her whole body ached.

Elvis lay on the floor next to her. She put her arms around his neck and cried into his soft fur. She needed help.

Scooting across the floor, she got over to the kitchen island and pulled her phone down from the charger.

After all his warnings, she hated to even call him, but she knew he'd come.

The call wouldn't go through. She prayed the text would.

Liz: Matt, I need help.

HER PHONE IMMEDIATELY rang back. "Hey, Liz. I'm still at the hardware store. Do you need something from here?"

"No," she said between strained breaths.

"Are you okay?"

"I'm hurt. I fell."

"I'm on my way."

She climbed up to her feet and tried to hop toward her bedroom, but she couldn't without causing pain, so she got back down on the floor and sat in front of the fire to wait on Matt. When she sat perfectly still, the pain wasn't quite as bad.

The front door flung open and Joe Don, Bubba, Billy, George Junior, and Glenn all ran inside. "What happened?"

"Matt called. He's on his way. Are you bleeding?"

"She's freezing cold," Bubba said. "Go get a blanket off her bed."

The next thing she knew she was huddled in blankets, and Joe Don was pushing a cup of hot chocolate in front of her.

She pushed it away. "I can't drink it." The pain made her nauseous.

"It'll help get you warmed up. Just try to take a little sip at a time." Joe Don put the mug in her hands. "Holding the mug will warm up those hands too."

Matt stomped through the door. "What happened?"

"I fell. I was collecting stuff to make a wreath. I thought I saw some mistletoe on the ground and I was looking up and caught my ankle in a root and fell forward."

Matt knelt beside her and laid his hand on her arm. "Did you hear anything pop or crack?"

"I don't know, Matt." She sucked in a sobbing breath. "It happened so fast. I was up and then I was flat on my face."

He scooped her up into his arms. "I'm taking you to the hospital. Bubba, get the door." He started moving through the room.

She laid her head against his shoulder. A hot tear ran down her cheek to his jacket.

"Thanks, guys." Matt helped her into the passenger seat, then ran around to the driver's seat and hit the road.

She clung to the door handle as he sped around the corner. "Okay, don't wreck us. We don't want to both be hurt."

He opened the middle console and rummaged around, then handed her a bottle of pain reliever. "Take two of these."

She took them, and then leaned her head back, trying so hard not to moan or complain.

He laid a hand on her leg. "You okay?"

She shook her head.

"Did you hit your head?"

"No. I don't think so. It's just my ankle or foot. I can't stand. It's like it's not there. It won't hold me at all."

"Okay. We'll be at the hospital soon. Hang in there."

The hospital was about a forty-minute drive, but thankfully the ER was empty when they got there. They checked Liz in and a nurse wheeled her straight back to triage.

Liz was grateful for Matt's help, but she was also happy he

hadn't come with her to triage, because when they tried to get her boot off she screamed out.

Tears streamed down her face now that she didn't have to act brave for him.

The nurse worked for a good five minutes trying to get Liz's boot off, but with every tug or pull Liz cried out. She couldn't hold it back. The pain was terrible. Finally, the nurse pulled out a big pair of scissors and cut the leather to free her foot.

It seemed like the second her foot came free from the boot it swelled to twice its size.

"It doesn't look good," the nurse said. "We're going to take you to X-ray. I need to be able to get up to your knee and get this sock off. Can I cut your jeans?"

"I don't care."

"I could get you a gown if you'd rather take them off."

If she could even get them off, there'd be no way to get them back on over a cast. The thought of riding home in a hospital gown with Matt was not appealing. "Cut the jeans."

The doctor came in. "How are we doing?"

"You're definitely doing better than I am right now."

He pushed and prodded and asked her a multitude of questions before sending her off to X-ray. Afterward, it didn't take long for them to confirm what she'd feared. She'd broken her ankle and a small bone in her foot.

When the nurse wheeled her back out, Liz had a soft cast up to her knee, a pair of crutches, a prescription for pain medication, and an appointment to see an orthopedist in a few days when the swelling went down.

Chapter Twenty-six

Liz shook her head. There was no way she was staying with Matt. She could take care of herself.

"It would be so much easier, and I have satellite television, and . . ."

"No, thank you, Matt."

When they got to the cabin, he carried her inside and set her up in the bed with her foot propped up on pillows. "It has to be above your heart so it won't swell. I have a flex-fit bed in one of my guest rooms. I can put you in the zero-gravity position and you'll be all set. It's really comfortable."

"I can prop it up on pillows. The nurse already explained all of this to me."

Matt sat on the edge of the bed. "I'd feel so much better if you were staying at my house in one of my guest rooms. You'd be a lot more comfortable. Plus, if you have trouble, I'd be there to help."

She closed her eyes. "All I want to do is go to sleep. I don't need help for that."

"That's the pain pill at work. They'll knock you out. I don't feel good about leaving you."

"Thanks for the rescue, but I'm not leaving here. Go home. You need to sleep tonight too."

"Keep your phone next to you, and call me. Or call someone. Anyone. If you need help. Don't be a fool and not ask for help."

"I promise I'll ask for help . . . if I need it."

He wrote down a list of phone numbers and set them on the night table, but she was already asleep.

When she woke up she was groggy. It wasn't until she tried to get out of bed that she remembered what had happened. As soon as she put her casted foot on the floor it ached, and it all came rolling back.

According to the clock, she'd slept either ten minutes or nearly twelve hours. It definitely hadn't been just ten minutes. She remembered Matt coming in to check on her several times through the night. And Elvis. Elvis had been here. Even sleeping on the bed with her at one point, unless that was all just a dream.

She got herself to a standing position. Elvis trotted into the room. With the crutches under her arms she could barely get herself propelled forward.

Using the crutches was a joke. She finally ended up putting them down, and using the bed and the dresser to push off and hop her way to the bathroom. It was just easier that way.

Her head was in a fog. There was no way she was going to be able to accomplish anything today. Probably not for a few days while she was on these pills.

A pang of guilt . . . or something . . . shot through her.

Was this the sign she'd been asking for?

Had her fall been some kind of warning? A catalyst to get her back on the right track?

If Matt had fallen on her property he might have sued her and she could've lost everything. She needed to make sure she had this place properly insured, with all the workers that were going to be around for the coming months, not just for the value of the home but for accidents like the one she'd had. Thank goodness she still had good insurance through work.

She should have had her phone with her, but it worked only about half the time anyway. She could've frozen to death out there.

That morbid thought left her feeling lonely and a little afraid.

Feeling a little lost, she picked up her phone and called her parents. Unfortunately, there was no answer, so she got back in bed.

A knock at the front door startled her. Who would be here? Only Matt really knew she was staying here, but that wasn't Matt's knock. Plus, he always announced himself when he knocked.

There was another knock and then a feminine hello. The front door groaned as it opened.

"Who is it?" Liz called out.

"Sorry to intrude. I'm Matt Hardy's sister. He told me about your fall. Can I come in?"

"I guess so. It's kind of hard for me to get out there." Between the pain and the pills she'd rather just go back to sleep.

A pretty blonde walked into her room. "I'm Krissy. I hope you don't mind me barging in, but when Matt told me about your fall, I just couldn't imagine being by myself if I were you."

She wore blue jeans and a fuzzy pullover sweatshirt with nautical flags across the front.

Liz lifted her leg back on top of the pillows. "I'm so out of it I haven't even noticed."

"At least they gave you something good for the pain." She lifted a large paper sack up in front of her. "I brought you some soup. I didn't know if you'd feel like eating, but I think something in your stomach will help you feel better."

"I *am* kind of hungry." Liz pushed herself up in the bed. "Thank you for coming. I'm pleased to meet you. Matt said you lived in South Carolina. She wondered how close they were.

Krissy dug two bowls of soup out of the bag. "Hope you don't mind if I join you. Maizey's soups are the best."

"Everything I've had from there so far has been good."

"Right? I love that place. Here." She gave Liz a bowl and a spoon.

Liz took a few bites, then looked at Krissy. "You don't really look like Matt."

"I'm his baby sister. I look more like my mom. He looks like my dad. I'm a teacher. School's out for winter break, so I figured I'd surprise Matt. Which I did, but he told me he's up to his eyeballs working on a project for you, and that you got hurt yesterday."

"There's so much to do. This is terrible timing."

"Matt will take care of the project. You just need to get well."

She thought about how he'd rushed to her aid, even carried her through the snow. Not just anyone would have done that, or offered their home. "Matt's a good guy. I'm so lucky that Maizey told me about him."

"He's the best," Krissy said. "Seriously, and I'm not just saying that because he's my big brother. If I ever meet someone as great as him I'm marrying him. There aren't many like him around these days. I know, because I've been looking high and low for one. Matt's honest, hardworking, smart, and not all that bad to look at if he's not your brother," she said with a laugh.

"I'm not much for guys with beards," Liz said, then slapped her hand over her mouth. "Oh sorry. Those pain pills seem to have dulled my filter too."

"Matt said you have a follow-up with an orthopedic surgeon later this week."

"Day after tomorrow I think. Dr. Teasdall or something like that, but I probably need to go back to Charlotte and find a good doctor." Suddenly she couldn't hold back the tears.

"Oh my gosh. Are you okay? Are you in pain?" Krissy put her bowl down and ran to Liz's side. "What can I do for you?"

"I'm sorry. I never should have bought this place. It can't be a good sign that I fell in the woods and broke my ankle. What if I froze to death? I was all by myself out there."

"But you didn't. This is just the pain medication talking." Krissy took Liz's hand. "I know I don't know you from Adam's house cat, but anyone could've fallen in this weather. Don't turn your accident into something bigger than it is."

"But there's so much to do before this place is anywhere near being ready for guests. I can't even do anything to help now. It's a sign. A bad sign."

"No it's not. It'll all work out. Just wait and see." Krissy straightened the quilt on the bed. "You're tired and stressed. Just give yourself a break. Well, not like another broken bone, but a rest."

Liz turned over onto her side away from her, and propped up the angel on the bed. Elvis had been up here sleeping on it again. Not that she minded. It was kind of sweet, really. Lying there, she felt as if she were on a slow-moving riverboat. It was starting to make her a little seasick. "You don't understand."

"Then explain it to me," Krissy said.

"I was praying for a sign that I was doing the right thing following this big crazy dream, then kerflooey, all of this happened." Tears blurred her vision. "I'm lucky all I ended up with was a broken ankle."

"You keep hanging on to that dream. Angel's Rest is a good dream. Trust me, my brother is the right guy to fix up this place. He can do anything."

She heard the words, but they didn't register in her foggy brain. It didn't matter anyway. "I need to go back to sleep."

"You do that. Just let me know if you need anything. I brought a book with me. I'm just going to snuggle in front of that great fireplace and relax for a while."

IT WASN'T UNTIL the next morning that Liz woke up. She was lying in bed reading when she heard Matt's familiar knock at the cabin door followed by the masculine hello.

"Hey," she answered.

"You've got a visitor." Matt came in, then stepped to the side, and Krissy walked over to the bed.

"Remember me?" she asked.

"I do. I thought you were a dream." Liz covered her face. "Oh my gosh. I'm so embarrassed."

"Don't be. How are you holding up?"

"I'm just doing a lot of lying around mostly." She let out

a sigh. "I do feel better today, though. I was so out of it yesterday."

"Better than being in pain," Krissy said. "I don't know if you remember or not, but you were worried yesterday about needing to go to the city for a good doctor, so I did some investigation on your Dr. Teasdall and it turned out he's highly acclaimed. You're in excellent hands right here with him. With Matt too," Krissy said. "I think you should stay put."

Liz flashed a glance toward Matt. She hated to talk personal business in front of him. "I'm really not sure."

"I know what you said, but come on, even if this doesn't end up your forever place, at least you'll have had a Christmas here with your dream. I mean, who wouldn't want to spend the holidays at Angel's Rest?"

"I don't know." She fidgeted with a broken fingernail.

Matt stepped toward the door. "I'm going to head back to the house."

"Thanks for letting me in," Krissy said. "We'll be fine."

Liz waited until she heard the front door close behind Matt. "What if I'm not? Fine, I mean."

"Just go with the flow for a little while. Don't make any hasty decisions." Krissy sat on the end of the bed and took Liz's hand. "I'm staying at Matt's for the holidays. I live down in Hilton Head on the beach. I love it there, but there's nothing like Christmas in Antler Creek." She got up and walked around the room and whipped back the drapes. "You might as well make the best of being laid up. Don't you think?"

The bulky soft cast looked like a Macy's Thanksgiving Day Parade balloon. Way too big to be one of her limbs. "I'm not going to be up for much of anything."

"That sounds perfect. Wait a sec." Krissy left the room, then came back in and thrust a bouquet of flowers in Liz's direction. "I brought flowers to cheer up the place."

I'm lucky to have such wonderful people in my life. "That was thoughtful."

"It's a little selfish too. When Matt told me about your project I was dying to hear all about it, but he just wants to talk beams and man-hours. I want to hear about the decorating and design."

Liz relaxed a little. Where else could you show up a stranger and be treated like this? "Thank you, Krissy. I'm glad you're here."

MATT WAS GLAD Krissy had shown up when she did. He'd suspected Liz was flustered, but he hadn't realized how close she was to throwing in the towel on this place until Krissy told him what she'd said to her. Taking that fall as some kind of bad omen was crazy. It wasn't a bad omen. It couldn't be. He wanted her to stay, and if he had any say in the matter she would.

He walked back to the cabin and knocked quietly on the door.

Krissy poked her head out. "She's sleeping," she said quietly.

"Good. It's you I wanted to talk to." He nodded for her to come outside.

She stepped outside, wrapping her arms around herself to stay warm.

"So, I'm worried," Matt said. "Is she really taking this fall as some kind of sign she's doing the wrong thing? She fell in the snow. It could've happened to anyone."

"I know. I told her to not think about that."

"Look. We're making good progress around here. You need to

talk her into staying at my place with you for the next week or so until she gets through the orthopedic visit and everything. I have a plan, and I think it'll make her happy. It should also prove she is on the right path."

"You like her, don't you," Krissy said.

He couldn't hold back the smile. "Things up here have been much brighter since Liz arrived. I'm not the only one who thinks that."

"So, she and I will stay at your house, and you and Elvis stay here?"

"Yes. And don't tell Liz, but I'm going to figure out some way to make things move faster and convince her this place is the right place for her. I really don't want her to change her mind."

She raised her hands. "Okay, I'm not going to ask for a bunch of details. If chivalry isn't dead, I'm going to let you prove it and surprise both of us."

"Good. Okay. Yeah. This will work."

"Oh, and she's never been a fan of beards, so if you decide to shave it off . . ."

He rubbed his hands across his chin. "I meant to shave it off at the end of November anyway."

"I know. It was for Dad." She reached over and kissed his cheek. "You're a good son."

"Thanks, Krissy."

"You owe me."

"Don't I always?"

"She's not going to want to stay at your house. I can tell you that right now."

"I have a feeling you can be persuasive."

"I've been known to be," she said lightly. "But she's stubborn."

"So make it happen. I'll help you get her over there tonight. The house is ready for y'all. I even stocked up on groceries."

"You knew I'd agree?"

"I had a hunch."

"Fine." She turned her back on him and went inside. Matt waited outside, praying things would play out the way he'd hoped.

It seemed like ten minutes passed before Krissy came back outside. "Hey, can you come inside with me for a minute? Liz wants to talk to you."

"Yeah. Sure." He followed her inside.

"You really want us to stay at your house?"

"Sure." Matt nodded. "Yes. It was my idea."

"Why?"

"Because you'll be more comfortable, and it will be convenient for Elvis and me to be here since we're working on the house anyway. You girls can enjoy a nice Christmas. Trust me, it'll work out for everyone."

Liz shook her head. "I can't let you do that. I should just go home to Charlotte. You can still use the cabin if you want to, but I'm not going to impose on you or your sister just because I got myself hurt."

"No. Your home is here, Liz," Matt said. "You said yourself this place made you feel like yourself. Home is *not* Charlotte. Antler Creek is your home."

Liz glanced at Krissy then back at Matt. "I really wanted Antler Creek to be home."

"This is where you're supposed to be," Matt said. "You know it." He held her gaze. "I believe it." He held his hand to his heart.

Krissy gave Liz a wink and a nod.

"Please," Matt said. "Consider it a spa week for you girls. You'll have the run of my house."

"See. How can we say no?" Krissy put her hands together as if she were begging Liz to give in. "Come on. It'll be fun. Hallmark movies and everything."

"I'll even come build your fires for you," Matt said.

Liz smiled. "And make us chili over the fire one night?"

"Every night if you want." Matt's eyes held her gaze.

"I guess we're moving" was all Liz said.

Matt didn't waste one minute, else she might change her mind. Within the hour he had her on his couch with her foot propped up on four pillows in front of the television with a mug of hot chocolate, compliments of Krissy.

Chapter Twenty-seven

Matt walked through the glass door next to the big barber pole mounted to the building with the iconic red and white helical stripes. The antique pole had been there since Howie Perry's great-great-granddaddy opened the shop here on Main Street back in the early 1900s.

One of the two old-fashioned reclining barber chairs was empty when he walked in.

"Take a seat," Howie said. "You're next."

Matt took off his jacket and sat in the chair, helping himself and adjusting the lever to recline.

Howie finished the teenager's trim and sent him on his way.

"Little off the top?" Howie asked as he walked over to Matt.

"Yeah, and a full shave."

"Thank goodness. You were beginning to look like one of those mountain recluses."

Matt rubbed his hand across his chin. "It's not that bad. I didn't miss having to shave every day." But if getting rid of it meant being more appealing to Liz, it was time for it to go.

Howie went to work, giving Matt the full hot-towel treatment. There was nothing better than a straight-razor shave.

When Howie turned him back to the mirror, Matt looked like his old self again. He ran his hand over his chin. It felt smooth as silk. That beard itched like crazy when he was first growing it, but growing a mustache or beard in November to help raise awareness of men's cancers was a small thing he could do after losing Dad. He was glad he'd done it, and he would every year. No matter what.

But if this bought him a few extra points with Liz, he wasn't against it either.

He drove over to the Creekside Café for lunch.

"Aren't you looking handsome," Maizey said when he came through the door.

George Goodwin let out a hearty laugh. "Finally back to your old self, huh there, Wolfman?"

"Was it really that bad?" Matt sat on his stool.

"Yes," Maizey said. "You having the special?"

"Of course."

"How's Angel's Rest coming?" George asked. "Heard that little gal took a nasty fall."

"She did. Broke her ankle, and she's taking it as a sign that maybe she shouldn't be working on this project."

"Well, if that isn't the craziest notion."

"Same thing I thought." He ran a hand through his hair. "I'm afraid she's going to throw in the towel. I need to buy some time."

Maizey stopped and leaned on the counter. "You two are good together. You and Liz."

Matt could feel the color rise in his cheeks, but he couldn't argue with Maizey on that.

"Flossie told me about you being at her cabin at the crack of dawn when they delivered the furniture. And all about your big bowling night. Met your match finally, didn't you?" She grinned big.

"Might have." Matt looked away, trying to not come across like a goofball with the big grin he knew was on his face. "I like her. She's smart. Pretty. Good people."

"So what are you going to do, boy?" George asked. "You better figure it out, because Buck took the first twelve-pointer I ever shot up there for her to use at the lodge. That thing needs a good home."

Matt had wondered where that thing had come from. It darn near took over the whole corner of her dining area in the small cottage.

"If we could make some really fast good progress, she'd have to see that it would all come together."

Maizey pushed two sweet teas in front of them.

"Y'all have already been working sunup to sundown, haven't ya?" George asked.

"We have." Matt took a sip of tea. "It's coming along good too."

"Would more people make it faster?" Maizey asked.

"Yeah. I could have a separate crew on each of the areas."

Maizey tucked her towel into the waistband of her apron. "This might be a crazy waste of time, but you need to do something that will make it feel personal to her. What if you decorated Angel's Rest for Christmas? She talks about those memories all the time. The town would love it too. I mean, if she abandons the project at least everyone gets one good last look."

Matt sat taller in his seat.

"I don't know how you could surprise her with that with her right under your nose," Maizey said. "Just a thought."

"That's it, Maizey. And she's not under my nose. Krissy's in town. I got her to convince Liz to stay with her at my house. I think you're on to something. Now we just have to figure out where I can find some cheap labor to help me." He'd stumbled upon enough decorations in storage over there to do a pretty good replica of the old days.

George picked up his phone and poked at numbers on the screen. "Hey, Jeffrey. It's your dad. Call me back."

Matt knew George was calling in the reinforcements. George's youngest son was at Appalachian State, and they should be getting off for Christmas break any day now.

Then George dialed another number. "Christopher. It's your uncle George. What are you doing for Christmas break?" He nodded, listening and mm-hmm'ing. "Well, why don't you pack up all four of you and come work on a very special project for a lady who broke her foot up here. Need some strong able bodies to string some lights and lend a hand. We'll put you up, and feed you." George let out a hearty laugh that almost sounded like Santa's. "Yeah, turkey and ham both. No problem. Bring your sleeping bags. Yeah. See you then."

Maizey was nodding like one of those dogs in the back of a car window. "I'll feed everybody. I can do that much to pitch in."

"That would be great, Maizey." Matt got up from his chair. "I'll check with Flossie to see if we can use the barn up on Mill Hill to house kids if we run out of room."

"She won't mind," Maizey said, waving a hand in the air. "I'll call and get it arranged for you."

"Perfect." Matt called Krissy as he was leaving to tell her the plan. Krissy was completely on board. "Maizey said that making Angel's Rest feel more personal to Liz would help her feel more connected. The lights are a special memory for her." He snapped his fingers. "You know what else is special? Her grandmother's quilt."

"What are you talking about, Matt?"

"She bought this quilt at the antique shop because it reminded her of the one she had as a kid. Blue and white. Counting Stars pattern, I think she said."

"Yeah, it's on her bed."

"Do you still do those barn quilts?"

Krissy laughed. "I haven't done a big one in a while, but I'm not that out of practice. I have my class make them for their families every year as a project."

"Can you make one to fit on the left side of the house there when you come in the lower driveway? In that pattern?" Oh man, this would be perfect. Not just a memory, but also something personal and just for her.

"Get the measurements and the board. If you get your guys to sand it and set it up out in your garage I'll work on it. Liz can't get around, so she'll never know."

"You're the best sister."

"I know. You're not so bad yourself, and I can do you one better. I still have my contacts from the North Carolina Barn Quilt Trail. I'll drop them a line. They love my barn quilts."

"Sis, if you can pull that off I'll owe you big-time."

THE NEXT DAY, Matt was keeping the original crew to task on the priorities Liz had set, but everyone else was pulling together to clean up the overgrowth and give the place a quick face-lift so that they had a decent canvas to decorate.

He went through the storage boxes and found all of the elves, then dropped off the ones that had the big "X" on the boxes over at Barney's Small Appliance Repair Shop to see if he could work any magic, then stopped back over at the barbershop. One thing for sure, every woman in this town would be making her husband come get cleaned up before the holiday. This was a good place to get the word out.

"You're back already?" Howie said, as he buzzed a razor over a young boy's head.

"Need your help." Matt filled him in, and now he had a drop-off point for all extra lights and decorations. "Thanks, man."

"Happy to help." Howie swept the hair on the floor into a pile. "I've got a ton of those old glass lights. Mandy insisted on going with the new LED ones last year. You can have them for keeps. They are just taking up precious space in my man cave right now."

"Sounds good. Call me when you've got something for me to pick up."

Matt stopped by Ginger's house and asked her if she could talk to the girls about possibly helping out too. She was more than ready to tackle the job. "Plus we can make cookies and hot chocolate for the help. Happy workers make better progress."

He had no doubt that was true.

MATT STOPPED AT the store and picked up a spiral notebook, then went back to the cabin and started sketching out designs and walking off spaces for them. He hadn't felt this alive in a long time. With a cup of coffee in his hand, he walked back to the house. He flipped on the lights and walked through the empty house. It was coming together, and they could make some significant progress, but Liz had to believe in this place. If it had been his dream he couldn't imagine letting go so easy. It was an accident.

He dragged a six-foot stepladder over in front of the window. He got two strands of Christmas lights out of his truck and plugged them in under the window. Then he ran them around the ladder from bottom to top. It had the right shape. He turned off the light and stepped outside. It looked like a Christmas tree—from outside no one would ever know it wasn't.

"And now we can begin."

Music. He remembered there being music. He called in a few favors with some buddies. An old boom box, CDs, and a ton of speaker wire should do the trick.

THE NEXT MORNING Howie showed up at Angel's Rest.

"Hey, Howie. I could have picked those up."

Howie carried two boxes stacked on top of each other. "Yeah, but I have a slow morning. I thought I could deliver them and give you a hand."

"Awesome. Thanks."

An hour later, George showed up with a van full of college guys. They piled out of that van like clowns from a VW bug. They were put on cleaning up the overgrown landscaping, and by the end of the day there was already a huge improvement.

"There'll be real work to do on the landscaping come spring, but for now it's cleaned up," Matt said to George.

"Yeah, but it does look better. If it weren't so darn wet we could burn all that mess. I'll have someone come haul it off to the dump on my flatbed trailer for you."

"That'd be great, George." Matt hated to look a gift horse in the mouth, but he had to know. "I know my motivation for this, but George, what's yours?"

"Probably not so different. That girl is stirring up memories from better days around here. She's been like a breath of fresh air. I like that. I liked the Westmorelands. They did a lot for this town. For all of us."

"They did."

That night George and Matt carried all the workers down to the Creekside Café for a buffet that would smack your momma's lips for her. After dinner, they took them all over to Flossie's barn, where things had been set up for them to get a warm night's sleep after some sledding and bowling.

Matt stopped by his house to check on Liz and Krissy and deliver two dishes of Maizey's banana pudding. He was a bundle of nerves at his own house. *Something is wrong with this picture.* He wasn't even sure if he should knock before he came in. He decided to knock and just announce as he entered. If Liz was asleep she'd be in the bedroom, and that was at the back of the house, so he wouldn't disturb her anyway.

Krissy poked her head out from the living room as he walked in. "Do come on in. We're breaking in the Hallmark Channel."

"Uh-oh. I didn't even know my TV got that station."

"It does now." Krissy moved to the side and let him in. "We've got company, Liz."

Matt walked in, and Liz was dabbing at tears with a tissue, her foot propped up in the recliner on top of a pile of pillows.

"I thought these were happy movies," he said.

She sniffled. "They are. They're wonderful." Liz tore her gaze from the television to him and almost choked. "Wow! You shaved? You look amazing." Clearly embarrassed by her overenthusiastic reaction, she pulled her lips tightly together beneath a grin. "I mean you looked great before, but . . . I like it. I mean without the beard."

Elvis walked over and lay at the foot of Liz's chair with a loud sigh.

"Thank you," Matt said. "It was just temporary." He didn't offer an explanation. That was personal. "Maizey asked me to bring this over. Banana pudding." He handed one to each of them. "She makes the best around."

"That sounds so good." Liz clicked the pause button on the remote.

"You doing okay?" he asked.

"I am. I'm a little anxious about going to the orthopedic surgeon tomorrow. I don't really know what to expect."

"I can understand that, but there's no need to worry. You can't change it, and you've got lots of friends to help you out."

"Thanks, Matt."

"You girls getting settled in okay? Anything I can do?"

"Not a thing," Krissy said.

"Thank you for the hospitality, Matt." Liz looked good in this room.

"You're welcome. So, chili tomorrow night?" He clapped his hands together. "I make a mean corn bread too."

"He's not kidding," Liz said.

"Oh, I know. He's an amazing cook," Krissy said. "Her appointment is at eleven, so we'll be gone most of the afternoon."

"Good. I'll have it ready for you when you get home."

Liz pushed herself up in the chair. "Matt, do you think the two of us could go over estimates and the project plan again tomorrow? I just want to think through some of it again."

"Sure. No problem." They'd already prioritized the kitchen, mandatory for a bed-and-breakfast, and the two cabins. That way she could have an income stream as they worked on the other things. It was a good plan, but if she wanted to talk he'd go over it a hundred times, because as long as she was reviewing that plan she was still invested in it. "Anything you want, Liz."

Elvis got up and walked out of the room, then came back with a pinecone in his mouth and dropped it in Liz's lap.

Liz lit up.

Who knew Elvis could be a wingman.

Chapter Twenty-eight

Liz woke up with a knot in her stomach. She hoped the news would be good at the orthopedic surgeon today. Surgery scared her to death. She'd never been put to sleep for anything, and she really didn't want to start now.

The soft cast was hard to maneuver around in, and she was lousy with the crutches. At least if they put a real cast on her she could put her foot down to balance herself. She was afraid she was going to break her other leg just trying to get around on the crutches.

Please don't let this mean surgery. The thought of surgery made her want to cry. All those years of team sports, cheerleading, and gymnastics, and she'd never broken more than a nail. Now, at thirty-two, she had her first broken bone. There wouldn't be a ski trip this winter.

Liz slipped on her jeans, since they were the only thing that would fit over the cast, having been slit up the side. "We're going to need to stop and get me some sweatpants," she called out to Krissy. She hadn't really thought about it, because she'd been in her stretchy pajama bottoms until today. "I can't get by with just one pair of jeans."

Krissy put her purse on her shoulder. "We can stop on the way back from the doctor. Are you about ready?"

"I think so."

The two of them made it out to the front porch, but then going down the stairs seemed a lot more ominous than going up.

"I think I'd better just sit on my butt and go down," Liz said.

"That'll work." Krissy spotted her to a seated position, then Liz bumped down the stairs one at a time. She was at the bottom stair when Matt pulled up in front of the house.

"Good morning. I wanted to make sure y'all got off okay," he said as he got out of Krissy's car. "Looks like you got creative."

"Whatever works," Liz said, standing up.

"Let me help you into the car."

"Thanks, Matt." She leaned on him and let him balance her as she slid into the passenger's seat of Krissy's car.

"Good luck."

"Thank you." She raised her crossed fingers, and Krissy started the car and headed down the mountain.

MATT WENT INSIDE and worked on the chili fixin's. He figured he'd make it now, then put it over the fire when they got home this afternoon. Then they could eat whenever they wanted to tonight.

He had a lot to do, and as much as he would like to share a cozy dinner with Liz and Krissy, there wasn't going to be time for that tonight.

Liz called when they were on the way back. "Good news," she said. "I don't need surgery. It's a stable fracture, and they've recasted me. I'll be in a cast for at least six weeks. He said it could be eight weeks, but I'm good at coming in ahead of schedule, so I'm banking on six."

"I don't think it works that way, Liz."

"Can't hurt to hope. I'll still be on crutches, but he said it could've been a lot worse."

"That's great news. When will you be back?"

"Krissy says the GPS is showing about forty minutes."

"Great. I'll be there to help you get settled back in."

"That would be great," she said.

He was relieved she was at least accepting his help now. That was progress.

When they drove up he was just taking the corn bread out of the oven. He shuffled the hot pan onto the counter and turned off the oven, then brushed his hands on his pants and ran for the door. "Hey there."

Liz was already trying to get out of the car. She was a headstrong girl, but then that was one of the things he liked about her too.

"Hang on. I'll help." He swung the door all the way open, and had her lean on his upper arm to get leverage to stand. "There you go."

She wobbled, then finally got the crutches underneath her and started moving forward.

"I like the red glittery cast," Matt said.

"The guy said it was Christmassy." She took a step forward. "Three twelve-year-olds and I are all sporting them this season."

"It is Christmassy. And youthful."

"A bright side to everything." Liz stood in front of the stairs, dreading the climb.

Krissy and Matt each got on a side of her and hopped her up the stairs to the porch. "This is a lot of work," Liz said, out of breath.

"Hang on. You wait right there. I have a surprise for you." Matt jogged inside and came back out pushing a deep red scooter. He had one knee on the pad and pushed off with the other foot. "Thought you could use this."

"Where did you get that thing?"

"Ruptured my Achilles in a skiing accident a couple of years ago. That's a yearlong recovery. This thing and I were inseparable for a while."

Liz pressed her lips together. "With the little basket and everything?"

"Yes. This thing will make your life so much easier. Laugh if you must, but you are going to find that little basket quite handy."

"I'm sorry. I'm sure you're right. Thank you."

"Let me show you how it works." He took her crutches and then lined the scooter up under her bad leg. "Just put your weight on the cushion and push forward with your other foot. Use the hand brakes to stop."

She moved forward a little. "Oh yeah. This is way better."

"See?"

"Now if you can just figure out how I can still make a snow angel I'll be set."

"I'll see what I can do." He gently held her arm as she navigated through the kitchen to her chair to make sure she didn't get tripped up. "Be careful when you cross to the rug or change floor types, this scooter will toss you off if you're not careful."

"Oh yeah, that was close," Liz said. "I guess I almost have to wheelie the front tire a little to get up on the carpet."

"Yeah, be careful."

Krissy took over getting her comfortable, so Matt went and got the pot of chili and hung it over the fire. "The corn bread is on the counter. The chili has cooked and simmered, really you're just heating it back up. Do you think you can maneuver the pot?"

Krissy nodded. "Yeah. I can handle it."

"I've got to run. I've got some people to meet up with tonight."

Liz felt her mood dip. She wasn't ready for him to leave yet. She'd hoped he would stick around and at least eat dinner with them.

"See you later." Matt left, and Liz sat quietly as Krissy messed around on her computer.

AT NINE O'CLOCK, the text chime sounded on Liz's phone. "Who could that be at this hour?"

Krissy looked up. "Can you reach it?"

Liz leaned forward and grabbed her phone with her fingertips. "Got it." She put in her password, and the message displayed. "It's Matt texting me. He asked if everything is okay."

"Well, answer him," Krissy said.

She texted back that things were going fine.

Then Matt asked her if she was still up, or had she gone to bed.

I'm still up, she texted back.

When Matt responded, she gulped.

"What's the matter?" Krissy asked.

"He wants to take me for a ride." She held the phone close to her. "What do I do?"

"Go with him. What's the harm in that?"

"I don't know."

"Why not?"

"Because it's complicated. He's working for me. I have a strict policy about dating anyone I'm working with."

Krissy sat there for a second, her mouth pulling to one side as if she was about to say something but wasn't sure if she should. "Look, this isn't my place to butt in, but—"

"You're going to?"

"Yes." Krissy licked her lips, and then pulled her hands into her lap. "Look, there's a spark between you two. You have to admit it. I get it. You've got this rule, but are you really just deeming the relationship not real so he can't hurt you?"

The words kind of stung. She hadn't thought of it like that at all, although it was true she was not ready to relive her divorce again. *Am I doing that?*

"But I'm focusing on Angel's Rest right now," Liz said. "It would complicate things for Matt and me to work together and—"

"You have too many rules. If you don't let yourself be vulnerable, you're going to miss out on the best parts of falling in love. You need to feel the wild abandon of those stuffy rules, and the rush of emotions that real love will shower down on you." Krissy paused. "Matt's a good guy. He would never hurt you. He will forever be your friend. It's just the kind of guy he is. Me too. I've grown really fond of you in this short time. So, just go have a good time." Her tone shifted from gentle to playfully demanding. "He didn't ask you to run away to Vegas and get married."

"You're right, although Elvis could officiate if he did." Liz laughed. "Gosh, Krissy, you've been so great. I mean, you came to spend time with Matt and instead you're stuck taking care of me. And apparently giving a free therapy session."

"Liz, don't flatter yourself. I love giving unsolicited advice, and trust me, this is not a bad way to spend winter break. I'm loving every second of it. Just text him back and tell him that you'll go for a ride with him. It'll be good for you to get out of the house. I know I'm his sister, so you think I'm biased, but he really is a good guy."

She lifted her phone and typed in, *Sure. Count me in.* Liz squeezed her eyes tight. "I can't believe I just did that."

"Let's get you dressed. Maybe some mascara?"

"Fine." It would feel good to primp a little. Liz rolled off the chair onto the scooter and zipped to the back of the house. Krissy showed up with her makeup bag and curling iron and went to work on her.

By the time Matt's diesel truck rolled up, Liz had decent hair and eyelashes. Krissy stepped back and looked at her. "You're ready, my friend."

Liz looked in the mirror. "Wow. That is better." She picked up on the handle of the scooter, turned it around, and headed back down the hallway.

Matt was walking into the living room as she sped by.

"Whoa!" He hopped out of her way. "Looks like you're getting along a little better."

"I am."

"Good. Let's go. Krissy, do you want to come?"

"Nope. I'm reading a book, and I can't wait to see how it ends."

"Great. I guess it's just you and me, Liz." He held the door as she maneuvered the scooter out to the deck.

She started to try to sit on the top step to go down and he came racing to her side.

"No need for that." He swept her up in one motion and carried her to the truck.

He set her down next to the door.

With his help, she hopped up in the front seat. "Where are you taking me?"

"You'll see in a minute."

"I'm not in any shape to snow-bowl." She was joking, but that had been an awesome night, and not only because she'd won.

"I don't know." He leaned forward and patted his hand on her cast. "I think it might be the perfect time for a rematch."

"You better be kidding." She swatted his arm. "That would not be fair."

"You're right." He rode out to the edge of town and then took a left on a dirt road off of Underpass Road. The dark road came to a stop in front of a pond. The moon shone bright, reflecting the silhouette of the trees on the water.

"This is so pretty." And peaceful. The water was so still.

"I've always thought this was the prettiest spot in town. There used to be a house over there on the other side of the pond. It burned down. All that's left of it is the old chimney."

"That's too bad. Who owns it?"

"I do."

She shifted in her seat. "You?"

He nodded. "It belonged to my mom's family, before she married my dad. They met and fell in love here."

"Right here in this spot?"

He nodded.

She let out a sigh. "That's so romantic."

"Yeah. It is. They had a big love. You know, I never once knew them to have a fight or harsh word to say to one another. Not once, and trust me, Krissy and I pushed their buttons once in a while. Nothing could tear them apart."

Except death. She wasn't that close with her parents. She ached for his loss. He still felt the void that losing them had left. She could see it in his face. "Why haven't you done anything with it? You should do something special in their honor here."

"I have. I saved it."

She smiled. "You did." She nodded, unsure of why he'd brought her here tonight, but happy he'd seen fit to share it with her. He made her feel special in a way she'd never experienced.

"I've got a surprise for you." His voice was soft, caressing her imagination.

Her lips trembled as he leaned toward her, but then he reached into the backseat.

She caught her breath and swallowed, embarrassed that she'd assumed he was going to kiss her. He tapped her on the head with a long narrow square box of something, then got out of the truck.

She touched her head where he'd just bonked her. "What was that for?"

He came around to the passenger side and pulled her door open, then grabbed her legs and swung her toward him.

Before she really understood what was happening, he was wrapping her left leg from hip to toe in plastic wrap.

"Are you crazy? What are you doing?"

"My little angel, we are going to make snow angels here tonight."

"What?" Was he crazy? "Oh my gosh. You've thought of everything. I love it!"

"You're welcome." With a *zip, zip, zip* he pulled the wrap around her leg again, then patted it so it stuck to itself. "I don't think anything is getting in here."

She couldn't stop giggling. It was the most innovative idea ever.

"Mission Snow Angel has commenced." He grabbed her and lifted her from the truck. "In five ... four ... three ... two ... one!" He laid her in the snow, and then plopped down next to her. "Let's do this."

She began flapping her wings and he did the same.

The tiniest snowflakes began to fall over them.

Liz let out an audible sigh, blinking away the snowflakes from her eyelashes. "This is fabulous."

"I'm glad you like it." He rolled over onto his side and propped his head on his hand. "I'm sorry you got hurt."

"Me too."

"It doesn't change anything, you know."

She closed her eyes.

"You're going to be fine." He dropped a soft kiss on her forehead, then stood and helped her stand, balancing on one foot like a flamingo. "Grab me around my neck."

She did, and he scooped her back into his arms and carried her back to the truck. He took his knife out of his pocket and cut the damp plastic wrap away, and tossed it into the backseat.

He walked around to the driver's side of the truck, and slapped the snow off his clothes before he got back in.

"Matt, this was amazing."

"Maybe we can make it our tradition." He sat there for a moment, then started the truck. "Maybe?"

She batted her eyelashes, hoping the tingle that usually happened right before tears fell was a false alarm. She couldn't imagine anything more magical. What she was feeling wasn't just from a good time. Something more had happened here tonight. This would be a wonderful new tradition—sans the broken foot, of course. But all she said was, "Maybe."

He took her back to his house. Krissy had already gone to bed.

Matt made cocoa and they sat in front of the fire without a word, just warming up and sipping the chocolaty goodness. She was sprawled out on the couch with her foot elevated on the arm.

The next thing Liz knew she was waking up on the couch.

She felt vastly better than she had since the fall. It took her a minute to put all the pieces together that she had fallen asleep while Matt was still here. Then she remembered making snow angels and lay there smiling.

Krissy walked into the living room carrying two cups of coffee. "Hey, sleepyhead. Did you have fun last night?" She handed one to Liz.

"Thanks. 'Fun' doesn't even begin to describe last night." Liz pushed herself up on the couch and took a big swallow.

"Nice artwork, too."

"Art?"

Krissy nodded toward the cast.

"What?" Liz leaned forward, trying to see what it said. "I can't see. Did you sign my cast?"

"Wasn't me. Looks like it was Matt." Krissy took a picture of it and handed her phone to Liz.

Matt had drawn the shape of a snow angel on her cast. Below the angel he'd written in perfect draftsman lettering,

Spread your wings and see how far you fly.
Angels will always spot your landing,
Matt

"THAT'S SO SWEET." Last night had been special. She hadn't laughed that hard in a long time, but the gesture itself had meant even more. It was thoughtful, and personal. "Wow."

"Wow is right. I wish someone would do something that romantic for me," said Krissy. "And you can't complain about his beard anymore either."

"He's really good looking, isn't he?"

"I told you," Krissy said as if there were no doubt at all. "Very."

"I'm glad I met him again. I wish I'd remembered him from back when we were kids. I have so many great old memories from being up here with my grandparents, but I'm thankful to be making new ones too. Like you."

"I feel the same way. Antler Creek was such a great town to grow up in." Krissy pulled her feet up underneath her. "Sometimes I can picture myself living here again, maybe running a specialty shop on Main Street in one of the new buildings with the apartments above. I think that would be fun."

"Really? Now that surprises me. I mean you saying you're a beach girl and all that."

"Yeah, but I'd love to sell candles and high-end linens. Specialty gifts. And nowadays you can have an adorable little storefront, but sell online so your marketplace is bigger. Plus with

Mom and Dad both gone, I hate Matt being here alone. I miss him way more than I love the beach."

"I always wished I had a big brother," Liz shared.

"So, you need to get Angel's Rest open to help build my customer base. Then I can buy one of those cute little buildings on Main Street and be your neighbor."

"I'll do my best."

"Or better yet, maybe we'll be family. I'd be a pretty awesome sister-in-law."

Liz waved her hands. "Oh no, don't go jumping the gun. I barely know your brother."

"Well, I happen to know he's been crazy about you since before you knew he existed."

Liz didn't know if Krissy was serious or not about moving back, but it sure painted a nice scene, and imagining Matt as part of the picture was very appealing.

Chapter Twenty-nine

All day long Matt couldn't shake the image of Liz asleep on his couch last night—her sweet face, and the gentle rise and fall of her chest as she dreamed. It hadn't taken her long to fall asleep, either. He'd just taken their mugs into the kitchen and when he came back she was out.

He wondered if she'd noticed the note he'd left for her yet.

He just hadn't been able to stop himself after spotting the permanent marker on the coffee table. He'd picked up the paper napkin to write on, and then the cast called his name. He gave angels the credit, but really he wanted to be the one to spot her every fall, every day, going forward. There wasn't one doubt in his mind that she was the thing that had been missing in his heart all this time. Liz made him feel whole again, even completed his attachment to this town that she loved as much as he did.

Who would've believed that a girl could wander into town from my past and change my whole future?

AT THE END of the day, Matt headed to his house to go over the project status with Liz. It sure was nice coming home to her in his kitchen sitting on a barstool looking like her old self.

"You know that leg is still supposed to be propped up," he said.

"I know, but I thought it would be easier to go over the project stuff in here on the island."

"No, ma'am. You don't want that foot to swell. Let's get you back in the chair. I'll print an extra copy and we can do it that way before that ankle starts throbbing again."

She rolled her eyes. "Fine." She shimmied down from the stool onto the scooter and headed back into the den.

He followed behind her, watching as she settled into the chair. "It's great to see you feeling better, though." Their eyes held, and for a moment he forgot what it was he was about to do. "Oh, give me a second and I'll print off the plan." His boots struck a steady rhythm against the reclaimed barn-wood floors.

Sorting pages as he walked into the room, he handed one set to her. "Here you go."

For an hour they went over each line item and updated progress where they could. Matt had also gotten a few more estimates, and they were able to fill in more of the dependent tasks and update the running totals. "I think we should be able to get everything done by the end of March with no problem at this pace."

She looked pleased. "That's really fast. I know it's a lot to do."

"These guys want to work. They're dependable too."

"If we could be done before summer, we'd start reservations already in the black."

"Folks are highly motivated to make this happen, Liz. It's likely to be a boost for every business in town."

"I hope so."

"You have to believe." Matt sat there quietly for a long moment. "I want to show you something. Will you come to Angel's Rest with me tonight?"

"Sure. I'd honestly agree to go just about anywhere to get out of this house right now. I'm going stir-crazy."

"I totally understand." He loaded her into his truck, and they drove over to her house without another word. Quiet with her wasn't awkward. It was nice. "I want to show you what else has been happening."

"What *else*? What do you mean?"

After he pulled in to the driveway he parked and turned to her. "Sit tight. I'll be right back." He pulled the keys from the ignition and ran up to the house, disappearing inside.

SHE WAS SITTING there waiting when all of a sudden colored lights shone through the front window.

"A Christmas tree?" *Why would he have done that?*

He came jogging back out to the truck.

"You got me a tree?"

"Well, not exactly." Matt climbed back into the truck. "It's the ladder. With lights on it."

"Awww. That's so sweet. It's awesome."

"I do what I can," he said. "There's more. I need you to close your eyes and keep them closed, okay?"

"I'm not sure I like this." She gave him a warning stare, but closed her eyes, then opened one.

"Come on. Humor me."

She placed both hands over her eyes. "Hurry. You're making me nervous."

He moved the truck, but not too far, and then stopped.

"Keep your eyes closed."

She heard the door open and close. Tempted to peek, she held her hands firmly over her eyes, trying to be patient.

He opened the passenger door. "You can open your eyes now."

She did and she couldn't believe what she saw.

Lights hung from nearly every single tree. Little lights. Big lights. Twinkle lights and colored ones too. Giant plywood deer, like the ones Pop used to make, frolicked under a spotlight next to a soaring forty-foot cedar full of what looked like a hundred thousand lights and great big ornaments that appeared to have been fashioned out of tinfoil pie pans.

Glancing from one side to the other, she couldn't take it all in.

Right in front of the truck, she spotted the elves. "Those are Pop's elves!" They worked in a Santa's workshop, painted in vivid reds, greens, and blues, and the elves were moving— hammering and turning their heads. "Matt? How did you . . . ?"

"It's been a town effort. Everyone has pitched in."

"Where did you find the elves? Oh gosh, is that the train too?" A loud deep steam trumpet tooted as it chugged by.

"Yes. The train. The elves. Lots of these lights were all in the boxes in storage in the other cabin. I was going to tell you, but then with the fall, and you were upset, and then I wanted to surprise you. The elves needed work, but Barney was able to get them going again. Those elves were always my favorite."

She glanced around in disbelief. It was like a dream, and suddenly she was fourteen again. She could almost hear Gram calling for her to come help, and Pop the way he laughed when he operated that train. She'd never realized it before, but Pop was like a kid himself when it came to Christmas and playing outside. "Why would you do all of this for me, Matt? You've had to be working day and night."

"Because I want to make you happy. I like seeing you smile, and you were meant to be a part of this town, Liz. Everyone thinks so. You've brought the Christmas spirit back to Antler Creek."

"I don't know what to say." She swept her arms out. "If my parents saw this all lit up like this, they'd change their opinions. This is already every bit as wonderful as it used to be. It can be done again."

His enthusiastic smile fell. "I take it they didn't think this was a good idea."

"No. They said it just sounded like a lot of work, and a waste of a good career." She turned and stared at the lights. "Oh, Matt, if they could see this now, they'd see what I see in Angel's Rest." But then she dropped her chin. "Who am I fooling. Then I fell, and I know what my parents would say. They'd say it was a sign for me to give up this notion, but they just don't understand how much of me is in this place."

"Liz, if your parents saw the sparkle in your eyes when you talk about this place, they couldn't deny it." Matt closed the passenger door and ran back around to the driver's side.

When he got in the truck he turned to her. "Look, I've kept all of our contracted work on schedule. I promise to continue to do so. None of this work has touched your budget. This project is personal. From me. To you. All of the cleanup and Christmas decorating has been the work of volunteers. Kids on Christmas break from college, neighbors, and friends."

"Christmas angels," she said with a smile. "I can't believe the way everyone has come together."

"I hope you're okay with all of this. I know it was a gamble on my part . . . but I really thought it would make you happy."

"It does. So much so. 'Happy' doesn't begin to describe how I feel. It's so much bigger than that. Deeper. The nostalgia of these memories . . . now everyone can enjoy them."

"There's one more thing," he said. "I hope you like it." He pulled the truck over to the left side of the house and turned on his high beams. "What do you think?"

"A barn quilt? Oh gosh, it's the pattern from my quilt." She turned to him, her mouth half open. "How did you?" She looked back toward the house. "Is that a trumpeting angel in the middle?"

"It is. Krissy painted it for you."

"When? That's impossible," Liz said. "She's with me all the time."

"Not all the time."

"I can't believe you did this for me. All of this." She pulled in a breath. "Thank you, and Krissy. The barn quilt is wonderful." Joy bubbled in her words, and shone in her eyes. "And all these people who've volunteered to help. This is mind-boggling."

"I wanted it to be more than just reviving a memory. The barn quilt makes this place yours. It's you, Liz. Not just continuing what your grandparents had. It's that and even more."

"How will I ever thank you?"

"There *is* something you can do. The town canceled the Christmas-tree lighting this year. The lights were damaged in the flood this past summer. It's a long story, but if we can finish this project and open it up for people to drive by like they used to when your grandparents were here, I think the town would love it."

"It could be the new Antler Creek tree-lighting tradition." She loved the idea, and how could she let the people that had volunteered down? That didn't seem right. Plus, it looked so pretty already. "How would we get the word out?"

"Roger down at the *Chronicle* could run something in the paper. But seriously. This is a small town. If it's one thing folks can do it's get the word out."

"That would be amazing." Her throat felt tight, and a tear slipped down her cheek. "It would be so wonderful. Something I've dreamed of." She could picture the cars lined up the mountain road. So many memories were coming back to life.

"Let's do it, then. If after Christmas you still have your doubts about reopening the inn, then at least you've lived out the memory of this place. And the town will have enjoyed it again. Besides, if you decide to sell, then the big holiday hoopla should help with that too."

"True." *How could I ever sell this place?* If the inn wasn't viable, she could still work and live here, not that she needed a house this big by herself, but something would work out. Wouldn't it?

"So we can do it?"

"Yes," she said. "Yes, let's do this."

Chapter Thirty

The Antler Creek Chronicle *headline read:*

LIGHTS AT THE LODGE AT LONG LAST

The article went on to say that for two nights only, the old tradition of the Lights at the Lodge at Angel's Rest was being revived. Beginning at six o'clock on Friday and Saturday night, neighbors and families were welcome to drive up Doe Run Road to enjoy the collaboration in celebration of Christmases past on the mountain.

THAT MORNING, LIZ and Krissy went to Spivey's Market and loaded the car with hot chocolate and baking goods to make cookies for anyone who came to see the lights, just as her grandparents had done all those years ago.

"We'll have to make the hot chocolate at Matt's house and take it over since there's no water in the house yet. We need a couple of those big construction-size watercoolers for the hot chocolate," Liz said. "Do you think we could stop by Goodwin's Hardware and see if they have some?"

"Sure thing." Krissy pulled out of the market parking lot.

When they got to Goodwin's Hardware, they went inside and George greeted them with a Santa-like hello. "Hello-ho-ho."

"Hi, George. I need a couple of big five-gallon beverage coolers to put hot chocolate in. Do you have some in stock?"

"All the way in the back of the store. There are a few different sizes. I've got one in the back room you can borrow too."

"That would be great. Thanks." Liz pushed off on her scooter, rolling toward the back. Krissy was in a half jog trying to keep up with her. They grabbed all three of the watercoolers, then went to check out.

As they waited in line, Liz heard a young man talking to Cindy at the register.

"We're exhausted and we're just trying to find someplace to rest. The hotels along the interstate have all been full. Do you know of anyone that might rent a room just for a night? My wife is sick, and the baby is fussy. I just need some sleep so I can get us the rest of the way to Florida tomorrow."

"I'm so sorry," Cindy said. "I wish I knew of something, but we don't have a hotel here in town. Let me call Pastor Mike to see if he can help you."

The man looked like he was out of options.

Liz felt so bad for him. She got out of line and went over to him. "Hey, I couldn't help but overhear." She extended her hand. "I'm Liz Westmoreland."

"Hi. Joe Harmon."

"Nice to meet you. I'm new in town too. I'm staying with a friend since I broke my ankle. It's not fancy, but I have a little cabin up on the mountain y'all are welcome to use tonight."

"Really?"

She watched relief flood over the man.

"I'd be so grateful," he said. "It's just me and my wife and little girl. I can pay you."

"The place is under construction. It's just a one-bedroom cabin on the back of the property, but there's water and electricity. You'll be warm and you can rest."

"Anything, ma'am. We're not picky. Thank you so much."

"Great. Let me get checked out here and you can follow us up. It's not far."

"I don't know how I can thank you enough. I'm going to go out and tell my wife. We're in the white Honda Accord."

"We won't be long." Liz smiled, feeling good about helping them out. She pulled her phone from her purse and dialed Matt's number. "Matt. Change of plans. I just told a family they could use the cabin tonight. Do you mind staying at your house with Krissy and me?"

"You what? Well, I guess it doesn't matter. Sure. Yeah."

"Great. I'll explain later. We'll see you shortly."

Krissy stepped up to the register. "That's why I love you, Liz. You're good to the core. Anyone else would worry that guy was up to no good."

It wasn't good. It was the right thing to do. That man was clearly trying to do the right thing by his family. He looked exhausted. She was thankful to be in a position to give him a break.

Liz and Krissy loaded the coolers into the car and waved the young family to follow them up the mountain.

When they pulled in next to the house, Matt came out on the porch and met them in the driveway.

The young couple got out of their car. The wife was pale. Joe whispered something to his wife and then raced to Liz's side.

"Ma'am," Joe said, "I can't afford something this fancy."

The thought almost made her laugh. A few weeks ago this was a gutted mess overgrown with years of weeds that had grown as big as trees. Matt had truly transformed things. She took a fresh look around. It did look good.

"Don't be silly. It won't cost you a thing. There's construction going on here at the house, but you'll be comfortable back in the cabin. You can see it from here." She pointed it out; with the gentle smoke pouring from the chimney, it looked even more inviting than the house.

"My wife is sick, but I'm not. I can help. Please at least let me help."

Matt walked up at that moment. "Matt, this is Joe." Liz offered the young man a smile. "He'd like to help out while his wife gets some rest so they can continue their trip to Florida."

Joe shook Matt's hand.

"Nice to have you on board."

"This is my wife, Maryanne, and our daughter, Holly. We're trying to make it down to Florida to my wife's parents' house. I promise we'll be out of your hair tomorrow."

"Don't you worry about that," Liz said. "Get her well. There's no hurry on our part. Take a couple days if you need."

"I'm a good worker," Joe said. "Electrical, plumbing, carpentry. I can do repairs too."

"Sounds like *you're* doing *us* a favor." Matt slapped the guy on the shoulder. "I can definitely put you to work."

"I'm going to leave y'all to get settled in," Liz said. "I need to get this foot up. It's starting to hurt again." She dug a piece of paper from her purse and wrote her phone number on it. "Call me if you need me."

Matt added, "I'll be around most of the time. I'll give you my number too." He turned to Liz. "Get on back to the house. I'll help these folks get settled in." He turned his back on the strangers and whispered, "This is a good thing you're doing."

"It feels good." She knew she wouldn't be rescuing people in situations like this if she opened the inn, but she did know that this place had been a refuge for a lot of people. Bringing families together. Offering time to unplug and enjoy nature. Time to get priorities straight, and do what really mattered. Matt seeing that too made her happy.

A Suburban pulled onto the property. Not just any Suburban. Dan's.

"Hmm. I wonder what he's doing here." Liz maneuvered her scooter in that direction.

Dan got out. He looked out of place in his Dockers and button-down shirt and tie. "I heard you took a fall."

She was a long way from Charlotte. The only people she'd called were Missy and Peggy.

"I had to drop off some paperwork to a client in your building and ran into Peggy," he explained. "She assumed I knew."

Why does that bother me so much?

"I told you this was no place for a woman to be alone."

"You never said that." Why did he have to be such a jerk sometimes? "And that's a chauvinistic remark even from you, Dan."

"You know what I mean." He hitched his chin toward the path to the cabin. "Who were those people?"

"Workers." She glanced back. Matt was walking the Harmons to the cabin. "And that's my contractor. He's walking that couple to the cabin. I'm letting them stay in the cabin until his wife gets well."

"Renting it out already?"

"No. Just letting them stay here. I ran into them at the hardware store. His wife is sick and they need some rest. All of the hotels for miles are booked."

"That's not a good idea. You don't even know them?"

She didn't appreciate his tone. "That's none of your business. Why are you here?"

"Thought I'd come and see if you were ready to come back to Charlotte, or at least see what all the fuss was about. Doesn't look like a dream house to me."

"What is that supposed to mean?"

"I'm ready to put this place on the market for you."

"Why would I do that?"

"I told you how risky this deal was. You said yourself there's a ton to do. Even in this condition we can probably quadruple your investment. If anyone can sell this place it's me."

She took in a deep breath, trying to not lose her cool. "Please stop. I'm not selling."

"You're right. That's my job." He raised his hands in the air. "I'll list it, and do all the work. I'll have it sold in no time."

"Lower your voice. You are talking crazy. I am *not* selling. I owe this dream at least a shot."

"A shot? Maybe you should come back for the holidays and think this through. You need a little space between you and this crazy dream of yours."

"It is not crazy."

"Look, I'm saying this as your friend. You can come with me to Mom's for Christmas dinner. I don't guess we'll be dancing in the New Year together this year with that bum foot, but I'll get the best champagne to celebrate your return. I know your favorite kind."

That didn't even sound appealing. "You probably should've called before you made the long drive up here."

"I did. You didn't answer." He was right. She'd been declining his calls for days.

"I'm perfectly at home here. I'm not going anywhere."

"Well, good luck then," he said.

"Thank you. I hope you really mean that."

He let out a huff. "I do. I'm not happy about it, though. I miss you, but I know if you're still this convinced you're going to make this happen, then you will." He walked over and gave her a hug. "How bad's the leg?"

"Just the ankle. I don't even need surgery."

"Thank goodness." Dan lowered his head. "I didn't mean to rain on your parade. I wasn't a very good friend."

"It's fine. You've never been good at change."

"You're right about that." He helped her over to Krissy's car. "Will you call and keep me posted?"

"I will. Merry Christmas, Dan."

"Merry Christmas, Liz. And good luck."

"Thanks."

Krissy turned the key in the ignition and waited until Dan got back in his SUV. "That seemed strained."

"Yeah. It was," Liz said. "But I set him straight. I was just remembering something Pop used to say. He'd always say that you couldn't find a new path without getting a little lost. I always thought he was talking about hiking. You know, literally finding new paths through the woods. I think he was imparting wisdom that pertains to what I'm going through right now too."

"Wise man."

"He was a good man." Memories of her grandfather warmed her heart. "I can't believe Matt has done all of this for me. Maybe not even for me, but for the place and what Angel's Rest used to mean to this town."

"You *are* paying him."

"I know, but the lights. The hospitality. That's all well above and beyond."

"True."

Liz wanted to do something nice for him. "I think we should put a Christmas tree up in his house for him."

"That's a great idea."

"Do you think we can do it by ourselves?"

"It'll be tricky with you in a cast, but probably. I can do the tall parts."

"I bet Ginger would help us. I'll call her and see if she'll meet us down at the tree lot."

LIZ PICKED OUT the perfect tree. Tall and not too fat. The guys at the lot must have felt sorry for her with the cast, because they insisted on delivering it and setting it up for them.

"Doesn't hurt to have three women shopping together on a tree lot," Krissy said to the others as the guys loaded up the tree and followed them to the house.

"Especially when you buy all your decorations from them too," Liz added. "They made a good sale on us."

It didn't take long for the guys to get the tree in the house and set in the stand for them. Liz tipped them, and then they got busy wrapping twinkle lights around the tree. Liz supervised, trying to make sure there were no dark spots by doing that squinty thing.

"It's perfect," Liz exclaimed. "Now time to decorate." She took the plastic lid off of the giant drum of ornaments they'd purchased.

All three of them went to work putting the red, gold, and green balls on the tree. It was the simplest tree Liz had ever decorated, but it looked beautiful.

In the living room, Matt had a big vase full of pheasant feathers. She raided them and tucked them into the tree in random spots, manning it up a bit. On the bookshelf he had four small sets of antlers. She hated to mess up his decor, but she took the antlers and tucked them into the leaner spots in the tree, instantly giving it a full and rustic look.

"This is gorgeous," Ginger said. "I feel like I need to go home and redecorate my tree now."

"You do not. I love your tree. Your little ones did a great job."

Ginger laughed. "It took everything I had not to move that big glob of ornaments they hung at the bottom. But they were so proud."

"It's sweet. I personally loved it." Someday she'd be happy to have a chaotic tree of handmade ornaments, none hung over three feet high. It would be just fine by her. "I have an idea. Ginger, can you go outside and see if you can gather about ten pinecones about the same size? I think I can make a tree topper out of them."

"Sure." The redhead ran outside and came back with her toboggan full of pinecones. "I brought ten big ones and ten medium ones. I wasn't sure which would work best."

"I wish I had a glue gun," Liz said, "but I think I can make it work with fishing line."

"Ah. Not necessary," Ginger said. "A crafter never leaves home without a few supplies in the trunk of her car." She ran from the house and came in with a pink plastic toolbox. "Ta-da."

"You're the best," Liz said.

"I'm just a neighbor being neighborly. You'd do the same for me."

"Count on it." Liz hoped she always would. The truth was she didn't even know her neighbors in Charlotte. In fact, she'd probably met more people in Antler Creek in the past two weeks than she had in her neighborhood in four years.

Liz plugged in the glue gun and went to work on the pinecones. She was able to fashion a star out of the medium pinecones. She tucked a couple of feathers into the star, then handed it to Krissy. "Do you think you can get it to stay on top of the tree?"

Krissy pulled a stool from the kitchen into the den and climbed up on it, then slipped the handmade star between the top branches.

"That looks so pretty," Ginger said.

Liz attached a hook to each of the big pinecones and handed them to the girls to spread out across the tree to tie it all together.

"He's going to be shocked," Krissy said. "He'll never believe we got this done so quickly."

"I hope he loves it." Liz took Krissy's and Ginger's hands into hers. "We did good."

"We did. I'm sorry, but I've got to get home and feed my kids," Ginger said. "Thanks for letting me be a part of this. Let me know what he thinks!"

They saw her to the door and she drove off.

"What a day." Liz sat on the couch and propped her leg back up. "I feel like everything was moving so fast, then it stalled when I got hurt, and now it's like we're going down the big hill on the roller coaster with our hands in the air screaming."

"But in a good way," Krissy said.

"The very best way."

Krissy turned to Liz, her expression serious. "Matt would take good care of you. This is more than a construction project for him. You know that, right?"

Liz dropped her head back against the couch. "It's so confusing. My head knows it's impossible, but my heart—"

"Your heart is smarter than that brain of yours. Trust it."

Liz's heart leapt, or maybe it was giving her a swift kick because she kept second-guessing it. If only she could believe it. "I can't risk it, Krissy. This is a small town. If something went wrong . . ."

"And if it didn't. Wow. I'd give anything to have someone look at me like he looks at you." Krissy squeezed Liz's hand.

Her heart pounded so hard she could barely swallow. If this was what real love felt like, it was scarier than she'd ever dreamed.

Chapter Thirty-one

When Matt got home it was after ten. He'd spent time after they wrapped up work at the house helping get the Harmons settled into the cabin, and then Barney had shown up with the train pieces. Matt couldn't wait to see if he could get the scene working the way Mr. Westmoreland had done all those years ago. They weren't really trains at all, as they didn't run on rails, but rather remote-controlled vehicles that looked like an engine, railcars with Christmas trees on them, and a bright red caboose. The handheld remote control explained the magical way the train made the big loop through all the lights without a rail. When he was a kid here at Christmas, he'd try to anticipate where the train would go next. He never could get it right. Now he knew why. He couldn't wait to play the same prank on the kids of Antler Creek.

Joe had tucked his wife and daughter in bed and come out to help. Between the two of them they'd rigged up the train and figured out how to preset a route. It worked flawlessly. They'd tested out the music and Joe had repositioned the speakers and rerun part of the wire to fix the ones that weren't working. They were wired for surround sound every step of the way. People driving through the lights would hear beautiful music as the lights captivated them along the ride.

Everything had come together, and without much time to spare. Tomorrow night people would flock to see the Lights at the Lodge at Angel's Rest.

Matt put Elvis in the truck and drove back to his house. He was sorry Joe's family had fallen on hard times, but they'd be comfortable and safe in the cabin. Being closer to Liz was no hardship on Matt either.

When they walked in, Elvis ran ahead, then crouched and growled, moving slowly toward the den then backing up.

"What's the matter, boy?"

Matt walked into the other room to check, and then stopped dead center in the room.

How did they do this?

Elvis braved up and walked into the room behind Matt, sniffing around the edge of the tree, then backing up again.

"It's okay, boy," he whispered.

Liz poked her head around the corner on her scooter. "Hey. I thought I heard you come in."

"You did all this?"

"Your sister and Ginger were a big help."

"It's great." Matt had never seen a Christmas tree look this good. "You're full of surprises, aren't you?" He stepped close to her and hugged her by his side.

"You like it?"

"No." He shook his head. "I don't like it, I love it." He moved closer to the tree. "Where'd you find that tree topper? It's the coolest one I've ever seen."

"I made it. Umm, full disclosure, all those pretty pheasant

feathers are from that vase in the other room. The antlers are from your collection too. I promise to return them after the holiday."

"No problem." He nodded. "Good use for them. I really love what you've done to this place." She was the one thing that had always been missing. Until this second, he hadn't been able to put his finger on it.

"I'm glad you like it. I wanted to do something for you." She moved her scooter over next to him.

"Thank you." He put his hands on the handlebars of the scooter. "How're you doing?"

She looked up into his face. "Pretty good. Not ready for snow bowling yet, but better."

"We may have to put our rematch off until next year."

"We can do that. Ink me in."

"Really?" He was almost afraid to take her seriously. "You'll be here?"

"Definitely."

He couldn't hold back a grin. Probably one that made him look like a goofball, but he didn't even care. That was exactly what he wanted to hear. He laid his hand on top of hers. "Good."

She held his gaze.

"The Harmons are nice folks," Matt said. "Joe stepped right up and pitched in. I didn't even have to ask."

"Good. I didn't get to talk to his wife, but when I heard him talking to the gal over at Goodwin's I knew I could make things better for them." She looked into his eyes. "I didn't think twice. I knew I wanted to help."

Matt knew that feeling. Sharing gifts was the best feeling in the world. "Joe wasn't exaggerating when he said he could do just about anything. He's been a huge help."

"That's great."

"I invited them to come over tomorrow morning for breakfast. It'll be a long day and with the lights tomorrow night I thought it would be nice for everyone to get together for a good meal."

"Great. What time will they be here?"

"I told them to come around eight. We'll eat at eight thirty."

"Sounds good."

They stood there in the silence, next to the Christmas tree.

"I better go get some sleep," she said.

"Yeah. Both of us. Good night, Liz. Thanks for the tree. It's beautiful."

"You're welcome." She slid her hand out from under his and scooted back toward the guest room.

No one had ever gone to this kind of trouble for him before. He pinched one of the boughs of pine, releasing the fresh scent into the room.

Wondering what kind of gift he might buy Liz to put under the tree, he turned off the lights and went to the other end of the house, where the master suite was. He wasn't used to having other people in his home, but tonight it felt comfortably full.

The next morning, Matt got up early to fry bacon and sausage. He took the dishes that had been his mother's and stacked them at the end of the island. He wished his parents were here to meet Liz.

"Hey, big brother." Krissy walked into the kitchen, dressed in jeans and a white sweater. "I'll get the coffee going."

"Thanks." He scrambled a huge batch of fresh eggs, then started making milk gravy the way Momma always had.

Joe and his family showed up, and he was just talking to them with Krissy when Liz finally rolled into the room.

"This place smells fantastic," Liz said. "Why didn't someone wake me?"

Krissy took the biscuits out of the oven and started dumping them into a breadbasket.

"We wouldn't have let you miss it. I was just coming to get you." Matt slid the huge pan of gravy onto the counter and put a ladle in it, then walked over to Liz and gave her shoulder a squeeze.

The smile she rewarded him with meant more to him than any paycheck.

With a happy heart, he spoke over the friends that had gathered. "Everything is ready. Y'all grab a plate and dig in. There's plenty here."

"What a spread." Joe picked up a plate and scooped eggs onto it.

"We can't thank you enough," his wife, Maryanne, said. She held her baby on her hip and a plate in the other hand. "That was the best night's sleep I've had in weeks, and now this?"

Little Holly cooed and clapped.

"I'm so glad you're feeling better," Liz said.

"Let me take the baby while y'all eat." Matt held his arms out for the little girl. "Come on, Holly. Want to come see me?" He lifted her in the air, then settled the giggling child on his shoulders, moving around the kitchen and then sashaying off into the den.

Chapter Thirty-two

Liz watched Matt from the kitchen. He was so at ease with the little girl, pointing out ornaments on the tree and singing Christmas carols along the way.

Seeing Matt like that had her imagining what it would be like to be a family with him.

Is there anything sexier in the world than a man with a child?

She fixed her plate, then took the spot at the very end of the island so she could balance on her scooter rather than try to transition to a chair.

Joe's phone rang and he stepped outside on the porch.

Not meaning to eavesdrop, Liz tried to focus on the conversation in the kitchen, but Joe's deep voice kept pulling her back. From what she could hear, it sounded like he'd been part of a mass layoff in Ohio when the factory where he worked lost a big contract. After four months of him trying to find a job, along with a thousand other locals, they'd been evicted from their home. He wasn't happy about going to Florida to stay with Maryanne's parents, but he was out of options.

She heard Joe say he felt like a failure for letting his family down. That tugged at her heart.

She regretted eavesdropping when she heard him tell the person on the phone about the kindness she'd shown giving them a place to stay. He'd referred to her as an angel, saying he'd repay her somehow.

Liz wasn't worried one bit about being repaid. She felt awful that he felt like he needed to work the whole time they were there. Maryanne was sick, but he'd needed rest too. She knew he was up late with Matt working on things.

Matt carried Holly back into the kitchen, but rather than stopping next to her mom, Matt brought the little girl over to Liz.

"She's so precious," Liz said.

"Thank you," Maryanne said. "She's such a happy baby."

"She is." Liz clapped her hands and held them out. Holly reached for her, and Liz took her into her arms. She smelled of baby powder and innocence. "You are so beautiful."

Holly grinned and giggled, drooling a little as she did.

"That looks good on you," Matt said.

Funny. I thought the same thing about you. She imagined what a Christmas would look like with colorful wrapping paper all around them as the baby managed her way through the pretty paper and overwhelming surprises Christmas morning would bring.

"You like children," Matt said with a smile as he sat down next to her.

"I do." Liz bounced Holly on her hip. "I'd always thought I'd be married and have one by now."

"Well, you had to get Angel's Rest first," he said with a wink. "I mean location is everything."

She laughed. "I guess." So many things felt right here in Antler Creek. "I'd like to get everyone together who has helped on Angel's Rest. The house project and all the Christmas stuff too. Do you think Maizey could cater it for me?"

"She'd be thrilled to. If there's one thing Maizey likes, it's a party," Matt said.

"I was thinking maybe something Saturday afternoon before the lights, since Sunday is Christmas Eve."

"Sounds perfect." Matt got another cup of coffee and warmed up Liz's. "We could do it here, but it might be more fun at Angel's Rest. The downstairs is in good shape and it would be nice for everyone to see the progress we've made so far."

"I love that idea. Nothing fancy, just an honest thank-you."

Matt handed her his phone. "Here's Maizey's number."

She pressed the button and Maizey's cheerful voice came over the line. "Hi, Maizey, it's Liz."

"Liz? I thought it was Matt's number that flashed up. Never mind. How are you doing with that bum ankle, dear?"

"Better every day. I have a favor to ask."

"Sure. What can I do for you?"

"I'd like to hire you to cater a little thank-you event this Saturday afternoon at Angel's Rest. Can you squeeze it in?"

"For you, dear. Anything. Anytime. Just let me know what you'd like to have, and how many people we're talking about. I'll take care of the rest. No pun intended."

"Great. I'll call you later with all the details." Liz hung up the phone excited to be able to thank everyone for their generosity. "Matt, do you have a list of everyone who has helped?"

"Better than that. I have all of their emails too."

"You're the best."

"I believe it's still *your* name at the top of that snow bowling scoreboard," he said. "That would make *you* the best."

His smile made her insides spin. She laid her hand on his arm. "Really. Just take the compliment. I couldn't have done any of this without you."

THAT AFTERNOON LIZ was dying to go help get Angel's Rest ready for the big production that night, but Matt insisted they had it under control. She'd loved the Lights at the Lodge when her grandparents had hosted it. It would be different without them, almost a little sad, but she couldn't wait to see how many people would show up.

She and Krissy sat at the kitchen island playing Scrabble to pass the afternoon. Unfortunately, Liz couldn't stay focused and had lost all three games to her. Something that never happened.

A puff of cold air filled the room as Matt and Elvis walked in.

"You girls ready for a great night?"

"We are," they both said.

"Staying here all day has been torture," Liz complained.

"Small price to pay to be out and play all night tonight." Matt closed the door behind him. "I can't wait for you to see it." He grinned wide, like a little boy with a big surprise that he was dying to reveal.

"I can't wait either." She had no idea what to really expect. It had been exciting to see the few things they'd done the other night, but it was nothing like what Pop and Gram had done. Now, that had been a real light show.

She'd already set her mind to not be disappointed, but rather appreciative no matter what with all the effort folks had put into it. Pop was no easy act to follow.

"Here's the plan," Matt said, rubbing his hands together. "It's a little after four now. Cars will start up the hill at six P.M. sharp. The sheriff blockaded the road for us."

"That's pretty special," Liz said.

"So, I need y'all to get the hot chocolate made and in the coolers, and be dressed and ready to go by five fifteen. It'll only take a few minutes to get to the house, but we'll need to set up."

"No problem," Liz said. "Come on, Krissy, let's start the water boiling then go get changed."

It didn't take long to get the pots on the stove, and then they took off back toward the guest bedrooms to get changed.

A few minutes later they were both dressed in layers and had their hats and coats ready to go. They stacked them by the back door, then made quick work of the hot chocolate in the big insulated watercoolers that would keep it warm for visitors that came to see the lights.

Matt carried the coolers out to the truck as they got each one filled.

The sun was setting as they loaded into the truck and headed for Angel's Rest. Liz rode shotgun and Krissy climbed into the backseat with Elvis. As they turned out of his driveway, Matt texted someone; then his phone pinged back.

"Who's that?" Liz asked. "Is everything okay?"

He patted her leg. "You'll see."

She gave him the stink eye. He was always up to something.

They took the side-pass road, and then Matt turned left back up Doe Run Road toward Angel's Rest.

Liz licked her lips, eager to see how things had shaped up. The corner post of the fence that ran the perimeter of the property now glowed with Christmas lights run among fresh pine roping. A wreath hung in the center.

"It's beautiful," Liz said. "There's an angel in the middle of the wreath! I love it." The angel, shaped like a snow angel, appeared to have been cut from plywood and sprayed silver. It reminded her of the other night when he took her to make snow angels near the pond. That was so much fun. Her heart raced much as it had when she'd been a little girl first seeing the lights.

"I can take credit for that one," Matt said, "but I think you're going to like what you see next even more."

He rolled down the windows. The cold air rushed in. Liz was getting ready to tell him to roll them up when she heard the music.

"Christmas music!" She spun around and looked at Krissy.

"This is great," Krissy said, bouncing in the seat and leaning up between the front seats.

Liz pulled her coat tighter and zipped it.

There was a glow up ahead. It started about fifty feet from the driveway, with white blinking lights dripping from the tall trees like snow or icicles. A row of colored bulbs was draped along the fence line in red, blue, green, and yellow.

Matt pulled up and stopped at the edge of the driveway.

To the left, with a spotlight shining on it, a sign had been nailed to two white posts with fancy finials. The sign was a dark green that matched the tin roof on the house. Trimmed in silver, a beautiful angel with detail that made her appear almost three-dimensional graced the center of the sign. The angel's halo was shiny gold, as were the letters in "ANGEL's REST" that flanked her on each side of her pretty white robe in a thick elegant script.

"Matt?" Liz's hands flew to her mouth. "How did you . . . ? Krissy?"

"That's not me," Krissy said. "That's real art."

Matt said, "Maryanne Harmon made that for you."

That didn't even make sense. "How did she? Why?"

"To thank you for letting them stay."

"How did she know? It's perfect. That angel looks just like Gram's favorite one from her collection. It couldn't be more perfect."

"You can tell her that." Matt moved the truck into the driveway, and everyone who was helping tonight was there, joining hands. They began singing "We Wish You a Merry Christmas."

The beautiful lights blurred into a rainbow through Liz's tears. *Gram, I wish you could see this.*

"Are you okay?" Matt's brows pulled together.

"Never better." She chased the tears from beneath her eyes with her fingers. "So good."

She saw Maryanne standing there, and opened the truck door to slide to the ground. "Maryanne? I can't believe you painted that."

Joe and Maryanne smiled at each other, and then Maryanne stepped over to Liz. "It was my pleasure. I'm so glad you like it. It's the least we could do for all your kindness. You have no idea how much we appreciate everything."

"The angel. She's perfect. My grandmother used to have one that looked exactly like that. I mean really. Exactly like the one you painted."

"I suspected that. Elvis brought me that angel. I couldn't figure out where he'd gotten it until I caught him in the act. There's a whole collection of angels in the cubby near the washroom. I guess Elvis was doing a little Christmas shopping of his own."

"In the cabin?" Liz asked.

"Where the water heater was originally," Matt filled in the blanks.

"Right! Elvis? You must've been the one leaving angels around since I've been here." Liz had thought they were signs from Gram there for a while. Or messages from heaven. In a way they probably still were.

Elvis bounded to her side at the sound of his name, and barked.

"I used to paint signs and do lettering on trucks before I had Holly. My dad taught me when I was little. I used to ride with him on Saturdays," Maryanne explained. "Lots of people prefer to buy the stickers these days. It's a dying art."

"You're a real artist. The lettering is gorgeous. So fancy and elegant. It's wonderful. I'll never be able to thank you enough." She hugged Maryanne, and then Joe. "Thank you both so much."

"No, Liz, thank you. You gave us more than a place to rest. You reminded us of the kindness in this world, and hope. You gave us hope again."

Liz couldn't even respond to that. She pulled in a stuttered breath.

Chapter Thirty-three

Liz stepped back and spoke loudly over the music. "Thank you, everyone, for all you've done. *Don't forget we'll be having the thank-you party right here tomorrow afternoon. I hope I'll see all of you here for that.*"

Everyone clapped.

Matt carried the coolers of hot chocolate over to a stand painted in red and white candy-cane stripes at the far edge of the half-circle driveway that entered above the house and ended below the house.

"The plan is to have people drive up Doe Run Road, then pass the first driveway to enter at the top driveway. I've got a couple flags to get them started, then folks should just follow along. Then they'll come right along the driveway through all of the lights, kind of idling through so you can serve them hot chocolate, then exit the driveway and head back down the hill," Matt said.

"Yes. That's exactly how we did it when I was a kid," Liz said. It was hard to believe this was all really happening.

"Liz, I don't think you've met George Goodwin's son Jeffrey."

Matt grabbed a tall lanky dark-haired boy as he walked by. "Jeffrey, this is Liz."

"Hi there. Thank you for helping."

"It's cool you're going to reopen this place. My friends and I have had the best Christmas break helping out here during the day and hanging out at Mill Hill at night." Jeffrey nodded toward his buddies. "We're glad Dad called."

Matt said, "You know Liz here broke my record on Mill Hill."

"Snow bowling," Jeffrey said with a laugh. "Oh, wow. That's not how you broke your foot, is it?"

"No. That happened after I was victorious. On a serious note, thank you. I appreciate your help so much," Liz said. "Y'all have been like a troop of angels showing up like you did. This is amazing."

"It's really cool," Jeffrey said. "We're helping tonight, but tomorrow night we talked my uncle into breaking out the John Deere and driving us up on his hay wagon so we can see it like everyone else."

"I'll have the hot chocolate ready," Liz promised. It was different seeing the lights from the hay wagon than it was from a car. Something about the nip in the air and caroling all the way up the mountain that made the lights seem that much brighter.

This whole place seemed to be meant to be. That she'd stumbled upon that auction the night before it went on the block was amazing on its own, but other things too. These guys giving up their Christmas break to help string lights. Joe and Maryanne happening into Antler Creek just in time. And Matt. She was ahead of schedule and under budget. Unheard of on this kind of project. And if she had been looking for a sign, there wasn't anything more plain than the sign Maryanne had painted with Angel's Rest right on it that this was the right path.

She and Krissy went over to the hot chocolate stand to welcome visitors. She hoped there'd be at least twenty or thirty. Everyone had put so much work into it. If no one came it would be such a shame.

Ginger drove up and her kids tumbled out of the car carrying boxes. "We brought cookies to give away," her littlest yelled as they all came running toward Liz.

"That's so fun," Liz said. "Thank you."

The little girl ran and jumped into Liz's arms, hugging her.

"Showtime," Matt hollered. The six o'clock train sounded as it rambled through town, just barely audible over the Christmas music, which was now being played loud enough to be heard down the street. And in three . . . two . . . one, all of the Christmas lights, the animated elves, and the train lit up and began moving. It was as if the whole place had just woken up.

Liz looked around in awe. Suddenly she realized there were snowflakes falling all around her. "It's snowing."

Krissy laughed. "Only over us. Look, it's coming from right there."

Sure enough, there was some kind of blower just behind a giant inflatable snowman wearing a blue scarf and waving. "He thought of everything." Liz sat sideways on the bench Matt had set up for her so she could keep her foot propped up. "I'll pour the hot chocolate, and you run them to the car," she said to Krissy.

"If we waited for you to hop over they'd only get a half cup of cool chocolate," Krissy teased as she walked around to the front side of the kiosk-style table. "I see headlights!" She bounced on her toes and clapped her hands.

Liz stretched to see, then balled her fists and punched them in the air with a squeal. "Awesome!"

She poured the first cups of hot chocolate. The beverage coolers were doing their job keeping it hot. Steam was still rising from the cups when she handed them to Krissy.

Krissy offered the hot chocolate, and Ginger and her kids raced to the car with their boxes of cookies, letting the driver pick out cookies for everyone.

Cars rolled by at a steady pace, and it was no time before Liz was opening another sleeve of cups. She wished she'd been counting cars.

"Thank you!" The carload of people waved and sang along with the music.

Everyone was having such a good time.

For two hours straight there wasn't a single break in the traffic flow.

Matt came over to the hot chocolate stand. "How are you girls making out?"

"We're almost out of hot chocolate."

"It's eight o'clock. They'll be shutting the road down, so the last cars will be coming through shortly." He held his hands up in the air. "What do you think?"

She high-fived him with both hands. He caught hers and pulled them in to his chest. "Did you really have any doubts?"

"Yes! I thought we might get like twenty or thirty cars. This? No, I never expected we'd get this kind of turnout."

Sheriff Wilson rolled by, his grandmother riding shotgun. The last car in the parade of visitors. "You did good," he said with a salute. "I've never seen the townsfolk look so happy. Then again I've only been here five years. This will be something to remember. I'll see you tomorrow night."

"Just like old times," Beverly called from the passenger seat. "Beautiful."

Krissy raced to the car window. "Have some hot chocolate. Thank you for everything."

He gave Krissy a double take, then glanced over at Matt. "Thank you," he said, taking the cup of hot chocolate. "I'm Grady Wilson."

"Krissy Hardy. I'm Matt's baby sister."

"Hope we'll be seeing you often around here."

"Thank you." Krissy turned around, her eyes wide as she looked to Liz, and the sheriff cruised down the mountain.

"He's cute," Liz said.

"Very. I'm tempted to speed down Main Street on my way back out of town tomorrow," she said.

"You're leaving tomorrow?" Matt asked.

"I am. I need to get home. I promised some friends I'd be back to see their little ones open gifts." She playfully shoved him. "If you'd hurry up and have some kids I wouldn't have to spend time with other people's."

He shrugged. "It's been nice having you around."

"Don't get mushy on me. I'll be back next week to spend New Year's with you."

Liz hadn't even considered that it might be awkward staying at Matt's without Krissy. "You don't mind me staying at your place without Krissy until the Harmons move on, do you?"

"I don't mind if you stay there for no reason at all."

"Thank you."

Joe Don walked from the top of the driveway carrying a big box.

"What's that," Liz asked.

"Ask the boss man," he said.

"Another one of your surprises, I suspect."

"You'll get used to them," Matt said.

"I hope not," Liz said. "I kind of like them."

"Let's go inside." Matt led the way to the house. Everyone filed in, and Joe Don set the box down on the floor in the living room. "Thanks, Joe Don."

"No problem. I'll see you tomorrow night," he said. "We're going to hit the road."

"Thanks for everything."

Joe Don let out a loud whistle. "Anyone riding with me over to Mill Hill, load up!"

The room pretty much cleared out.

Liz made her way to the hearth and sat down. "So what's with this box?"

"It's a comment box. I thought it would be a nice way for you to get feedback on everything. Maybe even convince you once and for all that you are the perfect fit for this town, and Angel's Rest has a place in these people's heart."

The box was painted white with a two-inch slot in the top. Simple holly leaves had been painted in each of the corners. She lifted the top. The box was full of letters and note cards. "There are so many," she said. "How did people even know to do it?"

"I might have started the rumor down at the Creekside Café, and our friend the sheriff passed out note cards to folks as they headed up to see the lights."

She took a card from the top.

Christmas Angels

*Thank you for bringing Christmas back to Antler Creek.
It feels like the old days when Lights at the Lodge shone
bright here every year. Please renew this tradition, and
keep it alive forever.*

The next one was in crayon.

*This is the first time I saw Christmas lights.
I love them. They make me happy.
The train is my favorite. You are nice. I'm eight.*

Liz blinked, and sniffed back a tear.

*Your grandparents would be so proud of you.
Everyone in this town is too. Thank you for coming home.*

Krissy fanned her face. "Okay, I think we'd better read these
when we get back to Matt's. It's cold, and I need tissues for this."
"I know. Me too," Liz said. "My tears are freezing on my face."
Matt bent over and picked up the box. "Let's go."
He helped Liz to her feet, and when they got outside, some-
one else had already shut down the lights and even put the hot
chocolate coolers in the back of Matt's truck.
"We've got an amazing team helping us," she said. "Thank
you, Matt."
"It's not me. You bring out the best in folks."

Chapter Thirty-four

Saturday morning, Matt made a big breakfast to send Krissy off.

"I'll never find a man that meets the bar you set," Krissy said as she took another bite of grits and gravy. She cut her eyes at Liz, and Matt pretended not to notice, but was happy to see her still trying to help him out with Liz.

Liz put a present on the table. It was wrapped in sea-foam blue, with a spiky silver bow that looked kind of like a sea urchin on the top. "Krissy, this is for you. I don't know what I'd have done without you through all of this. Thank you so much for your help and your friendship. I sure hope this is not going to be goodbye."

"You shouldn't have," Krissy said. "Matt, didn't you tell her we never do gifts?"

"I didn't have anything to do with this," he said. "Must have been those boxes in the mail she was getting. She's a resourceful one."

"I wish I could be as resourceful as you." Krissy slipped a finger under the edge of the paper and opened the gift. Inside the square box was a Sand Dollar Cove candle and a pendant just like the white-gold sand dollar Liz wore around her neck. "You shouldn't have." Krissy pulled her hands to her mouth. "It's just like yours."

"It is. I hope you like it."

"I love it."

"And someone told me you can wear it backwards so the poinsettia shows this time of year just to switch things up." She looked over at Matt with unquestionable love in her gaze.

"Thank you, Liz. You've been such a wonderful part of this visit." She hugged her. "You really are already like family. You're so wonderful."

"What about me," Matt said, feigning disappointment.

"You're always wonderful." Krissy turned her back to Matt and mouthed to Liz, *He's awesome. Don't let him get away.*

Liz blushed.

Matt looked suspicious of what Krissy had said. "Let's get you out of here before you stir up trouble."

"Me? Trouble?" Krissy rolled her eyes.

"Yes, you," he said.

"Well, before this troublemaker leaves, I have a little surprise for both of you."

Matt looked at Liz, who didn't seem to know what was going on either.

Krissy pulled a colorful flyer from her tote bag. "This is just the proof, but it does show that you're official."

"Officially what?" Matt asked.

Krissy handed the pamphlet to him. "Look. Then show her."

"You did it?" Matt's face lit up. "Liz, this is all for you, girl."

"What is it?"

"Krissy pulled some strings and called in a few favors. Angel's Rest is officially on the barn quilt tour."

"What?" Liz snatched the paper from his hands. The glossy paper showed a starred route with prominent barn quilts located throughout the state. There in Antler Creek was a tiny replica of the barn quilt on the side of her house, marking the spot for Angel's Rest.

"How did you?" Liz shook her head. "Thank you. Thank you both."

"This was all Krissy's doing."

"I couldn't have done it if you hadn't already put the barn quilt up."

"But I don't know when Angel's Rest will open," Liz said.

"No choice but to make it happen now. It's in writing," Krissy teased. "Plus, you've got us helping you. You can't go wrong."

"A team effort," Liz said, then wrapped her arms around Matt. "Thank you, thank you, thank you."

Krissy put on her coat. "I believe my work here is done." With a flip of her scarf she let Matt help her with her suitcase to her car.

He hated for her to leave. She owned the adjoining lot. He hoped one day he'd talk her into moving back too.

Liz waved from the door, and he watched his sister head off, then went back inside.

"She's great. I love your sister."

"She thinks the world of you too." If Liz only knew how much Krissy was pushing him to move faster with Liz, she'd probably run and hide. "By the way, there's something I've been meaning to talk to you about."

"What's that? You sound serious."

"It's none of my business, but I thought you'd want to know," said Matt, "but I was talking to Joe the other day and their trip to Florida isn't because that's where they want to live. It's their only option."

"I know they're in financial trouble," Liz said. "I feel so bad for them. They are such a nice couple."

"He's a hard worker too. Good at what he does. I don't know if you've given it any thought, but when you're ready to re-open the lodge you'll probably need someone to take care of the grounds and do odd jobs, especially the first year."

"True. There'll be a lot to set up and ongoing work."

"Well, it's just a suggestion, but they might be a good option for you. You could offer them room and board in one of the cabins, and pay a small stipend. It could work out for everyone."

She'd never considered having someone stay on the property. It would certainly take a lot off of her plate, and until the inn was making money, bartering for room and board would help her financially too. Pop had done well bartering for what he needed in this town. If it was good enough for him, it was good enough for her. "Do you think he might really consider it? I couldn't pay much in the beginning."

"I do. I don't think they require a lot of money. Their priority is their family. Antler Creek is a great place to raise a child. He seems to really like it here, and he's already made friends from working on your project."

"I'm going to look at my budget and see what I could afford. Once I get the place established I'd be able to better the offer, if it even worked out. We could do kind of a ninety-day trial. That way if they don't like it, or they aren't a good fit, no one has lost out."

Her wheels were turning. That was all he could ask: for her to consider it.

"You'd be their Christmas angel with an offer like that," he said.

"You're mine." She leaned in closer.

He put his arm around her shoulder, and looked into her eyes. Her lips were inviting; he'd thought of this moment a lot over the last few days.

As he moved in, a loud knock at the door startled them both. He stepped back, shaking his head. "Sorry."

"No." She closed her eyes and took a deep breath in. "It's fine."

He went to the door. "Grady? Everything okay?"

"Hey, man. I was just going to see if Krissy was busy. I thought she might want to ride along with me for a couple hours. See what's going on in town. I could show her around."

"She left a little while ago. She went back to the coast for the holiday."

"Oh. Sorry. I didn't know." He peered inside. "Hi, Liz. I hope I wasn't interrupting anything."

Just our first kiss, Matt thought. Just his luck.

"No," she said politely.

Grady shuffled his feet at the door. "If she comes back in town I'd love to get the chance to talk to her again."

"We'll let her know," Liz said.

Grady made an awkward descent back to his car.

Matt closed the door behind him and laughed out loud. "That was right bold. He's going to be bummed when he finds out she was only here to visit."

"Maybe she'll change her mind. Krissy did say she'd love to own a shop on Main Street. One of the ones with the apartments above it." Liz was already texting Krissy. "She just said she's half-tempted to turn around and come back to meet up with him."

"Really? Let me see that." Matt looked at her phone. "How about that. What is it about Angel's Rest that seems to pull people together? I've been trying to get her to move back forever."

Liz shrugged. "I have no idea, but whatever it is, don't mess it up in the renovation."

"I'll do my best." He stepped closer to her. "Now, where were we?"

His phone rang.

"Nah-ah. I'm not answering that." He leaned closer to her.

"Answer it. Go ahead."

The phone rang again. He cursed under his breath. "We missed our moment, didn't we?"

With a wrinkle of her nose, she nodded and said, "Yeah."

He punched the button on his phone and took the call, stepping away and turning his back to her at one point. "George needs my help down at the store. I've got to go see what's going on. Will you be okay here by yourself?"

"Yes. I'm getting around pretty good now."

"Be careful. I'll be back as quickly as I can."

Matt drove down to Main Street thinking about that almost-kiss. What were the odds he'd get interrupted twice in a matter of minutes? That was just plain wrong. She might think he was moving a little fast, but he'd had a crush on her all those years ago, and he hadn't forgotten that. It didn't feel that fast to him at all.

He pulled into the parking lot at Goodwin's Hardware. George's request had been cryptic, but whatever was going on, if he could help he needed to be here to do it.

Pastor Mike walked out of the store with a bucket of paint. "How're things going, Matt?"

"Never better."

"Really? How're things going with the woman you're going to marry? Does she even know yet?" Mike chuckled.

"No, but I'm more certain than ever now."

Mike quit laughing. "I'm sorry. I thought you were joking about that. I guess this is a merry Christmas for you then."

"It has all the makings of the very best." Matt walked back to the loading dock. George supervised as some college boys moved stock around to make room for the things people had on hold for the holiday and would come to pick up on Christmas Eve.

"Hey, George. What's so urgent?"

"George Junior. Come here. Tell him what you told me."

George Junior's face reddened. "Dad."

"Look, son, if Matt is getting serious about this woman he needs to know."

"What's going on?" *Is this about Liz?* "I need to know what?"

George Junior looked like he wanted to crawl under the pile of feed troughs that were stacked next to him. "I wish I hadn't said anything."

"Well, you did, so repeat it." George didn't look happy about whatever it was.

"That day the Harmons came. You were walking them back to the cabin when this guy in a Suburban showed up. He acted pretty tight with Liz."

Matt felt a jolt of unexpected jealousy.

"He was a real estate guy. He was talking about selling the house."

"Angel's Rest?" Matt shook his head. "No way. She loves that place."

"He said something about quadrupling her money."

"Are you sure?"

"Positive."

His heart felt like it had just landed in his gut. "I guess I would need to know that. I mean, I'm working on the contract for her. If she sells, that job could become much shorter. It could affect the whole crew."

"Like me, and I need that job," George Junior said.

"I know. Thanks for telling me. I'll figure it out."

Matt walked straight to his truck and drove off. He didn't know what to think. Well, he did know, but he didn't want to believe it. It just didn't sound like the Liz he'd gotten to know. Not ready to face her yet, he drove over to the pond, the one place that always brought him clarity, and sat there quietly trying to not take it personally. He was her contractor. Her project manager. Nothing else, no matter how much he wanted to be.

An almost-kiss didn't mean a thing. Maybe she wasn't sorry the kiss didn't happen.

The last time he was here at the pond he'd been making snow angels with her.

He got out of his truck and walked over to the spot where they'd lain there laughing. He hadn't felt that close to anyone in a long time. He relived every moment he'd spent with her. Had he missed a signal? An offhand comment that might have been a hint to her unloading the property?

Quadrupling your investment was hard to say no to, but surely she'd have told him. None of it made sense. Unless this was just all business to her.

He got back into his truck and stopped in over at the café.

"Where's Liz?" Maizey asked.

"Resting up for this afternoon and tonight." It wasn't a complete lie. "Just coffee, thanks."

Maizey slid a heavy white ceramic mug in front of him and filled it to the top. "There you go."

"Thanks." He sat there nursing his coffee and pretending to be addressing emails to avoid conversation as he passed time.

Someone slapped him on the back as they walked by. "Can't wait to see the lights tonight."

They'd better enjoy them, because there probably wouldn't be another display like this ever again.

"You rock, man. My kids loved the lights," Ginger's husband said as he went to the register to pay his bill. "They're home making more cookies to give away."

"You've got a really special family," Matt said. "Thanks for all the help."

"We're happy to be part of it."

Matt put his coffee down. He couldn't deal with this right now. "I'll see you over at Angel's Rest at two," he said to Maizey.

"We've got everything ready to roll."

Of course she did. Maizey always came through.

He drove back home, dreading facing Liz. He wasn't even sure if he wanted to ask her about what George Junior had overheard, because he didn't know if he really wanted to know.

He walked into his house hoping she was napping. No such luck; she was sitting in the den with the comment box and letters, cards, and money all around her.

"Matt! I thought you were never going to get back. These letters are amazing. There are even financial contributions. We'll donate those back into the town somehow, but seriously just the thought of it is mind-blowing."

"Yeah. Sure." He felt like he was an outsider all of the sudden.

"Look at this note. These people are from two towns over. They used to come to see the lights when he was just a kid. Now he's bringing his kids. Generations. My grandparents would've loved this."

"It's very special."

"So, I looked at the budget and went through the timeline. I think I can swing an offer for Joe to work for me. The list of projects is long and that will defray a bit of the contract work, paying him out of that budget for a while. I can have him clean out the other cabin. That one has a tiny second bedroom they can use as a nursery for Holly."

"It was just an idea," Matt said. "You have to do what you think is right."

"I went through the numbers and I think it'll work. In the long run I think it's the right thing to do. Once we get a bedroom in the house done or the other cabin ready I can get moved back and out of your hair too."

She wants to leave. That's telling. "Yeah. Whatever you want. You're the boss." His role was clear. He'd only been fooling himself. Carrying a torch from way too long ago that she never reciprocated. "I'm going to go jump in the shower. Then it'll be time for us to go over to the inn to let Maizey and her folks in to set up for the party."

"Okay. I'm going to go get ready."

When she came back out she was dressed in layers, and carrying an extra throw.

"Ready to go?" he asked.

"Yes." She scooted out to the porch and he helped her down the steps, then loaded her scooter into the truck.

He was quiet on the way over to the house.

"Was everything okay at George's?"

He shrugged. "Yeah. No problems at Goodwin's."

"You were gone a lot longer than I'd expected."

He didn't offer an explanation. He couldn't. He was too angry to even ask her if it was true, but then why would George Junior lie about a thing like that?

"Are you not feeling well?"

"You could say that." Truth was he felt like he'd been sucker punched. He'd been taken for a ride, and he didn't like that one bit.

"Do you need some medicine? I have—"

"No. I'm fine."

They pulled into the driveway at Angel's Rest, and Maizey's van was already parked in front of the door. He was thankful for the reprieve. It was hard to hold his tongue, and he didn't want to do or say anything that would ruin the lights for the community tonight. All he had to do was get through one more night.

Matt helped Maizey get everything set up.

"Everything looks so good," Liz said.

"I'm so glad you're happy with it," Maizey said. "If it's one thing I know, it's what people around here like to eat."

"I bet you do." Liz zipped around the room on her scooter. She was in such a good mood; it made him feel even worse.

"Matt, I hadn't seen the angel on the ladder tree. That's the one from the sign. When did you do that?"

"The other day when I first saw the sign."

"I love it."

"We probably ought to just take that ladder down. It's kind of

silly now that we have real trees and lights all around the house."
He didn't like feeling like a fool.

"No. I love it," Liz said. "It was such a neat idea."

He walked over and took the angel from the top and handed
it to her. "You should probably put this somewhere for safe-
keeping." He slid something from the top step of the ladder and
tucked it inside his jacket.

"What was that?" she asked.

"Nothing." He turned and went to help Maizey, sorry now
that he'd ever told her about the barn quilt trail.

Chapter Thirty-five

Liz couldn't figure out what was going on with Matt. He'd been fine this morning, but ever since he got back from George's he was acting strange.

"Hi, Liz."

She turned to see Joe and Maryanne walking toward her with Holly toddling between them.

"It's great to see you. She's really getting around better each day, isn't she?"

"I won't be able to keep up with her in a week." Maryanne looked tired at the prospect.

"I'm so glad you're here early before everyone else gets here. I wanted to talk to you. Right, Matt?" But when she turned, Matt had already walked off. "Well, we don't need him here, but he knows all about it." Liz laid out the offer to the Harmons.

"Are you serious?" Joe was delighted. "Honey, what do you think?"

Maryanne picked up Holly and held her in her arms. "I think you're about the kindest person I've ever met, Liz. Joe would do a wonderful job for you, and we love it here."

"I think it's too good of an offer to pass up," Joe said, then turned to his wife. "Your parents . . ."

"Will understand. They only want what's best for us. I love it here. Yes. We say yes," Maryanne said.

"I was hoping you'd say that. I was thinking you could concentrate on emptying out the second cabin and we'll get you set up over there. It's got a second small bedroom that you can use for Holly. It'll give you two some quiet time, and a place for her to play too."

"I'll get right on it."

"I'll have to help go through some of those boxes. I'm sure half of them will be trash."

"We'll help you," Maryanne said.

"I'm so happy. Thank you both. After ninety days we'll regroup and make sure this is working on both sides. If it isn't we can part ways with nothing lost. If it is, then we'll make it official."

Joe hugged Maryanne.

Meanwhile, the other folks had started filling up the room. People were mingling and eating. Maizey was the hostess with the mostest, keeping everyone well fed and spreading her own kind of cheer.

"Can I have your attention, please?" Liz tapped a spoon against her glass. "I just wanted to take one moment to thank you from the bottom of my heart. What you all have done here is amazing. Thank you for your craftsmanship, innovation, kindness, and your valuable time. You are all a part of something very special."

She scanned the room for Matt, but didn't see him. Where was he?

"Enjoy!"

Joyful laughter filled the air. You couldn't tell by looking around who had known each other before and who was brand-new to the group.

At five o'clock everyone helped Maizey get her stuff cleaned up and loaded back in the van to get down the hill before six. Joe Don and Bubba carried the coolers of hot chocolate out to the stand.

An hour later, the music played, lights were on, and everyone was in their place. A tingle of excitement coursed through Liz, and she hoped that people would show up again. Had everyone come on the first night? She could at least count on that one hay wagon of college boys tonight. That would be worth it too.

Headlights streamed up Doe Run Road, casting shadows along the road. As they got closer, cars lined up as far as she could see.

There was a steady flow of cars, trucks, and three hay wagons so far and no sign of it slowing down. The hot chocolate and cookies were going fast.

"Liz!"

She looked up when she heard her name. Dan ambled across the flower bed, then jogged across the driveway in front of a church van full of seniors.

"Dan?" She handed cups of hot chocolate off to Bubba, who was helping her tonight since Krissy had left.

"I sold it!" He ran over to her. "You never answer your phone anymore."

"What are you talking about?"

"I've been trying to call you. Missy has too."

"Missy?"

"Yeah. I had the perfect client for your house. We put in an offer with Missy on your house this morning. A good deal too, but she hasn't been able to get ahold of you. My clients are champing at the bit. You don't want to lose this deal."

"Really?"

"Yes. Really. I know. I was being a jerk about you leaving. I'm sorry. I was being selfish. I know if this is what you want you will make it work. I'm behind you. I wanted to prove that, so I showed your house this morning and doggone if they didn't bite on it. Chomp. Chomp. Full price."

"You're kidding?"

"Nope. I've got the papers right here for you to sign."

"How did you even get up here? There are cars lined up for the lights."

"Yeah. They're really pretty. My car is still in line. Missy is driving."

"You and Missy came up here together?"

"She's really nice."

"I told you that before."

"You were right. Are you even a teensy bit jealous we're together?"

"Not at all. In fact, y'all might really hit it off."

"I'm so glad you said that. I think so too. Here, sign these and I'll be out of your hair. Answer your phone!"

"Email me. I can get my emails better. I'll keep an eye on them."

"Okay. That'll work."

Liz handed the papers back to Dan, but when she looked up Matt was headed straight toward her and he didn't look happy. She raised her hand in front of Dan. "Excuse me."

She turned to Matt. "Is everything okay? You look upset."

His jaw clenched. "I am."

His voice was tight. "What's the matter?"

Maryanne swept in. "I need four hot chocolates," she said cheerfully.

Liz poured four and handed them to her. Matt and Dan stood there staring at each other.

"Sorry. Where are my manners? Dan, this is Matt. He's my . . . contractor."

"Oh, so you're the guy working on the place." Dan shoved his hand out. "I'm her best friend, and I was her go-to guy before she up and left me for this place."

Matt didn't look amused, and didn't shake his hand, either.

"That's not exactly how it was. Dan and I are good friends." She turned to Dan. "Can you help Maryanne with the hot chocolate for a minute, please?"

"This is cashmere," he said, referring to his coat.

"So don't be a slob, and it won't be a problem." She pushed a stack of cups into his stomach.

"Your Realtor?" Matt clucked his tongue. "How could you give this up so easy?"

"This?"

"George Junior heard your real estate guy say he sold it. I can't believe you'd sell it before we even got finished. I thought you loved this place."

"I do." She grabbed Matt by the arm and limped off to the side on her scooter to get out of earshot of Dan and anyone else, like George Junior, who might misconstrue something else.

"You sure had me fooled." His words were short.

Matt was upset, and she could see why. "Settle down. It's not what you think, and I don't appreciate you jumping to conclusions. Give me a chance here."

"Don't tell me your buddy Dan didn't come up here to tell you he sold the place. George Junior saw him with the papers."

"Yes. He did."

Matt's fists balled. He looked away. "And what about Joe and Maryanne. Why would you get their hopes up like that? Or mine? If George Junior hadn't told me, when would I have found out?"

She touched his arm, and his biceps tensed. "Matt, Dan didn't sell *this* place. He has an offer on my house in Charlotte. He's not the listing agent. Missy couldn't get through on my phone, so they drove up together to tell me that there's an offer on the table. A good one."

Matt's lips pulled together. "Oh."

"Yeah. And if I take that offer then I have no choice but to see this project through to the end. Which is what I thought we both wanted."

"I—"

"Look. I don't know what's going on with you. I appreciate everything you've done. This place. The work you've already done is amazing. But it's not only your work that's exceeding my expectations. It's you. You've made this feel real for me."

His jaw quit pulsing. "I knew from the time I saw your name on that ad that I wanted you to come back and stay in Antler Creek," he said. "I don't want you to leave."

"It was my dream. I've always thought I belonged here."

"What do you think now?"

"I'm happier than I've ever been. Even with a broken ankle. I can barely stand, and I'm less financially stable than I've ever been before, but everything I ever wanted is here in Antler Creek."

"Angel's Rest?"

"And you. And the possibilities."

"I'm so sorry I jumped to conclusions. I think I owe your friend an apology too."

"I understand. I feel vulnerable too. When I saw you holding Holly you were so good with her. Things that I'd never dreamed of started dancing in my imagination."

"Children?"

"Yes. Family, and so many little things. Snow angels by the pond. Traditions. Old and new."

"I know what you mean."

"I didn't have the least bit of Christmas spirit a few weeks ago." She held out her arms and looked around. Every light. Every decoration. Perfect. "This feels like Christmas." She reached for his hand, and he laced his fingers through hers. "Matt, thank you for bringing Christmas back into my heart. I wanted this place so badly that I'd lost sight of what is happening right now. This. All of it . . . matters as much as anything else."

Elvis trotted up with an angel in his mouth and laid it at her feet.

She looked down and laughed. Her priorities had completely changed, and the dream of running the lodge had a whole new meaning to her now. She picked up the angel and held it close to her heart. "It's not about a career change. It's a life change."

Elvis barked and ran to the front door and pawed at it. Matt and Liz walked over to get him. Elvis jumped and barked again. Matt laughed. "My wingman," he said to Liz, then pointed above the door.

"Mistletoe?" She shook her head. "The last time I went

running after mistletoe I broke my ankle. Please don't break my heart."

"I'd never." He kissed her under the mistletoe. A slow, gentle kiss. "This is the merriest Christmas I've ever had. Please spend Christmas with me."

"I wouldn't want to be anywhere else."

"I have something for you."

"What about the hot chocolate?"

Matt looked over at Dan and snickered.

Liz had to admit that Dan looked very awkward filling the hot-chocolate cups.

Matt said, "I think your buddy could use more practice. This will just take a minute."

He helped her inside. Over on the mantel he retrieved a red package. It looked like the one he'd taken from off the top step of the ladder tree.

"This is for you," he said.

The package was wrapped in pretty red paper decorated with small trumpeting angels and snowflakes, and a shiny gold ribbon and glittery bow.

She slid her finger under the paper one side at a time, careful to not rip it, then slipped off the top of the box to see inside. "Matt. This is a picture of Angel's Rest back when we were kids."

"Mm-hmm."

"I love it!" She looked closer. "You used this picture to duplicate the scenes just like Pop had done them. This is amazing."

"I told you this place was special to me too. I have a lot of great memories here. And pictures to help me remember them." He leaned in closer. "You're always looking for signs. Look closely at that picture. What do you see?"

She stared at the picture for a long moment, then looked up. "You're right there." She pointed to a young boy off to the side in the photo. "I'd know your smile anywhere."

"What else?"

She looked again, moving to where the light was better. "That's Pop standing just behind Gram and me." She ran her finger across the glass. "The way the lights are glowing behind him makes him almost look like an angel."

"If anyone should be an angel, it's him. I've never forgotten that night," he said.

"I remember it too. It was a magical night. All of them were good, but that night has always stood out to me. Do you remember the snowflakes falling that night? They were different. Dry powdery snow. We couldn't even make a snowball."

"I do remember. Liz, we can make so many more nights like that happen and share that kind of joy with others."

"I'd like that. I could never thank you enough for all you've done."

"Well, you could teach me to cast a fly rod as good as you."

"I haven't done that in years." She laughed. "I'm being serious here. You really touched my heart with all of this. You somehow brought all these people together to make all this happen." She placed her hand against her cheek. "I feel like I'm surrounded by Christmas angels."

"I'm glad you feel that way. Follow me." Matt started walking toward the back of the house.

Where is he going? She caught up with him. "Matt? What are—" He stepped to the side. It took a moment for it to register that it was her mother and father standing there in front of her. "Mom? Dad!"

"Hey, Liz," Dad said, holding his arms out to her.

"Dad? What are y'all doing here? Mom? I can't believe this."

"Matt called us."

She spun around and looked at him. "It's so good to see you. Merry Christmas, Mom and Dad. I told Matt if you saw Angel's Rest all lit up again you'd change your mind about it."

"Liz, the lights don't have anything to do with it. We just want you to be happy, and the sheer joy on your face is enough to let us know that something pretty special is going on here."

"It is, Mom. Dad. I've never felt like this."

Mom walked over and hugged her. She whispered into her ear, "Matt is a very special man. Don't you let him get away." She squeezed her tight. "I didn't believe this place could ever be the same without your grandparents here." Mom's eyes glistened. "You're so much like her."

"I couldn't have done it without Matt. He even let me stay at his house after the fall, and he stayed here in the little cabin."

"Do you live far from here?" Dad asked Matt.

"Not far at all. My property actually backs up to Angel's Rest. Just down and around the ridge."

"Wait a minute. The Hardys owned that property."

"Yes. That's right. I'm their son."

"Your dad and I did some hunting together." Dad shook a finger toward Matt as he looked at her. "Liz, this is a good kid. His dad is a great guy."

"He passed away last year. Meeting your daughter really helped me pull my bootstraps up after that. It's been a rough year."

"I'm sorry, son," her dad said. "I hadn't heard."

Liz's mom said, "My father-in-law always said the right things would happen in their own right time. You can't rush it or force it. Matt, we can't thank you enough for contacting us so that we could be a small part of tonight. This is really special, what you two have done. Clearly this was meant to happen. I'm sorry I wasn't more excited for you when you first called us, Liz. I hope you'll forgive me."

"Stop it, Mom. I know you were just trying to help, and ultimately it was my decision."

Matt stepped closer to Liz and put his arm around her waist. She turned and looked at this man who truly put everyone before himself. She had no idea how he kept her so off balance, but she sure hoped she got to spend a lifetime figuring it out.

Dad came over and hugged her. "Your mom and I are going to head on out. We're staying in Boone. You keep us posted, and let us know how we can help with getting Angel's Rest ready. We don't head back to California until Thursday. Let's spend some time together."

"I'd like that," said Liz. She slipped her hand under Matt's arm as she watched her parents leave. "Thank you, Matt. That was so thoughtful of you. I can't believe you got them to come. They haven't been back in years."

"They love you. I think a part of them died when Angel's Rest closed too. You were just the only one that was willing to do something about it."

"You're the best thing that has ever happened to me, Matt Hardy."

"I don't know about that, but I do know that I'd like to spend every Christmas with you . . . forever . . . if you'll let me."

"I like the sound of that."

"And you'll always be safe to spread your wings and fly under the mistletoe with me."

"You'll spot my landing, won't you?" She looked into his eyes.

"Always and forever." He reached into his pocket and took out a small velvet bag. Not big enough to hold even a quarter.

"What's that?"

He fumbled with the small bag, then tipped it over, the contents falling into his hand. "I know that sand dollar is special to you, but I thought maybe a trumpeting angel like the one on the new sign might be too." He placed the pendant in the palm of her hand.

"I love it, and I love *you,* Matt."

"I've been in love with you for so long." He kissed her forehead. "Merry Christmas, my special angel."

CPSIA information can be obtained
at www.ICGtesting.com
Printed in the USA
FSHW011557250919
62382FS